Also b

Stonewall

This unforgettable historical nove
losses, of famed Civil War genera
Preston, the "Poetess of the Confederacy.

"John J. Dwyer makes one of the great heroes of American history accessible
to modern readers."

—*The Daily Oklahoman*

"Stonewall is truly a fascinating figure and Dwyer's novel explores him
beautifully."

—Brock and Bodie Thoene

Robert E. Lee

The mighty sequel to *Stonewall* tells the blood-and-thunder saga of Lee, leader
of the South in war and peace, his beautiful daughter Agnes, and the Lee family.

"I still savor with pleasure reading *Lee*. So much good and truth, so well told."

—Clyde Wilson, professor of history
University of South Carolina

"Dwyer has an uncanny way of communicating the richness of real, godly
Christian leaders. He paints a picture that is so vivid, it is hard to erase."

—Veritas Press

The War Between the States: American's Uncivil War

Was it truly a "civil war"? This acclaimed 700-page epic unveils the causes,
people, events, and consequences of America's greatest tragedy. The book
features more than 530 illustrations, over two dozen paintings from renowned
historical artist John Paul Strain, nearly 100 biographical features, and a free
online study guide for students, parents, and teachers.

"*The War Between The States* is the best textbook for the high school,
preparatory academy, or junior college I've ever read."

—Roger D. McGrath
retired lecturer in history, UCLA

"Judicious, clearly written, suffused with Christian knowledge and understanding,
The War Between the States: America's Uncivil War stands out a mile."

—William Murchison
Radford Distinguished Professor of Journalism
Baylor University
former senior columnist
The Dallas Morning News

www.bluebonnetpress.com

When the Bluebonnets Come

When the Bluebonnets Come

For Alec Forsythe-
Best wishes,
John Dwyer

John J. Dwyer

Bluebonnet

Published by Bluebonnet Press
P.O. Box 1105
Norman, OK 73070-1105
www.bluebonnetpress.com

Page design and composition: Scott Suckling for MetroVoice Publishing Services
www.metrovoice.org

Cover image: *The Seen and the Unseen*
by Brenda Robson
bruthrobson@aol.com

Cataloguing-in-Publication Data is available from the Library of Congress

ISBN 978-0-9768224-1-7

Printed in the United States of America

*To the saints whose heavenly choruses used to bless us
from across the fields that were Texas, while their little wood church
still stood, down Slate Rock Road between us and the Trinity.*

"Oh, when I was in love with you,
  Then I was clean and brave . . ."
—A. E. Housman

One

When I was young, we lived down Shiloh Road, way out from ever'body.

Paw Paw Gremillion said that a hundred years ago and more it come down to one vote between Austin and our Cotton Patch for capital of Texas. Course I also heard him tell it was Bristol, south of us a few miles, that almost won.

Anyhow, I expect you think you know who won. Maybe not. If you ask me, we never had near as many crazy folks as Austin. We did have our share.

I remember Annie Lee nickerin' as my daddy put the bridle over her head. It may a been 'cause the horseflies were bitin' extra nasty that day, bitin' ever'body—horses, people, pigs, dogs, cats, cows, 'possums and snakes too, probably. But she stood true, all sixteen hands of her, when he threw the blanket and saddle over her back, and even when he buckled the cinches under her girth, and he wasn't even givin' her any oats.

Then is when I watched him swing high up into that saddle in his jeans that always smelled of the land he loved, even when Mama just washed 'em, and his boots that looked the same the whole time I knew him, which wasn't long enough.

And I remember him smilin' that white smile that always made me feel safe, even though I knew it was not all smile behind his blue eyes. It could turn hard and final as the twisters that came over from tornada alley.

Then he had my little white hands in his rough big one—rough shore for a preacher—and I was flyin' up to that saddle myself and the butterflies were flutterin' in my tummy and somewhere a little girl was gigglin' with a delight she had no reason to think would never be quite as full or free again.

Even though I never once saw him wear spurs—he said if anyone needed spurrin' it was the man who used them to claim rights with his horse he hadn't earned—it always shook those butterflies all up when the horse broke into a canter 'cross the pasture.

Daddy used to say when you got back to the land, you got back to God. And, my, was there ever land.

I am not sure that if you have never galloped through a meadow of wavin' buffalo grass then over a rise to see an ocean of bluebonnets stretchin' far as you can make out in the sunshine that you have really seen the whole hand of God the Creator at work.

There would go that giggle again, almost a screamin' sort of giggle now as we would go down the path between the bluebonnets, and my tummy would be tryin' by then to climb out of my mouth, but I didn't want it ever to stop.

Sometimes I would manage a peek up and sure enough there would be his broad shoulders and the straw Stetson with the sweat stains around the band. I cannot say if I ever saw one of those hats (he had a whole herd of them, in the closet, on the hat rack, out in the garage, even out in the stables and the barn) come off that long oval head with the short thick brown hair they pushed down, even when the 50-and-60-mile-an-hour winds came, or the jagged hail the size of baseballs or the locust swarms or when some low-hanging bough of a live oak thumped him.

And, yes, those hail stones were big as baseballs, because one of them split my forehead open once and I can show you the little scar to this day. Daddy said it wasn't a scar at all, but God's kiss to heal up where I hurt. I reckon God must've set some kinda kissin' record on Daddy and that was only on the outside. Somewhere a long time after I figured out He must've had to kiss my Daddy a lot more on the inside even than he had on the out.

I used to be afraid of those live oak boughs I mentioned, and got to where I even shrieked warnings to him. It amazed me he could be so fine a rider in other respects yet still manage to run under so many of those low-hangin' boughs. My conviction on the matter was strengthened when I heard Mama scream at him to stay clear of the low-hangin' boughs of the live oaks and realized she shared my concern.

Sometime after he was gone and the concrete and the apartments and Dallas had come, I figured out why he always laughed when he went under—or through—those low-hangin' boughs and that Mama was only part scared for us and plenty more mad.

When I make it to the upper sanctuary, one of the first things I'm gonna ask God is why He only let me figure out so many things later when I could've used them earlier.

Anyhow, up our hill we'd go, the one with the Indian paintbrushes glowin' coral-red off to the side and the last live oak at the top. Then Daddy would pull rein next to the live oak and step down. At least I assume he would pull rein, though he hardly ever seemed to do it with our horses, they just seemed to know when he wanted them to stop.

Now when I was real little, I remember he would feel shamed if he didn't have his Justins on the ground before the horse's hooves all were. But I may not really remember that, it may be just from the home videos or Mama recallin' how he was just wantin' to act like Jeb Stuart, even after he was older than Jeb was, when that Yankee who was runnin' away shot him after Jeb was out of bullets.

His mustache looked like Jeb's too, in those paintings he had of him taken from old photographs and where they added color. Jeb's beard always looked like it was fixin' to catch fire, sorta rusty-lookin'. I heard it called ginger and cinnamon, too, in the books Daddy read me, and tawny, though I never remembered at the right time to look up in the dictionary what that meant.

But maybe the comparison is poorly-drawn, because comparin' Daddy's mustache to Jeb's beard in those paintings, where they probably added a stroke or two for dramatic effect, was like comparin' horse apples to oranges or a Shivy (that's Texan for "Chevrolet") to any other truck. Daddy would like to have had a beard to make the comparison more even, I'm sure, but Mama drew the line about half an inch below the corners of his mouth, and she would like to have drawn it higher than that. Still, it was a mighty orange-lookin' mustache for a man with brownish hair and I expect it would have been a fine-lookin' beard as well if allowed to prosper, which it never was beyond early on the Lord's Day.

Funny, if Daddy hadn't grown his mustache we'd never have known that other color was hidden in there. Just like if my hair didn't get out in the sun without a hat, we'd never have seen it come out there either. What really adds to the peculiarity of it all is that my hair is yellow, not brown, till that secret hidden part comes out. It's always there, though, just waitin' to come out.

That's as fishy to me as how it gets passed right along from me to someone else, which it did, from one hidden place to another to another to another, down a long, long line, never bein' seen at first, but just comin' out when you least expect it.

And besides, we're Celts.

Now this one particular time after Daddy swung me down off Annie Lee, he pulled his pocket knife, not his huntin' knife, out and walked to the live oak. He carved somethin' into the trunk, which I had never seen him do before.

I remember that when I walked over to see what it was, a little breeze puffed up from the north meadow, sweeter than the first good spring rain.

"Ah," he said with a smile, closin' his eyes and drinkin' it in, as he did the things men did not make, "Texas perfume."

That's what he always said when the wind caught the scent of a whole pack of bluebonnets just the right way and brought it straight to us, the way it did not often do, not nearly as often as you would suspect it would when you were there and ten thousand bluebonnets were there and the wind, not such a factor in our part of Texas, snuck in to make a show.

I did what he did, breathin' it in, sweet to my nose as those little bite-sized chocolate candies with the white and yellow fillings in them are to your tongue and mouth.

"Yeah, Texas perfume," I said.

When I looked up at him, he was starin' out over the blue, the red, and the green again.

By then, I was at the live oak, where a redbird had lit and where I saw he had cut a cross of the Christian sort deep into the bark. Above the narrow horizontal part of the cross and separated by the longer vertical one were the initials "ES" and KS."

Ethan Shanahan and Katie Shanahan. Now I know that what I felt then was that my soul was full and I loved him with my whole heart.

"Oh, almost forgot," he said, stridin' back to Annie Lee. He pulled something from the saddlebag and brought it to me. It was my King James Bible. "Surprise in there for ya."

I opened to the Psalms, where there was a brand new bookmark—the brightest and prettiest and sweetest-smellin' bluebonnet I had ever seen or have seen since.

"I'd never pick one—and you better not either," he notified me, "but that little puppy Jeb had it hangin' out his mouth and it seemed none the worse for wear."

I expect if my face lit up half as bright as my heart was, it looked like the sunrise breakin' over the Trinity River Valley.

"It's awesome—and it still smells good too!"

Right then a bell clanged in the distance. That was the outside world's manner of intrudin' on our own, better, one.

This would have been the place in the book where Jeb Stuart would yell, "To horse!" We were in the saddle and back down from the live oak in seconds.

"Yah, Annie Lee!" Daddy hollered, for himself, not the horse.

Paw Paw was waitin' by his brass clanger, which he'd hung years before on a rawhide strap from an elm branch, hammer in hand. It wasn't often he got to bang that old thing, but when he did, he hit it like a Comanche medicine man beatin' his war drum. "Say, buddy, we got a rabid dog over 'round the west pasture," he huffed, like if he was the one that galloped a half mile over the earth for the first bell clangin' in nearly a year. "He's already killed some of McCain's chickens, and they say he's headed this way."

He had quite a bit of Shrimp Gremillion on his shirt, but I'm sure not as much as our Labradors Jake and Daisy had in their bellies as they watched the proceedings from the shade side of Paw Paw's double-wide. After a minute, one of those nasty horseflies must have bit Jake right through that thick white coat because he lit right up off the ground and shook. I thought it might be a good time for him to scamper over and jump into one of the horse-waterin' troughs the way he did when he was showin' off to Daisy and that little puppy Jeb, but he elected just to go find him another shade spot. There is a point that can be passed where you have eaten so much Shrimp Gremillion that you just aren't worth a hoot for a spell. I expect the same principle would hold true for a dog.

Only then did I see that Paw Paw had my daddy's Winchester 30–30 and a box of shells. He pitched the one up to Daddy, then the other. We knew enough about the old days to know if it weren't for his gimp and his rheumatiz and the "incidents" he refused to admit were bunches of little strokes, and the table-muscle he'd put on, and his three score ten and then some, Pierre Richard Gremillion would not be clangin' a bell for anyone to go clear a mangy renegade off his land.

"Oh, Daddy, please be careful!" I screeched as he gave me a hand down.

Then he was up there squeezin' in one long dread-lookin' shell after another—Daddy was always partial to that 30-30 because he said it had a "real big slug behind it"—and pumpin' one into the chamber. "I will, sweetie," he said. "Now you run on inside and practice your piano."

"But—"

Holdin' the Winchester in one hand, he did indeed jerk the reins with the other to turn Annie Lee and he rode away, off toward the west pasture. Jake must have taken out alongside him, because I heard him shout, "No, Jake, go back boy! Go back!" as I stalked poutin' toward our house to do my blasted piano.

Jake barked, but he did stop even though Daddy rode on.

Then I felt Paw Paw's thick arm around my shoulder and his breath and shirt smelled like there was quite a bit more Tabasco in that Gremillion than usual.

I don't know if it was that or havin' to practice that blasted piano or Daddy ridin' off after a wild dog with his 30-30 or maybe just bein' tired since I had been doin' a lot more for Mama, or maybe even a combination of all these, but those were sure tears in my eyes.

I have since figured out it usually is a combination gets after us in life.

Two

"kindly" (kind'le) *adj.*: expressive of a sympathetic, helpful, or benevolent nature or impulse: *a kindly interest.*

"kind-ly" (kin'-a-lee) *adj.*: sort've, in a manner of speakin', pretty much, if not most of the way true.

This is prob'ly good a place as any to say that not ever'thing I am going to tell you did I see with my own eyes. In fact, not ever'thing did I even get from what someone else saw. There is a third category that has to do with things as they may or may not have been, but should have been, and prob'ly were.

That is a tradition among many dangerous groups, all of which I am a member. They would include, as already mentioned, the Celts (most especially the particularly combustible mixture of Irish, Scots-Irish, French, and more Irish who passed along all their secret stuff from their hidden places to me), as well as Southerners of the unreconstructed sort, Presbyterians of the Old School variety in a New School generation, and Texans.

Texans would be those whose state is always the first one those powdered-and-primped TV news actors light up in red during the Presidential elections when all the other states so far are lit up in blue.

For instance, I didn't actually see Daddy gallopin' heck-for-leather across the west meadow, then the gently-slopin' McCain pastures, as the cows and cowbirds and trees watched him and a buzzard soared overhead.

Nor did I see him charge up and over that hill other side of the McCains. But I know he did and you aren't gonna change my mind about it, so don't try. Remember what groups I'm part of.

Now that is understood, let me tell you that when Daddy crested that hill other side of the McCains, he saw an expanse explode across his sight wide and far as the one I saw with him and Annie Lee, but with somethin' else than just bluebonnets.

Maybe a hundred yards ahead, he saw two of the McCain boys standin' over a mangy-lookin' dog they had peppered. A couple hundred yards farther, on the two-lane, asphalted farm-to-market, he squinted to make out one of the biggest Cadillacs and one of the longest Mercedes' he had ever seen, and several suited men climbin' out of them.

He pretty much figured right off where they were from, because he had seen their kind plenty before. He galloped down the far side of the hill, sparin' the mangy dead dog barely a glance. Dogs of all sorts, even mangy dead ones, were common as biscuits and gravy in eastern Ellis County. Such vehicles as he now saw were not, and he had lived there long enough to know that when vehicles which cost that much money showed themselves out there, they were in search of more money.

Seein' the men confirmed they were the sort with more money than folks from Cotton Patch or Bristol or Ferris would ever have, and they were doomed to be less satisfied with it. In fact, just when they got up to about where they were supposed to be satisfied, they realized they were so miserable they must need to get some more to be happy like they thought they were gonna be when they got to this point.

My daddy knew none of the scoundrels would ever stop clawin' for more, but they would come to one of several ends. Some of 'em, wily as a coyote (that should be said ki'-oat not ki-o'-tee) you hear away off ever' night but never catch a peek at in the day, would just keep right on makin' more and more till they left it to the kids they kept right on seein' less and less as they made it.

Quite a number of 'em would lose it—sometimes more than once—and have to work all the harder to get it back. Ever'body that trusted 'em, of course, would never get anything of their own back except their singleness from a furious spouse or maybe somethin' new, like a fresh kind of cynicism they hadn't quite known before their supposed buddy let 'em in on the supposed deal of a lifetime.

Others of 'em would kind-ly go up and down till they just stroked on out, droppin' dead in mid-step, leavin' the little lady (whichever one they were currently then hitched to) with just a mite of responsibility Junior League and the Kappas or Thetas or Chi O's didn't prepare her for.

So far, Cotton Patch Mayor (and City Council President) Ben Coltrane was kind-ly shimmyin' back and forth between those first two categories, with just enough heavy-starched orneriness to maybe ward off the third for awhile yet.

Then there was that Clint Granger of "The Bubble," also known as Highland Park, richest section of Dallas and second-richest in all of America. He came from oil money a couple generations back.

You know what they say about how the kids of the man who pulls himself up by his bootstraps and gets rich never have the sand their daddy had, because they get given to them what he had to fight and claw for? Well, that was sure enough true about Clint's daddy and his granddaddy. And even though Clint's daddy was a lush and a skirt-chaser, he did grow up just enough to be more discreet than he had been in his younger days when he flunked out of Princeton then cheated his way through UT Austin. Leastways, they let him keep payin' his dues at the country club in Highland Park. Plus, he at least understood he was nothin' compared to his own daddy, "Galveston" Granger, the East Texas wildcatter. And he didn't really want to be, since for a man he hardly ever saw and sure never knew—though he had met two of Galveston's secretary-wives)—he pretty much hated him.

Whereas young master Clint actually had a notion about himself that he was cut from the same tough, smart mold as his granddaddy. Well, he did play some good football at SMU till he wrecked his shoulder and that old Methodist school dedicated to circuit-ridin' gospel preachers got the first death penalty in the nation for cheatin'. That means the NCAA killed the whole program—dead—for two years. That means they didn't have a team for two years—and not much o' one since.

Dead. Dead, dead.

Sometimes even a true Texan has to admit it ain't always a Yankee conspiracy.

That bein' said, Clint wasn't cut from the same mold as his granddaddy, as you'll shortly learn firsthand—or somethin' of the sort—from me.

Those other Dallas suits with that Granger and Mayor Coltrane were just junior jackals runnin' with the pack. Yeh, "jackal" does seem a bit harsh, doesn't it? Ever read Woody Guthrie's poem about Pretty Boy Floyd? Ole Woody allows as how one man might get you with his gun, but another man'll do it with his fountain pen. Ole Woody never saw an outlaw take a poor man's house from him, but he saw a heap o' houses taken from the poor folk. Sorta like the Grangers and how they helped get that levee built south of the Trinity in Dallas, where the poor folks', mostly black, homes were.

The suits were so jacked up with their new lodestone they didn't take notice of the dead dog or my daddy.

"Yes sir, once we widen the road here, this is definitely the best spot in the whole county," that Granger said, turning to the others. "You boys agree?"

"Yeah, Clint, this is great," puffed one of the junior jackals with a trophy wife, a trophy ex-wife, and a trophy "administrative assistant" to fend for.

The other junior jackals nodded their agreement, and that Granger, smilin' the more, sucked in a hefty breath of bluebonnet country. "And how can you beat this country air?" he crowed. "This reminds me of my daddy's deer leases down in the Hill Country." He turned again to the rest of his pack. "See what I mean, though? Good drainage—" He cocked an ear over his right shoulder. "—you could almost hear the interstate from here if the wind's blowin' right; it's close to Dallas, but not too close; and we've got a mayor on our team here with the vision and foresight to make it happen."

Mayor Coltrane nodded. After all, it was quite a privilege to be allowed to spread-eagle one's own county out for a Granger, and one who had only added to the family fortune—at least the main family fortune, the one that had tightroped its way through the divorces and the paternity suits and the F.B.I. investigations.

"Gotta hand it to ole Shorty," that Granger just rolled on. "He's got a nose for the deal like no one I ever saw. He's forgotten more than most the big dogs up in Dallas will ever know."

Then was when my daddy rode up, but it was prob'ly that Winchester more than him that caused that Granger's eyes to widen just a shade.

"Afternoon," allowed Daddy.

"Afternoon," said that Granger.

"Howdy, Mayor Coltrane," said Daddy.

"Hello, Ethan," said Mayor Coltrane.

"Where y'all from?" asked Daddy.

"Dallas," said that Granger.

"Figured as much," Daddy said with a smile. "What do you have in store for this pasture?"

That Granger and the others passed around some looks. Sporting a nod from Mayor Coltrane, he said, "Well, let's just say Ellis County is about to become the fortunate recipient of an economic and employment boon."

Now it always amazed me how, for a man I assayed to be very honest, my daddy could be so happy without smilin' sometimes, then sport a smile so long in the presence of human rodents. "Well, let's see," he said, "We already have as many WorldMarts as we can probably support. They put the horse track in Grand Prairie. Hmm. You boys don't look as though your fixin' to start a new church. Mayor Coltrane? You're my councilman. Do you have some good news for us hard-pressed taxpayers?"

The good mayor offered no concrete evidence of bein' comfortable either with this conversation or the appearance of my daddy. "Ethan, I believe we'll have some good news for our district at the next City Council meeting," he rallied. "That would be on Tuesday the ninth, and I'd invite you to attend."

My daddy smiled as the other men awaited his response. "Thank you, Mayor," he said. "Good seein' you men, but we've a rabid dog to check on over here. Oh, no need to fret yourselves. Couple other boys already shot him. Good thing it's still just haymow out here and not the middle of a mall or somethin', I guess."

Then he tipped his hat and turned ole Annie Lee. "See y'all later," he said.

"There rides the pastor of our little Presbyterian Church, Clint," announced Mayor Coltrane a moment later.

Now this lit up that Granger. He turned and spied a half-smile on the face of one of the other Dallas men. It sparked him into a smile too, then a chuckle, then a belly laugh, which the whole group shared as they climbed back into their cars. "A pastor! He'll love us," he said as he got into the back seat of the Merc. "We're gonna give him somethin' that'll fire up his whole church. It'll be the greatest thing ever happened to his collection plate."

"Let's hope it doesn't *hurt* his collection plate," Mayor Coltrane opined.

"Then maybe it'll help his confession booth business," that Granger said. "Dickinson, you're a Presbyterian—do y'all do the confession booth deal?"

Dickinson swore an oath, then revealed his shock there was anything besides Baptists and Church of Christ folks out there anyways.

Three

Truthfully, I can't imagine Cotton Patch ever bein' capital of Texas. It had a couple thousand people fifty years before I was born, and it has a couple thousand people now.

The town square, though, has always been kind-ly pretty, in an old-fashioned sorta way, especially when they hang all the lights at Christmas.

Gentle hills kind-ly rolled all 'round the Shanahan spread. Couple miles west of us was Catlett Bottoms, which I used to like mostly because it made my tummy flutter when Daddy jumped his truck over the crest of what we called "Tickly Hill." He only did it in his truck because Mama wouldn't let him do it in "her" van. Now I like those bottoms 'cause they and they alone stopped the trailer parks and Dallas from stampedin' all the way to the Trinity River Valley behind us to the east.

Things flattened out quick once you moved west. Used to be, with the mesquite and locust trees mostly cleared out, the lands around the farm-to-market over to Cotton Patch and Interstate 45 were pretty much what you'd expect—cotton fields, along with maize, corn, wheat, alfalfa, coastal bermuda, buffalo and prairie grass, and even some sunflowers, not to mention horses, cattle, chickens, a few goats, sheep, and hogs, dogs of ever' breed and especially of no breed at all, and a brick—or more likely frame—farm house hither and yon. That, and all manner of elms, hackberries, and pecans, particularly along the creek bottoms.

Folks were mostly poor in Cotton Patch, but not too poor to play football, politics, and church. That reminds me how my daddy used to say that even though the Lord God created all things, He ordained—but was not Himself the author of—evil in this world for His own purposes. Turns out, unbeknownst to any of us, evil was about to have itself a heyday around Cotton Patch that early evenin' in summer that we sat suppin' around the table on our back patio deck.

Now I won't comment on that table, other than to say it was a pretty good table and that I always thought that Jeff Foxworthy joke about how you know you're a redneck if your lawn furniture used to be in your livin' room hit a little close to home for me. Fact, it wouldn't take the nose o' those white yellow Labs of ours to prob'ly scout out a piece or two that qualified somewhere out on the property at any given time.

What I mainly remember about how that meal started is that Mama was servin' up that French bread she never let me have enough of, and I think venison steaks, too, that my daddy and our friend Mr. Posey shot down around the Byrd place near Bracketville the season before, and corn on the cob to go along with the carrots, potatoes, cucumbers, okra, radishes, tomatoes, green, hot, and sweet peppers, black-eyed peas, squash, and pinto beans from our own garden. But to me, all those were chores to get done, hurdles to clear if you will, in order to qualify for gettin' a second chunk of that French bread.

The other thing I mainly remember is the sweet harmony of the singin' voices that came waftin' through the cedars and the pastures rollin' away to the east behind our place, the Shanahan place.

I heard 'em first.

"Listen!" I blurted, since no further French bread seemed immediately available to occupy my mouth. "There they are. Right on time."

"What's that they're singin', Pookie?" Daddy asked, a cob of corn jammed half into his mouth, that rusty mustache polishin' the kernels he hadn't yet eaten. Pookie was just one of the names he had for me. Where most of them came from, I do not know.

I listened close as the singin' faded with a shift in the wind, then got clear again. "Believe it's *Were You There?*" I said.

"Believe you're right," Daddy said, noddin' and chompin'. I swear, I saw that man derive more pure delight out of things like corn on the cob and cold watermelon, and a clear starry sky the night of the winter's first frost, and even ticklin' me and turnin' me upside down and shakin' me, than other folks got out of havin' the whole world at their feet. Me, I suspect it was those Scottish Covenanters his mama came from. PBS says those fellas were bluestockings and killjoys, but that's the sorta mischief you can expect to be spawned by tax dollars. There was so much those tough folks didn't do, seems they crammed all the pleasure would have come from those things into the simple things they did.

"They sure sing pretty, don't they, Daddy?" I said.

"Yes, they do," he said.

And that is when the cell phone on the table that had previously been located other than on the back deck rang. Mama answered it as Jake and Jeb the puppy advanced toward the table. "Hello?" I heard her say in her sweet way.

"Y'all get back," Daddy scolded the dogs, shielding his vittles. "You'll get yours later. That's all we need is another dog around here to feed," he aimed toward Jeb the puppy.

More barking sounded from over near Paw Paw's.

"Well I guess the smell is out now," Daddy grumbled, a smidgen before Daisy lumbered up onto the deck, her thick tail swattin' over tableware like a crackin' whipcord.

"Daisy!" I called to my favorite, the one I had personally picked four years before from a mixed litter of ten black, brown, and yellow little balls of fluff.

"You get back too, Lazy Daisy," Daddy said, shooing her away, "you're already wearin' an inner tube around you."

"Daddy!" I exclaimed, offended and near slappin' him.

But whatever was comin' through that little phone had upset Mama somethin' awful. "Oh no, I can't believe it," she said into the contraption, tears in her eyes. "That's just horrible. Yes, we'll figure out how we can help. Yes. Thank you, Lily."

She clicked off and began to cry.

Daddy leaned over and put his arm around her and asked, "What's wrong, honey?"

"That church out on Harvest Road, the black folks, Macedonia Baptist—" she began.

"Yes, Pastor Jasper's church," Daddy said.

"George Washington Carver Jasper, Daddy," I corrected him.

"—somebody burned it down," Mama finished.

"No, not a church!" I think I shouted.

Then Mama and I were both sobbing.

"First the Gomez store and now a church," Daddy said.

"But why, Daddy, why?" I demanded. "Why would anybody burn down a church?"

Before he could answer, Mr. Scott Posey pulled around the side of the house on the old gravel entryway in the largest and certainly the shiniest new pickup truck I had yet seen in my nine years of life. That is not to say I had not seen other, large, shiny pickup trucks of Mr. Posey's. But even Daddy, who had driven pick-em-ups since he was 13 or 14, whistled at this one. (And by the way, just because he whistled didn't mean he would have driven that thing even if Mr. Posey had given it to him.)

But Mr. Posey was jolly, liked by just about ever'body, real successful, and one of my daddy's best friends. He was certainly his most faithful supporter on the Session, or board of elders, of our Cotton Patch Presbyterian Church. He was handsome, too, even if he had made a habit of takin' an extra helpin'—or two—of chicken fried steak and mashed potatoes with gravy when they were offered, which was often around Cotton Patch. And if they weren't offered, he would sidle over to Dee's Cafe and offer 'em to himself off the menu.

"Howdy," Mr. Posey said as he got out of his truck and started toward us, sportin' his newest cowboy hat, madras shirt, jeans, and boots, like always. "Oh, I'm sorry, I came at a bad time."

He turned and started to leave.

"Scott Posey, that never stopped you before," Mama said, sniffling.

"Yeh, we need to talk with you anyhow," Daddy said.

Mr. Posey went from bein' happy as a meadowlark in spring to lookin' like he'd just heard a tornada blew down Dee's, which was in fact fixin' to happen. "Oh?" he said, his face flushin' crimson.

"Yeah, say, you want some venison?" Daddy offered. "It's the last o' what we got last fall."

"Oh, no thanks," Mr. Posey said, lookin' kind-ly relieved. "I already ate—say, that does look pretty good. Good as those tacos we made from the backstrap." Then he did the smart thing and took off his hat (they didn't make him do that at Dee's, but Mama did at her table, even the one on the back deck) and sat down. "Yeh, sure, I'll take a plate. Just a small piece, though."

Daddy knew Mr. Posey and was already through the door and back into the house.

Mama wiped away tears with a napkin. "I'm sorry, Scott, but Lily Witherspoon just called and said that black folks church out on Harvest Road was burned down last night."

"You mean somebody torched it?" Mr. Posey said.

I thought Mama was gonna break out cryin' all over again, but she just nodded.

Mr. Posey couldn't say anything. It was maybe the first time I ever saw him upset at heart. For a moment there, no one said anything. Then I caught the singin' again on the wind.

"*Deep River*," I uttered, but I don't know if loud enough for anyone to hear.

Then Daddy reappeared with a Corningware plate, glass, and utensils for Mr. Posey, along with our fat, furry cat Puffy. How a cat could survive as long in the country as Puffy did, and look puffed-up as a blowfish to boot, is a deed I haven't yet figured out. We never had another cat make it more than a year, and we had a bunch of 'em. One of Jim Slade's hounds carried one off one day for a late snack, fetched him right off our gravel entry road, he did. Course, next time my daddy happened upon that dog trespassin' on our property, and bullyin' one of our puppies to boot, he caught him on the fly with the blade end of a weed slinger from over sixty feet away. Flung it like a tomahawk, he did. That must've taken somethin' out of that mutt, 'cause shortly thereafter he was dumb enough to get his final comeuppance under the business end of Spud Tatum's '69 Dodge Ram. Anyhow, Puffy looked ready to make his own bid for venison.

"Here I thought I had big news, and a church gets lit up," said Mr. Posey.

"You've got news?" Daddy said.

"Yep, and it ain't much better than the church news," said Mr. Posey.

No one said anything then, as the final strains of *Deep River* faded away.

Fortunately, Mr. Posey had his appetite back pretty well by now after the tragic bulletin of thirty seconds past. As he piled food onto his plate, he announced, "Well, ole Shorty Anderson's gone and done it this time." Tearin' into that venison like an ole Comanch' comin' upon a chuck wagon out in the Llano after a lean huntin' season, he continued, "He's sellin' that hundred-acre patch of his over on the farm-to-market to—you're not gonna like this at all, Ethan—"

"Well let me have it, Scott!" Daddy fairly hollered.

"Why, Ethan, he's sellin' it to some Dallas-types fixin' to build 'em a horse racin' track," Mr. Posey said.

My daddy didn't know what to say to that.

Mr. Posey kind-ly let out a half-burp, the sort that would've been considered a full-fledged belch at home. However, since he was a guest on our back deck, it only qualified for partial status, and he did his best to cover even that meek effort with, "Say, Katie darlin', could you hand me another chunk o' that bread? That's good stuff."

"Here?" Mama said. "But why here?"

Just then, Mr. Posey had what I swear was near a whole slab of that French bread I was pinin' for more of, stuffed in his face. But he rallied quick-like. "Even considerin' it was Shorty, they evidently felt land was too high north of Dallas, and that the growth is finally comin' this way," Mr. Posey said.

I remember I was watchin' Daddy's face real close on this one. After all, it was like they all forgot (it's pronounced fuh-gott in our part of Texas) I was even there and they were talkin' like it was just adults trained and qualified to handle such challenging new information.

"I don't guess I know what to say at this point," said my daddy.

Mama clasped his hand and said, "Now honey, since when have you ever not known what to say about anything? Everything will come out well in the end."

After all, that was what Presbyterian theology told us. Real Presbyterian theology, not this milk-and-water, many-roads-to-heaven fiction. Sometimes the good end happened in this life and when it didn't, well, things'd get squared in the next. That was why I needed to hear about Jeb Stuart and General and Mrs. Lee and their daughters, and Travis and Crockett and Susannah Dickinson too, all of 'em on the losin' not the winnin' end in this world, and I'm sure it was why Daddy knew he needed to tell me of 'em, too. One way or another, good was gonna win out and bad was gonna get hammered into the ground.

Daddy thought over Mama's words for a minute and I guess when he gleaned what he needed from 'em, that is when he winked at me. And that is when I knew ever'thing would indeed come out well in the end.

"Say, Lorena, you couldn't spare another chunk o' venison by chance, could ya?" Mr. Posey inquired.

Four

My daddy always said city folks drove themselves crazy—and not just Yankees, but Texans, too—because they had lost the rhythms of life. Birth, life, death, resurrection. Summer, harvest, winter, spring. Life always ran in cycles, he said. You might not know ever' time when they were comin', nor for how long, but you could bet they were. And just knowin' that helped keep you ready to deal with whatever came your way next. But most folks never quite got their halter around that fact.

Course, Mama would've said that was the Celt in him talkin' again.

I regret to say such afflictions have long since spread to many country folk as well. I didn't usually share Willie's politics, but I always admired his singin' mightily. I guess *My Heroes Have Always Been Cowboys* hits all real Texans close to home. But I have lived out there amongst 'em my whole life and there are some rough edges to most real cowboys I've known that the sandpaper of life seems to only have made worse.

Most of the cowboys I know will ride into hell to lasso the devil for you if they find you're in a bad way. Once that bad way's over, though, don't expect your average cowboy to mosey back with any help, lessin' your huntin' for disappointment and maybe more of a bad way than you started with. Daddy always believed those old Hollywood tales where the cowpoke rides off into the sunset at the end. It's just that he said they were supposed to be showin' up for work or spendin' time with their kid or comin' home from the bar right when they headed off for the sunset.

I don't remember how far on I was when I realized a lot of these fellas with their ten-gallon Resistols, Red Man and Copenhagen, and scarred knuckles were pretty much just drinkin' coffee with their buddies or "checkin' on their cattle" ever' day while their wives or girlfriends were gettin' several kids ready for school, then speedin' half-cocked down the farm-to-market doin' their hair and puttin' on the war paint a woman has to have when she works ever' day in a high-rise office somewheres in Dallas.

Then those ladies'd speed back home to slap down supper for a mess o' kids that'd been gettin' fed how they came from swampy soup and apes in the classroom, and four-letter words on the playground all day—while her "man of few words" hurried to get to his leather easy chair for that night's ESPN lineup.

Now I've seen enough o' Dallas and those high-rises from the inside to know that there is a word for a man that'll let his lady go there ever' day while he meanders about his fields—there is a word, and it ain't hero.

Anyhow, one bright late-summer mornin' when the cotton bolls had gone to openin' and the old flatbeds and pickups rumbled down the farm-to-markets, stacked high with baled coastal and alfalfa hay, not to mention that good-for-at least-somethin' native Johnson grass, Daddy took his old Shivy pick-em-up into town, the sad strains of *Red River Valley* on the radio. He saw ole Cass Mastern diskin' the soil for to plant him a winter cover crop, prob'ly wheat or rye grass, prob'ly not oats any more. He waved out the window to Cass, and Cass waved back, like he had a hundred times before.

Daddy knew how uncontrollable that black land over toward Cotton Patch could be, how one summer the heat and drought'd bankrupt the Cass Masterns and the next spring it would rain so much you could end up after plowin' with nothin' but gullies deep enough to put a house in. But most folks, even in Texas, live in cities now, so hardly anyone ever gives such things a thought anymore.

Then it occurred to him how big was the Texas sky and how many folks' bones must've bleached under the same blazin' sun to win this hard land to the gospel. Daddy pondered such weighty matters often, I reckon too often as it turned out. He also pondered the folks whose bones bleached as they lost the land to the other folks. He wondered how many bones of either type would've had to bleach out if those God gave the gospel to had lived it out better, even when it cost 'em, instead of pullin' out their guns. And Daddy had lots o' guns and would've used 'em in a New York second if anybody came across our threshold.

My ole Granny Gremillion used to say she reckoned too much thinkin' can drive a person stir-crazy.

Daddy saw a redbird perched on Dirk Kelly's fence post, then he pulled into Cotton Patch and over the tracks. It always amazed me how I'd occasionally hear the whistle of a train through my open window late at night in spring or fall. I asked Daddy where could it be comin' from and he never knew of any tracks closer than Cotton Patch—up Shiloh Road, over Catlett Bottoms, across the hills and fields, all the way to the interstate—eight miles away. How in the world could that sound travel so far, starry sky or not? But sure as the turnin' of the earth, I heard it, many a time. What a long list of questions I'll have for the Lord if He'll hear 'em on that great day, or later.

Anyhow, as Daddy crossed the town square, he passed Jose Guiterrez, ridin' his old bicycle. Short and stocky, the little workman's hard-drinkin' and womanizin' had given him forty-five years' worth of lines on his thirty-five-year-old face. Daddy smiled and waved, but it took Jose a moment to focus. When finally he recognized Daddy and smiled and waved back, he nearly fell off the rusty and rickety two-wheeler.

Daddy parked over by Dee's, which was usually a wise place for a pastor to park if he was aimin' to find the people. Right when he opened his door, there was Will Hankins comin' out.

Will had come from humble beginnings out in Hood County forty-six years before. His folks, even the short spell they were together, never amounted to much, and Will didn't for a long time either. If not for his rough charm and rugged good looks, I doubt he ever would've snagged Sallie Beth Sibley. But ain't that how it seems to work with so many of those goat-ropin' good-for-nothin's? Another one o' my questions is gonna be why He made so many sweet girls who paid no heed to the sweet boys, but chose instead rakes and ramblin' men unworthy of 'em.

Anyhow, Sallie Beth had many charms, not least which she won Miss Ellis County, and somehow these combined to pretty much straightin' out Will's less savory inclinations. He even got to be a respectable fella with her money, and even made her a little more. And despite bein' a pillar in the community, he had a conscience, too.

(If you ask me, which no one has, he was still just a coffee-drinkin' cattle-checker who had more cars—and trucks—and nicer ones than his less-well-married counterparts.)

Will brought just a bit of a chicken-fry-and-mashed-potato belly out of Dee's with him, a toothpick in his mouth, and a sheaf of newspapers folded under one arm. Somethin' had him riled.

"Why, howdy, Will," Daddy said.

"Ethan, you heard?" Will said.

"Heard what?"

"That rascal Shorty Anderson's done it now. He's gone and sold—"

"I know, for a race track."

Will just stared at him, a cock-eyed look on his face. "You know that ain't all," he said.

"What do you mean?" Daddy said.

"Well Ethan, it's gonna have a casino, too."

Daddy looked as if he'd just been cold-cocked with a two-by-four.

"Folks move out here—other folks stay out here—to get away from the city, then they bring the city out here to us," seethed Will, who had brought himself out there from Abilene when he was nearly thirty.

"Well, can they just do it, no matter what folks say?" Daddy said.

Will brandished his newspapers like a saber. "Not if I have anything to say about it—and I do, 'cause I'm on the City Council," he said. "We'll get the schools and the churches and the good folks of the land after this, and we won't *let* it happen. We can't!"

My daddy thought that was a good thing, 'cause he sure didn't have time enough to add fightin' a race track and casino to his pastorin' schedule.

"We've got families and kids to raise around here, and—oh, I've got to fetch Charlie Settle and get to the School Board meetin'," Will exclaimed, lookin' at his watch. "They're talkin' 'bout them crazy new history textbooks again tonight."

He started to hustle away, then turned back. "I swear, Ethan, next thing you know, they're gonna be teachin' our kids we *deserved* to lose at the Alamo."

He walked away some more, then turned back again and pulled out a newspaper for Daddy. "Oh, here's the new paper." Then he did it all again—stoppin' and turnin' that is—this time sayin', "By the way, I know you're partial to coconut cream, but don't leave there today without gettin' a dish o' Dee's apple pie. Best ever. For you, she'll prob'ly tack on an extra scoop o' Blue Bell, no charge." He clutched his stomach in sure-enough pain. "But heed my advice—one piece of pie's enough."

Daddy laughed and said, "Alright Will, thanks for the warning."

He watched as Will made his way across the chugholed street to an old two-story office buildin' fronted with peelin' paint and a sign that said "COTTON PATCH PRESS—THE CONSERVATIVE VOICE."

Meanwhile, the upstairs window of an ancient two-story coffee-colored building across a pot-holed alley from the newspaper office was slit open just a few inches. Smoke billowed from it like a chimney, or chim-i-nee as Paw Paw Gremillion called it. Blinds hung over the glass inside, but someone with a long fat cigar parted them just a shade, looked down toward Daddy for a second, then closed them again.

❊   ❊   ❊

Daddy, Mr. Posey, and portly old Reverend George Washington Carver Jasper stepped through the ashes of Reverend Jasper's church. The name "Macedonia Baptist Church" still shone, faded and splintered, on the singed little wooden sign out by bumpy asphalt country two-lane. No one spoke until a mockingbird cried his protest from a honeysuckle bush not far distant in the otherwise peaceful country setting.

"She was a lovely old church," Reverend Jasper said, low and sorrowful.

Then appeared Mrs. Charles Tollett, "Miz T" to Cotton Patch folks then and now. Miz T—to a little girl like I was back then, Miz T was about the closest thing to . . . well, I reckon her own actions'll show you who she was better than me blabbin' on about her, which

25

I have done to many folks on many occasions. Anyhow, good decade older even than Reverend Jasper, she steered a tricky course with her cane. Reverend Jasper's eyes opened right wide when he saw her. How well, or if, she saw him, I couldn't tell you. Those black sunglasses of hers were about as thick as Jake's and Daisy's winter coats.

"Why Miz Tollett," Reverend Jasper sorta stammered, "I didn't see you."

"Ain't right, ain't right a'tall," said Miz T. Those words she did not speak to anyone one in particular as she meandered through the rubble. "Pastor Ethan, Mr. Posey," she said from behind those black coke bottles, "y'all take off your hats in the Lord's house."

"Yes ma'am," they said, and I promise you, they could not get them off fast enough.

"Pastor Ethan?" Miz T said. "Same folks what burned out the Gomez store?"

"We don't know yet, Miz T," Daddy said.

She caned around another minute or two, then sidled off. "Sorry I am for the—good—folks of this here church," she said.

The men watched as she ambled off down the road on foot.

"You need a ride, Miz T?" Mr. Posey called after.

"She doesn't need a ride, Scott," Daddy said.

"Yes sir, she surely was a lovely old church," Reverend Jasper repeated.

Five

I reckon now's good a time as any to tell you that my daddy had some kinda temper when he got his fire stoked. Bein' the daughter of a pastor, I expect I had enough of a dog in the fight to say we all expect our ministers to be so dad-blamed Godlike and perfect while we all go crazy around 'em that if they're human men at all they must have a mighty fire that boils up in 'em, if they don't kick the dog or beat the wife or somethin', none of which Ethan Shanahan ever did on his worst day.

Now in lookin' back, it wasn't the fire that came to bother me as much as it was that little simmer of his that seemed to keep the embers not outright ablaze, but more aglow, oftener than I like to admit.

Havin' said that, I never saw anything stoke my daddy's fire like that old church bell up top our Cotton Patch Presbyterian Church. Ug-lee it was, rusty and jagged and who knows why it was even still up there. Shoot, the church itself was beauteous, if a might frayed around the edges by time. They built it back in 1925 and those old bricks might've been a little shadowy around the edges, but that building still stood like a rock fortress. The stained glass windows looked alright too, even though they were mostly imitation by then. Withal, it looked just fine on that little corner lot at Bowie and Church Streets, tucked inside a cluster of elms and pecans and, alright, I'll admit it, cottonwoods.

One blazin' hot July day that year it all happened, Daddy was back up there rasslin' with that old rusty church bell like he didn't have a flock in the world to pastor. I swear, he fought that vile hunk o' scrap iron with no less desperation than ole Jacob did that angel, and with even less success.

The long and the short of it was the cussed thing wouldn't ring and hadn't for over 50 years and no matter how lit up my daddy got, he wasn't about to roust it from such a long slumber.

"Ah—this—danged—doggone it," he fumed as he trifled with it. Those were about as profane a words as you'd hear him say. Now occasionally you might catch wind of a few others, but only when he thought no one was in ear shot. Seems as God's the only One sometimes a pastor can be a human bein' around.

When he nearly tumbled off the roof, he slung the bell away and fell hard onto his rear, the sweat just a-drippin' off his tanned face. "Silly, stupid," he sputtered, motionin' out over the dumpy little town. "Why do I get Your stupidest sheep?" Then he huffed and puffed and looked up into the shimmerin' sky, more white than blue. "Are You really there?" he called out. I'm glad I'm not the only one supposedly a respectable Christian who has entertained such thoughts from time to time.

That is when he looked down at the sound of what turned out to be a shiny, loaded new "sport utility vehicle" pullin' up next to the church lawn. Out stepped Clay Cullum, a handsome young man with blue eyes and an olive complexion, the finest pedigrees in shirt, slacks, and Italian shoes, and intoxicating cologne, twenty-four years old. "Pastor Shanahan?" he called up.

"I guess that would be me," my daddy said.

"I'm your new intern, sir," the handsome young SUV driver announced.

Now Daddy hanneled that one a sight better'n I would have. He just stared down at him.

"You're Pastor Ethan Shanahan, right?"

"Well, I didn't order a new intern."

Clay shifted his feet. "Well—hmmph—they sent me."

"Who's they?"

"Presbytery."

"Pres . . ." Daddy mumbled. "That figures."

Then Old Man Taggart thought he would help my daddy out by breakin' into hootin' laughter at the both of them from his front porch swing across patch-riddled little Church Street. Clay shifted some more and blushed this time for good measure.

"Alright, hold your horses," Daddy said. He walked to the roof ladder, glarin' at the bell as he passed it. Downstairs, he shook hands with Clay, then gave him a strange look.

"Clay Cullum, sir," said Clay.

Daddy's eyebrows arched a shade. "Uh-huh. So Presbytery sent you?"

"Yes sir. You don't have to pay me."

"Well that's good, son, sure is, since I can't even pay me."

Old Man Taggart erupted into fresh laughter.

"So what do you—and presbytery—aim to see happen around here, son?" Daddy inquired, doin' his best to ignore Old Man Taggart, who represented a prime example of those folks about whom Daddy had only moments before been disputin' with the Lord up on the roof.

"Well, I want to learn how to be a preacher, sir," Clay said with no apologies.

That seemed just the cue for my daddy to make for his Shivy. "Uh-huh," he said. "Well you come to the wrong place, then."

"What?" Clay said, as though it had been suggested he wasn't his generation's Jonathan Edwards after all.

"You want to learn some pastorin', I expect we can fix you up," Daddy said. "I never seen folks needed more pastorin' than this bunch around here. But you want to impress folks with fancy preachin', then step up to the next biggest church soon as you do, you can just move right along back to Dallas."

"How'd you know I came from Dallas?" Clay said, feelin' less Edwardsian by the moment.

Old Man Taggart howled at this, in order to confirm the sentiment. Clay turned scarlet.

"You ain't never gonna fix that bell, Ethan," Old Man Taggart hollered.

"You got a bell up there?" Clay asked, his manly respect spying an opportunity to reappear. When Daddy nodded, Clay proclaimed, "Well I spent two summers travelin' around fixing them."

Now it was Daddy who blushed, accidentally glancin' the last direction he soon wished he had—right toward Old Man Taggart, who roared with new gales of laughter. Daddy sighed, feelin' licked in more ways than one. "Well, come along to the house then," he said to Clay. "My wife'll want to feed you."

*　　*　　*

Later that evenin', when we were back out on the land, after supper and feedin' the animals and such, Daddy sat in Great-grandma Miller's scuffed old pine rockin' chair like he did ever' night, that old amber lamp of Paw Paw's with the stained shade over his shoulder, and he rocked and he read to me as I lay under the covers.

Many a night I would sit atop the covers as he read, some I would move all about, actin' out the scenes he read. Sometimes, if the story was good enough, I might be inspired to initiate attempts at takin' the book right out've his hands and readin' it aloud myself while I moved about and performed the scenes. Usually, however, that would result in somethin' along the lines of me bein' turned upside down and shook out like a sack of cropped oats into the feedin' trough, leastways up till the time I was about seven.

This particular night as I recall, I was tired and I just lay under the covers in my pajamas, or probably my OU Sooner t-shirt and shorts since it was summer. Course, it could've been the OU shorts and one of my Tweetie Bird t-shirts, maybe the one where Tweetie's standin' there with that big ole yellow head and scowl on his face sayin' "Who asked you?"

Daddy finished his readin' for that night and closed the book. It was one about General Lee, 'cause I remember his rugged handsome face adorning the cover. It was that picture right after the War, the one where his eyes look sorta sad and resigned, but still defiant. I like that picture of him the best. That might've been Flood's book about his last years, the ones in Lexington after the War.

"Did Jeb like Mary Custis?" I asked, my brow furrowed.

"Well, they were friends," Daddy said.

"What about Agnes?" I said. "Wasn't she the prettiest of all General Lee's daughters?"

"Well now, they say Annie was prettiest," he said, "though there's no pictures of her, 'cause she lost that eye when she was little."

"I remember," I said, noddin' but thinkin' really that there was somethin' amiss. "Didn't Jeb like any of them?"

"Well—" Daddy began.

"Y'all say the prayer, Katie, your daddy has company," Mama hollered from the dining table, where she was still sittin' with Clay, who had taken her at her word to eat till he was full. Sakes, poor fella must've had no money to buy food with the last couple days, he ate so much. Least that's what I thought at the time.

Speakin' of time, Daddy looked at his watch and his face corkscrewed up a smidgen. I knew just what he was thinkin'. He had already gone past my bedtime, so as to finish that chapter about Jeb—you know, I guess maybe that wasn't the Flood book about General Lee's last years, because Jeb was gone by then—and he hadn't remembered to do Shorter Catechism with me. Yes! I thought to myself in triumph. No Catechism tonight—thank you Jeb Stuart!

So as not to ruin this run of good luck, I didn't throw a pillow or anything else either at Daddy as he walked out of the room after kissin' me g'night. "Night, Mama!" I did shout.

"Night, baby," came her voice.

"Tomorrow night I get to read," I squeezed out as Daddy made it to the hallway.

*   *   *

Next day, Daddy took Clay on a tour of the Cotton Patch town square, which appeared in those days pretty much as it must've half a century before, except that the buildings were half a century older and more of 'em were empty.

As they walked along the sidewalk, another of our colorful locals, Jefe, jogged by, his tree-trunk thighs causing him to clunk from one foot to the other. He had hair kind've like you see on those old pictures of Geronimo and Sittin' Bull and Stand Watie and those other famous Indian war chiefs, long and dark, down past his shoulders, and muscles like they probably had too. Course, Jefe was a Mexican, not an Indian—excuse me, he was a hispanic, a non-English-speakin' hispanic. Lamar and them ran all the Indians out've Texas way back. Actually, they gave 'em a choice—leave or die. It was the same choice the Comanche and Kiowa had been givin' the Texans. It tended to simplify life much more so than it is now, either for us Texans or the Indians, who are now up in Oklahoma, among other places.

Anyway, Jefe was sportin' that Walkman that seemed to have grown out of him just like his long hair, along with his weightliftin' gloves, various other wrappings and braces, an unbuttoned vest, shorts with strips of leather hanging from them, black socks, and high-topped tennis shoes.

Remember, like I said before, I'm tellin' it to you like it really happened, even if I wasn't there at the time. And this part about Jefe, that's not in the "way it should've been" category, it's in the way it was category, 'cause I'm not at all sure Jefe was anywhere near the way he should've been, him or a passel of other folks in Cotton Patch, includin' quite a few who spoke English, or some Texas variation of it. Some of whom Clay met that very mornin'.

"Mornin', Jefe," Daddy said with a nod. Jefe nodded back as he passed.

Daddy and Clay caught just a glimpse of a bent-over, cane-wielding old man wreathed in cigar smoke, as he ducked into a buildin' up ahead.

"Who's that?" Clay asked.

"Sam Houston 'Shorty' Anderson," my daddy said, "banker, cattleman, oilman, and the richest man in Cotton Patch and maybe the whole county."

Then is when a handsome, strapping young man of seventeen or eighteen, fair-haired, blue-eyed, and a couple inches over six-foot tall, stepped out of the *Cotton Patch Press* newspaper offices and directly into their path.

"Howdy, Jed," said Daddy.

"Hello, sir," said that young man.

"Gettin' interviewed again?" said Daddy.

"All-County team, sir," said the young man, without airs.

"Why I saw you're on the *Morning News* and *Star-Telegram* national blue chip teams," said Daddy.

"Yes sir," said that young man.

"Alright then, we'll be cheerin' Friday night," said Daddy.

"Thank you sir."

Daddy and Clay watched him climb into a dark late model Ford pickup and drive off.

"Jed Schumacher?" Clay blurted.

"Yep," said Daddy. "Season opens this week. Little Cotton Patch takin' on a Dallas team that went to the 5A state championship last year. Pretty much because of Jed."

"Special kid," said Clay.

"Yep," said Daddy.

"Most of the scouting services list him one of the top five senior running backs in the whole country," said Clay.

"Oh, you know your football," Daddy allowed.

"I know OU football too," Clay said, lookin' at him.

Daddy's eyebrows arched a tad. He looked across the street.

"Controversial as that topic can be around these parts," Clay proceeded.

"Let's see what kinda pie Dee's has today," Daddy said, startin' across. "Most folks favor their pecan, and I'll admit it's mighty fine, but I'm somewhat partial to the coconut cream. Hope she made some today."

They did not see the upstairs window of that ancient coffee-colored building slit open again, smoke cascadin' from it. Someone sportin' a cigar—a long, fat one—parted the closed blinds. His beady eyes, wary and alert like a coyote on the hunt, followed Daddy and Clay.

And they could not hear that voice utter, low and growlin': "Mess-kins."

Six

Now if you ever have a hankerin' to figure out if someone's a native Texan, ask 'em what part of the day comes after dinner. You're likely to hear somethin' like "evenin'" or "nighttime" or, for the fanciful or those with airs, "a beautiful sunset."

That's because those folk not native to Texas is a powerful majority, nowadays even among those who live in Texas. In fairness to those other folks, however, without them we would not now have ice hockey or as much in the way of operas or symphonies, and we sure as shootin' wouldn't have anyone to cut the rich folks' grass or to ride your rear bumper, speed, wave the "number one" sign but with the wrong finger, and generally make you miserable on the freeways in Dallas and Houston and elsewhere.

Course, we also wouldn't have a bunch of Christian Republicans favorable to my way of thinkin' on most issues in offices from the state house clear down to the outhouse. However, I tore up my Republican membership card, the plastic one with the elephant on it, years ago, when that wily ole Democrat Bill Clinton started havin' us bomb schoolbuses and hospitals in Serbia and the Republican leaders said we needed to fight a more "ferocious" war than that. I still have not figured out how much more ferocious you can get and still be fifteen thousand feet up in the air, out of range of anti-aircraft fire even if they had any to shoot at you, which they pretty much didn't.

Then when one of our fine "conservative Christian" magazines featured one of those fifteen thousand foot flyboys' picture on its cover and told inside all about what a hero he was, well I just repeated my previous action, the part about tearin' it up and tellin' 'em when they telephoned at supper time that heck no, they wouldn't get any more of my money. And if I wasn't an Old School Presbyterian preacher's daughter, I wouldn't prob'ly have held the line at sayin' "heck."

Anyhow, speakin' of supper brings me back finally to my original point, which was how a real Texan knows good 'n well you don't wait till nighttime to eat dinner, you're sensible enough to eat it when you should, in the middle of the day (which for some folks is later than it is for a real Texan anyhow).

That means it sure isn't evenin' which follows on the heels of dinner, it's afternoon.

And that's the second part of this test. If I asked you when breakfast was, before noon or after noon, what would you say? That's right, before noon. As opposed to after noon. Same goes for when you get off work, or when a Mexican takes his siesta. It's *after* noon, not after *noon*. We just put it together in Texas and we get *after*noon. 'Cause it's after.

You remember that temper of Daddy's I told you about? Well, late that same afternoon he was introducin' Clay to folks around the town square, the thought of that temper was boilin' up in my head like a skyful of black cumulonimbus in August when it ain't rained since May, which is not part of the "how it should've been," it's part of the how it has been way too often around Cotton Patch.

I was never ever supposed to get out on the road myself, but Jake took out after a jack rabbit and Jeb the puppy took after him and I took out after him and next I knew I was out front of the Rodriguezes' a couple hundred yards up Shiloh Road from our front gate. I snatched Jeb the puppy up and turned to head back, noting that Daisy had joined the procession. Jake was off in the woods across the road chasin' his jack.

Then is when I heard shoutin' from the Rodriguezes'. I looked back at their little wooden house. Paw Paw always called it a ramshackle house; I liked that word so much I'd ask him what kind-ly house the Rodriguezes had when he drove me by there, just so I could hear him say "ramshackle" again. It was set back from the road in a grove of elms with some peach and pear trees off to the side.

For some reason, I forgot momentarily about my Daddy's temper boilin' up and I stopped. Jeb the puppy started whimperin' and squirmin' in my arms, and snappin' with his teeth at a fly that was buzzin' around his soft white head. "It's the Rodriguezes arguin' again," I told him.

Except this time they were screamin', worst I'd ever heard 'em. In Spanish too, though they always yelled in Spanish. When you live in Texas—the real Texas, out on the land with the people of the land, not the concrete jungles that ole George Grant calls the "Geography of Nowhere"—you learn some Spanish as you go, even when you're young. And I could tell some more of the words besides, from the Latin Daddy made me learn in home schoolin'.

It was the Rodriguezes I first heard the word "cerveza" from. Even before I knew what it meant, I knew it had to do with bad doin's.

When I heard somethin' break inside there, I took off runnin' like I was that young man Jed Schumacher himself, in a full sprint, outrunnin' all the opposition, ready to run over any of 'em I couldn't outrun. Daisy had to hoof it to catch me, though she was totin' along a hogshead full of Paw Paw's cookin' in that tub belly o' hers. Then Jake caught us, barkin' and stinkin' like he got into somethin' that had no business showin' itself anywhere near Shiloh Road.

I turned onto our gravel entry path and was halfway down it when I decided to stop and walk just like I owned the world, which at that point in my life, livin' out on the land, the only child of Lorena and Ethan Shanahan, lots of animals to boss, I still pretty much thought I did.

When I got close to the house, I saw Daddy through the window, leanin' over and kissin' Mama. I didn't see that so much, I wanted to see it more, but when I saw it right then I felt like I must surely not just own the world, but be the luckiest girl in it. Course us Presbyterians—us real ones, remember, not the watered-down sort—we don't really call it luck, nor fate nor fortune neither. It's Providence, don't you see. Foreordained and predetermined, from before the foundation of the world. Even the black-eyed Susans Jeb the puppy was chawin' on after he'd jumped down.

That'll be another of those questions I ask the Lord if I get the chance. You know, why some folks get mamas and daddies like I got and why some get different sorts, or no sorts a'tall.

I think that is the day I began to think about that.

*   *   *

That Lord's Day that rusty old bell was quiet as usual up on the roof of our church. It wasn't quiet inside, however.

Daddy was baptizin' little Ellie Blevins, but that wasn't what was the commotion. No, it was Ellie's older brothers Ezra, who was five, and Joshua, who was three.

"And I baptize you, Ellie Blevins, in the name of the Father, of the Son, and of the Holy Ghost," my daddy was sayin'.

Ellie was pretty much just starin' at that pretty cream-colored robe and emerald-green stole Daddy wore during worship services. Now as you might expect, a lot of folks in Texas think such trappin's are just for the hoity-toity. But at least some of 'em around Ellis County way know better now, thanks to my daddy.

There's no one you'd less likely catch in anything besides his boots and jeans and hat in normal comin's and goin's. But not during Lord's Day services; and he could tell you how what he wore was not to impress anybody, but that they were the robes of office. He knew his Bible good enough to back it up, too, as I saw him do one day outside Dee's with a certain new young red-headed preacher boy who thought bein' in town for a week was long enough to tell about the big church he was gonna build up on the hill west of town and how if the Presbyterians intended to reach anyone in Cotton Patch they had best start by "meetin' 'em where they are." And that included dressin' like 'em and ever'thing else.

Course that only went so far with young Pastor Fancy Britches, 'cause that Beemer he drove into town wasn't your standard drivin' fare among the trailer parks stretchin' west from Mockingbird Valley along the farm-to-market halfway to Ferris.

He did, however, begin to meet them where they were. One evenin' while my daddy was helpin' crazy young Ricky Sikes out of his wheelchair to change his messy underpants after the two "ladies" who had been helpin' him had got him to cash his welfare check, got him drunk and what-all, then skedaddled from town with the money—to get married we heard later (to each other)—while Daddy was spendin' his Saturday night on that high and mighty plane, Fancy Britches was bringin' the joys of salvation down on the Trinity Bottoms to the 14-year-old daughter of his new church's piano player. That is when I finally figured out how Texas could be maybe the most pro-life, antiabortion state in the country and have about the most abortions of any state in the country at the same time.

I have also figured out along the way that sorta thing happens a lot with folk that hear "The Call" when they're sixteen or seventeen and get themselves "licensed to preach" while they're still in high school— or at least of high school age—but not necessarily attendin' any church themselves, and certainly without the pompous airs it takes to wear any robes of office.

It also happens that they don't tend to then find themselves an honest line of work. They just hang their shingle somewheres else and open 'em up a new branch to sell more of whatever potion it is they are currently peddlin'. But then I hadn't figured all that out, so I was quite amazed when my cousin' Emma in Mississippi told me at a family reunion the next summer how this flashy young fella sportin' a flashy young Beemer had showed up one day, built himself a church overnight, got on the local radio, and all the ladies fell in love with him.

This time, it turns out, he was sparkin' his piano player herself, which turned out not to be so smart, 'cause she had a husband who was a salt of the earth farmboy with no pizzaz but lots of love for her and that she loved and broke down and cried to about it. Well, he did his husbandly duty and he went and he shot Mr. Fancy where his britches should've been.

Now I don't know if that was a legal thing to do in Mississippi— what the good ole boy did, that is—but it darn sure is in Texas. And when that Mississippi prosecutor was insulted that anyone would expect him to do anything more than make sure the County Coroner's report was accurate, I was reminded anew of why Mississippi is one of my favorite states, Hollywood and PBS notwithstandin'.

So while Fancy Britches was pushin' up daisies somewhere around Hope, Arkansas (I might've known that), Daddy was pronouncin' the New Testament Covenantal sign and seal of baptism on little Miss Ellie Blevins. But as I said, it was Ezra and Joshua who flat stole the show that day.

Myself, I was sittin' in my usual seat on the second row, left center. Mama, I believe, was workin' the infant nursery that day. I confess, I and most of the congregation were strugglin' mightily not to look at those crazy little brothers.

Ezra had him a tattered black cowboy hat on, checkered cowboy shirt, red bandana, short pants, and black cowboy boots. He kept tryin' to buck loose from his mother, Mama's friend Sara Lee Schreiner, but his daddy, Dr. (Luke—no foolin') Blevins, corralled him and yanked off his hat. I could barely keep myself quiet, bein' a preacher's daughter and all. Besides, Clay was standin' next to Daddy, holdin' the silver water plate, and I could tell in his eyes he wanted to laugh too.

Meanwhile, little brother Joshua had himself a jacket or blanket or somethin' wrapped around his neck and hangin' down his back like a cape Superman or somebody would wear. He had on Western-style suspenders and was standin' next to Daddy while he held Ellie. Then Joshua and his cape scurried under his mother's long skirt. Dr. Blevins yanked him back out into daylight as the congregation took it all in.

When the baptismal water began to flow off Ellie's bald little head, Joshua held up his hand to catch the trickling liquid. When some of it ricocheted into his face, his mouth commenced to sputterin' so loud that the whole crowd—all 60 or so of us—looked right at him.

When I saw that ole blue twinkle in Daddy's eyes, while he was readin' from the Book of Church Order, I knew if I didn't put my hand over my mouth I was gonna embarrass the whole Shanahan family and that Sunday dinner would be no fun at all that day.

Seven

Our little Handy Dandy "Super" Market in Cotton Patch had some things, mind you, quite a few in fact. The only difference between them and the bigger stores in Dallas and the suburbs was Handy Dandy's didn't carry anything I wanted.

Of course, if they hadn't had five items in their whole store, they would've sold lotto tickets. That's one of the biggest bones my daddy always had to pick with Texas. Oh sure, we usually show up in red on those Presidential scoreboards, and we're known for holdin' to the old ways, the good ways.

But Daddy said way too often we don't hold to 'em, we just hold to 'em a little longer than the next fella. Take sideburns and long hair and all the other zany things the hippy-types did back when Daddy was a kid. Well, he said when that stuff started out in California and New York City and wherever else, Texas mocked it, spit on it, and pronounced it Communistic and downright un-American. Same when those folk started doin' their drugs and their free love and all.

Lo and behold if Texas didn't go and get Communistic and un-American within two or three years. And now, as I said, we're right up there at the top in those categories none of the states want to be at the top of.

Anyhow, we were the same way about all this gamblin' stuff. The usual out-of-state suspects tried for years to get big-time "legalized" gamblin' into Texas and the preachers—W. A. Criswell and the like—stirred up the folks and threw those out-of-staters back out-of-state, where most good Texans would say they belong anyhow.

Then one day Dallas and others decided they should be "cosmopolitan" (all that meant was a dirty magazine when I was growin' up) and "international cities" and the like. And it was downhill from then on. Pretty soon the stores were open on Sunday, the Dallas Cowboys were more popular than church on the Lord's Day, and you had race tracks, slot machines, and lottery games.

Like in Handy Dandy's that Tuesday *after*noon when Daddy and I walked in. Now more often than not, a Texan still knows what's right, even if he doesn't do it. Sorta like ole Dr. Dabney, one of those fellas whose likeness Daddy always kept on the wall in his office, who said the difference between the North and the South in the War for Southern Independence was that the South still believed there was such a thing as original sin.

Perhaps that is why they were sellin' lotto tickets right and left at the checkout counters inside Handy Dandy's while they had signs in their front windows that said "No Track/No Casino/No Way." (Course, I expect a less generous person could suggest darker motives, such as they just didn't want the competition.)

Pretty soon we were standin' in one of the checkout lines. Right there in front of us was a lady plump as the cluster of children shoutin', whinin', hangin', and standin' all about her were skinny. They were blonde, dirty, barefoot, and runny-nosed, too. Meanwhile, she was rummagin' through a purse that was almost as hefty as she was.

"How much you say them Texas Two-Stepper lotto tickets are?" the lady asked.

"Ten dollars each, ma'am," the checkout girl answered.

Then is when that woman emptied her money onto the checkout counter while the line cued up behind us.

"You need two more dollars to have enough for two Texas Two-Steppers and three Lone Star Expresses, ma'am," the checkout girl answered as one of the little boys wiped his nose on his sister's shirt and she started crying. I guess since she was smallest of the five, she didn't have anyone to wipe her nose on.

"Hmm," the lady said, worried a sight more about gettin' those lotto tickets than she was about the line growin' behind her. The seriousness of her dilemma was not lost on her. "Well, if I buy four boxes of Twinkies instead of five, will that be enough?"

"Mama—my ear *still* hurts," said one of her other little boys who didn't know enough to grab his sister's shirt, though my cousin,

42

who mopped the Handy Dandy floors up at night likely would have appreciated if he did.

"Hush, Bobby Jack," the lady said. "We'll be home in a minute and I'll tend to ya, darlin'. Besides, we gonna win enough on tonight's games to buy us the whole drug store if'n we want it," the lady said.

Between all the cigarettes and Mountain Dews and Twinkies and lotto tickets that lady bought, I reckon she could've used a winner.

*   *   *

Cotton Patch has its own City Hall, if you can call it that. It sure wasn't built to hannel all the folks showed up that night for the most important City Council meetin' anyone could remember. The main room, where the council and the like met, and which took up most of the little one-story building, was packed out. They took up all the seats, they stood around the walls, and they sat in the aisle and on the floor up front.

Mr. Posey, my daddy, and his deacons—Dr. Blevins, Carlos Romero and Jim Langtry—sat in a row near the front. Not far away was that Clint Granger. Daddy saw many other familiar faces around the room, too, like Miz T.

Daddy could not think've too many places he'd less rather have been that night. He assayed the collective intelligence of Cotton Patch folks none too highly, but he knew even they weren't stupid enough to go for this foolishness.

But Mr. Posey was fired up for it for some reason and wanted him to go, and Mr. Posey was a good friend, the only elder he had, the biggest financial giver in the church, and he bought Daddy a new suit, ties, and boots when he thought he needed 'em, whether Daddy wanted him to or not.

Two long tables connected to one another ran across the front of the room. There sat Cotton Patch's seven City Council members: Mr. Posey, Reverend Jasper, Will Hankins, Mayor Coltrane, Maria Rivera, Garth Chisholm, and that dashing young black pastor *Doctor* Xavier D. Carter, whom I did hear referred to as "elegant."

43

I found out a long time later that Azusa Street Seminary, from where Doctor Carter received both his master of divinity and his master of theology degrees, was a figment of somebody's—maybe his—mail order imagination. He paid $49.95 for each degree, which were sent him after a, er, female friend of his filled out the tests they mailed him. A few years later, with the advent of the internet, they started e-mailing the tests and degrees. (The internet, it can now be said, has done wonders for what Daddy called the A.E.R.— the American Entrepreneurial Religion.)

I know it always stung my daddy to see sidewinders like that with "Dr." in front of their name, when it was all Daddy could do to get a degree from that Presbyterian seminary of his that gave him the right to put "Reverend" in front of his. They actually expected him to learn the Bible and Greek and Hebrew and what-all there. My Irish gets up when I think how the source of the good Doctor's degrees was not found out till long after he was gone from Cotton Patch and my daddy was too.

Fact of the matter is it was that fancy man that was speakin' right about then.

"So with the greatest respect as always for Mayor Coltrane here, and all he has done to build this town and this county, I say to the financial vultures and big-money men from Dallas and wherever else—take your filthy lucre and your tainted jobs somewhere else!" he thundered.

You'd have thought he was preachin' from his pulpit over at the First Deliverance Tabernacle of God in Christ by the number of amens fired up by that audience, especially Doctor Carter's "loyal parishioners," over 80 percent of which were of the female persuasion. For someone that hated filthy lucre as much as he did, he had one of the nicest collection of drivin' cars I ever saw. Fact, he was the only man in Cotton Patch, at least then, before Dallas came, that had cars you couldn't tell apart from the cars in Dallas. (I don't reckon that red-headed Fancy Britches with the Beemer as havin' stayed long enough to count.)

"Cotton Patch and Ellis County have done exceptionally well without you up to now," Doctor Carter boomed, grabbin' him a chorus of witnesses, "and I expect we'll go on doing exceptionally well, especially once we see your license plates disappearing back up the interstate in a northerly direction."

Well now, that was all she wrote. Our little City Hall meetin' room nigh exploded in clappin', cheerin', and screamin'. Neither Mayor Coltrane's shouts nor his gavel could be heard. And that ole Clint Granger's face was darker'n a Texas Blue Norther in January.

Afterwards, Doctor Carter sashayed out the door, a covey of well-wishers swirlin' about him. A fresh group, again largely of the female variety, lay in wait for him outside, most of 'em dressed just classy enough to be reckoned as church folk, and just trashy enough so's you knew they had a lot more'n Jesus on their mind.

Anyhow, they just cheered and cheered him. He acted real humble, the same sorta humble those Hollywood glamour boys act with crowds of fans when they're really tryin' to impress some pretty lady.

Then Doctor Carter saw Reverend Jasper and he got really really humble, almost hangdog humble. He paused and straightened to his full five-feet-nine inches (includin' three inches of shoe sole), givin' the crowd time to note his hangdoggedness and quiet themselves accordingly. "Words cannot express the sorrow I experienced upon learning the news of the wretched atrocity perpetrated against your dear little church, George," he said, more hangdog and elegant than any present had yet seen him. So humble was he, it seemed it took him a whole minute to get that one sentence out. The only thing longer than the *l*'s he spoke were the *r*'s that rrrolled and rrrippled from deep within him, up through his chest and throat, and out his spearmint-sprayed mouth. "We have already added you to our own church prayer tree."

Actually, I reckon it was good to say such, since most of the folks that used to go to Reverend Jasper's church now went to Doctor Carter's, including most of the classy-trashy ones that didn't have husbands, but did have babies.

"Why thank you, Pastor, thank you, sir," said Reverend Jasper, all solemn-like, wantin' to believe the hangdog and all was real.

As if to settle that matter, a cluster of classy-trashies blurted out, "Ooh—Doctor D! Doctor D! Oooh, ba-by!"

Then a whole new round of applause broke out for the popular, humble servant of the Lord.

It wasn't too far away that Granger and Mayor Coltrane ducked into a long dark Rolls Royce Silver Spur. "That silky-tongued medicine man has been a bur under my saddle ever since he brought his slimy circus to Cotton Patch," he announced in a heartening show of statesmanship.

"We didn't lose nothin' tonight, Ben," that Granger said. "We just learned what we need to do to win."

Why I expect that wily coot already had up his sleeve what he planned to do. Like I said, even if his daddy hadn't learned his lessons from old Galveston, that young master Clint sure enough had, "administrative assistants" and all.

Eight

I expect I'd be in the minority in this day and time in holdin' that livin' in the city comes out way on the short end of the stick in the comparison to livin' in the country. Like I said, your cats won't live as long and the fire ants and buffalo gnats'll chew the socks off you, but at least the sky's lit up at night from the stars and not the Toyota and Ford dealerships and the freeways.

That is how it was one night late near the end of August as Daddy headed down Shiloh Road in his Shivy for home. If it was like a lot of nights, especially those when the moon was full and high, he'd roll the windows down, shut the headlights off, and kind-ly savor the land as he drove, like he would a seasoned slab of venison backstrap or a plate of barbequed quail.

This particular night, I believe he was partakin' of Bob Wills and His Texas Playboys and *San Antonio Rose* on that ole pickup radio. That would not be an unsafe bet, anyhow, since not many evenin's would pass without KBEC spinnin' that selection, and somethin' from Marty Robbins and Merle Haggard and the Man in Black too, as well as Loretta and Tammy and Patsy, lessin' Waxahachie Indian football was on. Remember, they went off the air at 11.

I remember Daddy sayin' one time how Shorty Anderson had told him, back when they were still friends, how he'd seen Bob Wills and His Texas Playboys in person one time, up at the Ritz Theater in Muskogee, Oklahoma, just after the war (as the World War II generation called their "Good" war).

Daddy said Shorty swore to him that back in the '30s and '40s, Bob Wills and His Texas Playboys were ever' bit as popular as the Glenn Millers and Tommy Dorseys townfolk listened to, and even in California. Shorty had said he actually got to meet Bob Wills after the show and he was as nice a fella as you could imagine. Then later he

47

heard he wasn't so nice when he was likkered up, which kind-ly took the place after awhile of him not bein' a star anymore.

Lot of that goin' around still, seems like—the likkered up part.

Speakin' of which, Daddy passed Jose, who was weavin' somewhat on his bicycle, and turned onto the gravel road leadin' to our house. I had had one eye out for that ole pickup for an hour or more, and when I saw it comin', I charged out and flagged him down. "Daddy! Daddy!" I shouted.

"What are you doin' still up?" he said, just as the announcer on the radio said, "Comin' up on eleven p.m. and the end of another broadcast day from KBEC 1390, Waxahachie."

"Daddy, Lucy's in going to foal!" said I, happy for that and happy too to have a bona fide reason to by gosh still be up at 11 P.M. and no way to be in trouble for it.

"Yeh?" Daddy said.

He wheeled off the main gravel path and down the side one that looped around toward the stables behind the house to the east as an owl hooted high up in one of the cedars.

It was a spell later, after midnight when I was in bed, that Doc Gibbs the veterinarian shook his head and stood up in the stable. "I'm sorry Ethan, Lucy's fine, but I couldn't save the little one," said he.

Daddy was quiet for a minute, then his first words were, "This is gonna be awful hard on Katie. It's the third one we've lost like this. Sometimes . . ." Then he lowered his head and shook it real slow-like, and his words just kind-ly trailed off into nothin'.

The next mornin', I knew what it was the second I saw his sad face poke into my room. I shook my head and got real mad at him and ran past him like it was his fault and out the back door, barefoot and all, and as much further as I could get before I caught me a needle thorn in my left heel.

Then is when someone who wasn't a Southern lady would've shouted out the worst word or words she could pull to mind, but since I was saddled with that sometimes weighty legacy, I just sat down and bawled a spell.

Jeb the puppy came up to me then to cheer me up, but he mostly made me just madder at God and ever'body because when he licked me I could tell he had been lickin' the cow's faces again, but at least just their faces.

Like I said, cats don't last long out there and lots else too. It takes a person a while to figure out about those cycles I spoke of to you earlier. But then you know they are comin' sure. They are comin'.

*   *   *

Folks love bein' an expert on Texas, especially if they aren't Texans. There are many ways they can signpost their ignorance, with so little effort they themselves don't even know they've done it.

One way is to become an expert on how backward Texas is on matters of race; that is, skin color. You'd think they already went and printed in the Farmer's Almanac that hispanic Texans hate black ones and black ones hate Asian ones and white Texans hate all the above, as well as certain other whites besides, that hail from Northern latitudes.

Now there is a thing called history for which today's computer-mousin', channel-clickin' folk have a curious empty spot in that portion of their brain God created to hold history facts, and the lessons learned from them.

Since that spot is empty, this worldful of intellectual pygmies would not know of such as the Nueces Strip, the minor difference of opinion the Father of Texas and his eldest son had in 1861, what day were James Fannin and his men murdered, and Cynthia Parker.

If you don't believe me, ask for a show of hands at your next party of who all knows who is Rip Ford. In fact, if you're a Texan yourself and you know who is Rip Ford, raise your own hand and pat yourself on the back. Congratulations, you're one of what those fancy folks at the universities call an "endangered species"—you're a Texan in more than just claim.

For all these reasons and a bunch more, the Texan who is a Texan—of any color—does not give one hootin' h—- how others judge his ways or his history.

Withal, seems to me the best way to hannel that skin color deal is the best way to hannel most things—Christianize the folk, then let them work it out, without the surrogate god up in Washington or wherever buttin' in. Shoot, seems like half the folks I know in Cotton Patch have one white parent and one Mexican—excuse me, hispanic. I should think even the folks out in California might call that good race relations.

Which brings me to Graciela Rodriguez.

*   *   *

Jesus said the Sabbath was made for man and not man for the Sabbath. And I say that as a second-generation Old School Presbyterian who wouldn't go to a movie on Sunday even if there was one that wouldn't curl the scales off a lizard to watch and hear; and I sure don't watch the Dallas Cowboys on Sunday either, even if they're winnin', like they used to do.

Those cows we passed that fall morning headed for church saw it my way too. The two in question were about as excited as I expect you could get grazin' all day on dry grass in a field where the tanks are usually more bleached out than these girly-boy high school football players with their blonde-"tipped" hair. The white boys look even more foolish than the blacks and hispanics when they do it. American males now "tip" their hair blonde and shave their bodies, while American females lift free weights, show off their muscles, curse like sailors, and go fight in our wars. Hmm.

Anyhow, I didn't know what fornicate meant then, still probably couldn't spell it without this fancy "spellcheck" contraption, but I've noticed God didn't make most creatures in the country where they had to know how to spell that word to know how to do it.

Same with the horses and the dogs and the ever'thing else I saw doin' that deal along the way out there. In the country, you see that sorta thing and you know it's normal, it's needed, it's God-blessed. And you don't run sick at your stomach from the whole notion and you don't make a public spectacle out of it either.

Now I expect these city kids that learn of it from the magazines and movies, well no wonder they drive mad and crazy around their freeways all the time.

The next afternoon after Lucy had lost her baby, my daddy pulled his old Shivy up front of the Rodriguezes. Graciela, who was petite and I thought the prettiest lady I'd ever seen around Cotton Patch, met him out in the junk-strewn front yard. Daddy saw the tears streakin' her face. She could not hardly look him in the eye. He doffed his hat like he always did around a lady and like gentlemen and cowboys used to do. "Mornin' Graciela," he said.

Loud snores rumbled out from the house as a mockingbird sounded off from the woods tangled up behind the Rodriguezes. Daddy looked toward the clapboard house, then back at Graciela, whom he noticed was coverin' her mouth with the back of her hand to stifle more sobs.

"Well, alright then," said Daddy.

She led him into the house.

There, Eduardo Rodriguez lay sprawled face down on an ancient tattered couch, flatter'n a centipede on a shady rock. An empty pint of whiskey lay on the floor next the couch and empty beer cans littered the room like corpses on a lost battlefield. In here, his snores were a pain to the ear.

"Eduardo," said Graciela. "Eduardo. Please, dear, you have a visitor."

"Que?" he sputtered. "Que esta?"

When she touched him, he roused to semi-consciousness.

"It is Pastor Ethan," she said. "He is here to—"

"Uh? Que?" he sputtered some more.

When his bloodshot eyes finally focused on Daddy, his legs swung onto the floor and he flew to his feet.

"Eduardo—" she began.

Even though Daddy knew Spanish pretty good, he couldn't tell what all bad Spanish words came flyin' out of Eduardo's mouth then, which is probably a good thing. But for a man who was as asleep as Eduardo must've been to be snorin' loud as he was, he sure seemed to wake up in a hurry, since right when my daddy tried to say something, he whipped out a knife.

"Eduardo!" Graciela shrieked.

Now she was plenty awake, which became obvious real quick, because no matter how much Spanish Daddy knew, he couldn't have told what she was sayin' unless he'd been weaned on the language, I promise you. I guess to make sure ole Eduardo caught her drift, she shouldered her way between him and my daddy and stuck a finger right up into his face.

"I'm leavin'!" Daddy said, raising his hands like you do when it's the better part of valor to surrender and fight another day, or, like in cases such as this one, maybe no day at all. "Just settle down, alright?"

The fire in Eduardo's eyes dulled and the knife just kind of seemed to lower itself, then he slumped back onto the couch. I guess then is when Graciela saw her eight-year-old daughter Blanca, my friend, standin' in a doorway, and realized she had witnessed the whole thing. She pulled her into her arms, then commenced to start a good cry.

That'll be another of those questions I'll ask God when I get up yonder. Why do You let the little children see such as that, and worse besides, like Blanca my friend saw?

Nine

"pitcher" (pi'chxr) *n*.: **1.** *Baseball.* The player who throws the ball from the mound for action by the batter. **2.** Someone who goes out and raises the money for a new real estate deal. **3.** Something you take with a camera.

"picture" (pik'shxr) *n*.: What folks outside Texas call something you take with a camera.

The first time I saw the words was on that hand-carved little wooden sign that hung over the counter of the Cotton Patch General Store. But I saw them a passel of other places too when I was growin' up, so many that I wondered if it came from somewhere in the Bible, or at least the Declaration of Independence or somethin'. I don't think that's near as half-cocked as some of the things I hear people say come from the Declaration.

You could fill a grain silo with the foolheaded things I've heard said in my life in Ellis County, but "Life is too short to spend in Dallas" ain't one of 'em. Neither is "Out here, we don't call 911," carved on a nearby sign that also featured the likeness of a Colts pistol. Just a few feet off to the right of the sign was a life-sized cardboard cutout of John Wayne blazin' away with his six-gun. The Duke guarded the entrance to the back room. There, an enormous Texas flag covered almost the entire rear wall.

Fronting our Lone Star flag, amidst a herd of mounted deer and elk heads, some big as Boone and Crockett 10-pointers, Normie Valentine was pickin' the notes of *I Walk the Line* on his shiny guitar. Sage and mustachioed, Normie was prob'ly the closest thing we ever had around Cotton Patch to our own local troubadour.

A few feet away, his fellow geezers Huey, Newy, and Scooter huddled around the domino table. They were all accomplished cattle-checkers and coffee-drinkers, and Scooter could play a mean breakdown on his fiddle, too. Behind them, ole Arvel Jenkins, the best mechanic in a locale teemin' with mechanics, sat on a packin' crate and guzzled an RC (they must've been out of Big Red and Mountain Dew that day).

Then there was Tater Tatum, on the long side of forty, younger than the others, whittlin' a cedar stick over top a pile of oat sacks.

"Well I be switched. I'm beat deader'n a hammer again," Huey announced.

Newy put an amen to that with a choice tobacco shot that rang into the stained brass spittoon ten feet away.

Then my daddy stepped into the store, kind-ly grimfaced, a load of somethin' under one arm.

"Ethan!" Scooter hollered. "Come own back."

"How's ever-buddy?" Daddy said, noddin' at the Duke as he passed.

"Sit down Ethan," said Scooter. "Huey here's just tellin' us how all-fired good a race track'd be fer us—and he cain't imagine anything this side o' paradise itself good as a true-life casino."

"Would it be like them over to Louisiana, Ethan?" Huey asked.

"Why I expect it would, Huey," Daddy said.

Huey nodded at Newy like he just reeled in a 50-pound channel cat on a 10-pound test line, and Newy rang home another amber missile.

"Hot dog, I knew Ethan'd know," said Huey.

"You reckon we might git us a dog track throwed in as part o' the deal, Ethan?" Tater asked in what, for him, would have to be considered an uncommonly insightful burst.

"Sakes alive, Tater," Scooter objected. "Why Ethan, you'd think he'd be satisfied with his ole cockfights of a Saturday night."

"Whatcha got there, Ethan boy?" Arvel asked, prob'ly since he was through with his RC.

My daddy's face looked like it did last time he saw Mama serve up brussels sprouts for supper, which she loved and he couldn't tolerate.

He cleared his throat and his face kind-ly twitched a mite. "Aimed to put up one o' these 'No Track, No Casino, No Way' flyers here if you'd oblige me," he said, pullin' one from the wad under his arm.

"Heck Ethan, Cody up there owns the place," Scooter said, eyein' his dominoes.

"Well, he said ask you boys and whatever you said's fine with him," Daddy said, sorta quiet.

"Where them casino boys from, Ethan?" Newy asked with his first words of the conversation and his most important of the day.

"They from Dallas?" Scooter asked, suspicion on the edge of his voice.

All Daddy did then was kind-ly arch his eyebrows a tad. I guess that must've been part of that secret domino language I never could figure out; those fellas seemed to say more around there with fewer words than anyone I ever saw.

"H--- yeah put it up, Ethan. Put 'em up all over Cotton Patch," Huey pretty much shouted, seemin' to forget that just a minute before he was boastin' about a casino.

"Shoot yow, Ethan. Gimme a wad o' them to put up for ye," Tater said, gettin' up for the first time from his pile of oats. Guess he forgot about his dog track.

Arvel cackled out loud and put his old straw hat on to leave. Even though he never opened his mouth wide enough when he cackled so's you could see where-all he had teeth missin', you still knew he was laughin'.

None of 'em knew it was Mr. Posey raised cane for all our church officers, even my daddy, to take flyers around like that. Daddy had thought about just throwin' his bunch in a trash can, but he'd learned the hard way, and often, that Scripture about bein' careful to be a teacher in church 'cause you're held to a higher standard by God. So he figured if he pitched those flyers, sure enough someone'd see him do it or find the flyers or somethin', just like the time he caught him a ticket for speedin' in front of his own church and that ole biddy Mrs. Sanders, who always sat right up there on the front row with her blue bird's-nest hair-do, God rest her soul, saw him and reported it to the deacons.

Meanwhile, Newy racked up his loudest ring yet just before he grabbed his own handful of flyers. Right then, Normie shifted over to *Turkey in the Straw,* as if to celebrate. Hangin' one on the cityfolk'll do that for a country boy.

*   *   *

One of the many benefits my daddy occasionally mentioned about livin' in the country was that when you heard gunshots, you knew it wasn't a crime bein' committed, but people were shootin' maybe at jackrabbits, squirrels, or flyin' game, or even a careless coyote, and prob'ly at things like pumpkins or scarecrows or dirt or the occasional signpost. (The quickest I ever saw anything catch a load of buckshot was when they put up the new "Drive Friendly—the Texas Way" sign out on the interstate.)

I guess the liberals would say it is all part of that "Southern Gun Culture."

We had two straight days of rain that summer heavy enough it washed out the levee over by Witherspoon Bottoms, between us and Cotton Patch. That rain sat on the farmers' maize for nearly two weeks, so the farmers got to replant their maize. That is why the maize was high and red and ready for harvest not in June or July, but one early September day when Daddy was ridin' Annie Lee down Shiloh Road and I was ridin' Billy our sometimes-obedient shetland. I was scannin' the hill to our right when I spotted it. "There's one, Daddy!"

"Yep," he said.

"There's another!" I shouted. I had seen a lot of critters out there, but I had only ever seen llamas at the State Fair in Dallas, until the two I saw now munchin' away on bermuda and Johnson grass up that hill. They led me right into my next question. "Are all rich folks divorced, Daddy?"

"No, Pookie. Why'd you ask that?"

"Well, Mama said the lady doctor who owns the llamas is," I said. "And the lawyers who own the big red house with the white columns are too."

Right about then we crested a gentle rise that gave us one eye-opening view of the Trinity River Valley. I wouldn't want to know the menu for the catfish that lived in that river (if any still lived there), but the bottomland spreadin' out from it was sure enough able to take your breath away certain times of the year, such as the time we were lookin' at it then. In the spring, though, the Lord laid a carpet of bluebonnets down that started up where we were, at the bob-wire, and spread clear to the bottoms. Now that was a sight, even for country folk.

The only thing kept it from bein' a pitcher good as Eden itself was that ole tractor stuck down there, right in the middle it all.

"Old Man Harper's tractor gets rustier ever' year, doesn't it, Daddy?" I observed.

Guess I got the Eden idea from Daddy, 'cause he used to call that tractor the "Sin" tractor. He said it marred the otherwise-perfect beauty of that valley just like their sin ruined the perfect beauty of Adam and Eve and their garden and all us that came after.

It was those cycles got to Old Man Harper. One year he got the bright idea to plant potatoes down there in that bottom land. Well, so many came up he couldn't get 'em all out of the ground, thousands of 'em—leastwise accordin' to Paw Paw's method of calculatin'—small as marbles almost. Then he tried it again the next year and he got his tractor stuck before he could even get 'em planted, then a three-month drought and sixty straight hundred-degree days cooked the ground brown anyway, even in the bottoms.

Like I said, it's still a hard land, Texas is, though you wouldn't know that just drivin' from your house in the suburbs to your neighborhood WorldMart Super Grocer.

"What are those lights way over yonder you can see from the house at night?" I asked, motionin' across the valley which separated us from Kaufman County.

"I expect that's Scurry and Rosser," he said.

"Are those towns?"

"Yes."

"How far away are they?"

"Oh, I reckon from our place, eight or ten miles as the crow flies," he said.

"And we can see their lights at night?" I said. "I mean, they sorta twinkle like little stars and such."

"Well, we're on high ground, highest in the county," he explained. "Paw Paw had it checked with the A & M folks when he first moved out here over forty years ago. It's one reason we don't get as many snakes as some folks. There's nothin' between us and those little towns but farms and the Trinity Valley."

"How far is the closest town to us this side of the river?" I asked.

"Course, Cotton Patch, but Bristol's 'bout the same distance south of here, but it isn't a town," he said. "Then there's India and Ferris and Palmer. And Crisp, where Ernest Tubb was born. But Crisp isn't really a town either. Course, neither is India."

"There's a lot of places around here that aren't really towns, aren't there?"

"The country still carries over more from the old days than the city," he said. "And in the old days, most folks, leastways around here, got along fine without a lotta towns."

"Daddy, are all rich folks mean?" I asked, pressing right on from my line of llama questioning.

"No—" he started.

"Take that Shorty Anderson," I said, my mouth as usual workin' faster than my ears. "Why does he hate you, Daddy?"

"Ah, he don't hate me, darlin'."

"Doesn't, Daddy," I pointed out, "he *doesn't* hate you. Well he sure acts rude when we see him."

"Shorty's family helped found our church," Daddy said.

"They did?" was what I said, but it was a pretty wimpy sign of what I was thinkin', which was somethin' along the lines of how I would've quicker expected those two llamas to have started that church than kith or kin of Shorty Anderson.

"That's right," Daddy said, noddin' and lookin' out over the valley. "Shorty grew up in it, and, well, for different reasons, he was always friends with the pastors the church had. When I came on, he was real friendly and he gave me this expensive new car."

"Was that 'cause he fancied you or 'cause he thought if he was nice you'd do what he wanted?" I asked.

"Little bug, you definitely got your brains from your Mama's side of the family," Daddy said, a half-smile bringin' out the crow's-feet around his eyes. "Well, I was young and way too proud and I sold the car to help us pay the church's bills and feed some folks down in Peru after an earthquake."

"You did?"

A longhorn steer mooed from a pasture in the valley down below. I realized the wind must be blowin' from the southeast, toward the Gulf, which made me wonder if weather was comin'. You could've never heard a steer from down there otherwise.

I noticed Daddy glancin' at the sky toward the southeast too, which made me feel even smarter than I already did. "Anyhow, Shorty got real upset," he went on, "and I reckon he had cause to be. But he tried to get me removed as pastor and that didn't go with Presbytery, so he left our church and hasn't set foot in any church since so far as I know."

"Do you like the Presbytery, Daddy?" When he talked about those fellas around me, it was usually good, but when he talked about 'em when he didn't know I heard, it was usually bad. I had already learned that what folks, even daddies, say when you're not around is more what they think.

"Well," he sorta stammered, "there's some good men on there, and some good friends, too."

I kept in mind that he was sayin' these things right to me, so he clearly knew I could hear what he was sayin', when I allowed, "What does man-pleaser mean, Daddy?"

"Man-pleaser?"

"Yes sir, man-pleaser," I said. "I overheard you tellin' Mr. Posey one night on the phone when I was in bed but couldn't sleep that the Presbytery was 'nothin' but a bunch o' man-pleasers.'"

I'm pretty sure he kind-ly blushed a shade on that one, which told me that he must have really thought those Presbytery fellas were man-pleasers, because I hardly ever remember my daddy blushin' the whole time I grew up.

"Well, first of all, man-pleaser means someone who is more concerned about sayin' or doin' what will make him look good with folks, as opposed to with God," he said, pushin' his straw Stetson up off his forehead a nudge. "And second, I shouldn't have said that, even in private—which I thought I was, Nutmeg."

Then it was my turn to blush, with the look he gave me with those blue eyes, which sorta lit up like that sometimes in a queer way that made them seem almost like they'd been plugged into an electrical current or somethin'.

Nutmeg, you see, was one of those silly names he always called me which neither he nor I ever had any notion whence they came. They just seemed to strike his fancy when he heard one of them as somehow capturin' the sense of what he thought I was, I guess. Nutmeg and Pookie and Puppet and Bird and Little Bug, and even Mutthead—and Headmutt, when I complained about Mutthead.

Sometimes now, even when things are pretty fine, all tolled, I wish so bad I could hear one of those words that I feel like cryin' if folks are around, and sometimes I even do cry if folks aren't.

Anyhow, lotta times what your daddy says to you with his first fleeting expression or reaction to a question tells you all you were askin', and sometimes even more. Not that the words which follow aren't important, but once you know ever'thing is still okay, you can commence to plannin' ahead for your next statement, which in this case, overlookin' the Trinity River Valley that day with the hint of weather in the air was, "Daddy, can we ride over and look at the emus?"

Ten

I expect that was the most pickups and cars parked at the Cotton Patch Presbyterian Church since the old days, when folks in the country still cottoned to covenants and creeds, and confessions and catechisms.

In case you didn't know, all those good "C" words help protect us from ourselves. It's good to be reminded that Christ was "Begotten, not made" and He "descended into hell," and that God created all things of nothin' "in the space of six days"—morning-and-evening, 24-hour days, just like ole Moses said, not days that last "ages" or "epochs" or have those between them or make up some sort of "literary framework." It keeps men, includin' smart theologians, from bringin' their fashionable innovations to God's Word.

Anyhow, the pickups and cars stretched both sides of chug-holed Church Street for blocks, and ever' other street near the church too.

It seemed Jefe was the only one in town not packed into our sanctuary that night, and he must've thought about that as he jogged past all those pickups and cars.

Mr. Posey had shown up half an hour late at Dr. Blevins's for a root canal and that made them about the last two to get to the church. They hustled up the scuffed old steps as cheerin' sounded from inside, which is not somethin' you hear ever' day at a Presbyterian church of the Old School.

"Zig Ziglar's the greatest motivational speaker in the country," Mr. Posey huffed as they got to the door. "I saw him once at Reunion Arena in Dallas. There were twenty thousand people there. It turned my whole career around."

"He's a fine Christian man, too, they say," Dr. Blevins said.

Inside, ever' seat and ever' foot of standin' space was covered with folks, includin' the balcony, which was usually roped off. Miz T sat right up front, not far from some of the city councilmen—Will Hankins, Garth Chisholm, and Reverend Jasper. I reckon they were there, along with Mr. Posey, to show the leaders believed the same as the folks and would vote accordingly.

"These folks have stuck a friendly-soundin' name on this bidness," said Zig Ziglar. "They don't even call it gamblin'; they call it gamin'. Well, let me tell you what kind of game you'll have if you let this into your town."

Now if you never heard Zig Ziglar talk, you need to get one of his tapes. I liked hearin' him say just about anything, but when that deep rollin' voice said he was from Yaa-zzooo City, Mis-sis-sip-pi, I expect the Lord Himself, with a voice like the sound of many rushin' waters, couldn't have bested ole Zig by much.

I loved to hear him talk about his "Redhead" too, even though if you've ever seen a pitcher of her, she didn't look like just any redhead, she looked like she prob'ly stopped quite a bit of traffic before she stopped ole Zig dead in his tracks for the next 50 years or so of their lives.

I heard somebody say once Zig had a voice that was "mellifluous." That's right, mellifluous. I would love to have heard Zig Ziglar say that word, mellifluous. His voice seemed to me like it could've churned butter or melted it, I'm not sure which. Maybe it could've done both.

But on this night, Zig was in to talk about one of the other many subjects besides Yazoo City and the Redhead that he was an expert on, and that was the ills and evils of that Great American Pastime and favorite sport of the American people, gamblin'. First he got ever'body to laughin' like he could do, whether it was a group of muckety-mucks on Wall Street or a bunch o' fellas who had more fishin' poles than ties and no suit coats at all prob'ly. Which was more along the lines of what we had that night, and any other time, at the Cotton Patch Presbyterian Church.

By the time Mr. Posey and Dr. Blevins arrived, however, Zig, in the finest Southern Baptist tradition, had made the folks laugh, then he had made them nearly cry, and now he was in the process of firin' 'em up to go to war.

"You let this in here and you'll have the sort of game four million Americans were addicted to 10 years ago—and twice that many are today," he continued. "Look around you. With a crowd this size, I can virtually guarantee you someone in this sanctuary, maybe right next to you, already has a gamblin' problem—and someone else will if you let this thing in.

"But it's just me I'm hurtin', you might say," he said with a smile and a shrug. "Oh? This is the sort of game whose addicts—that several million I mentioned a moment ago—average $75,000 in debt apiece they don't pay their neighbors and friends and service providers—and families. The sort that includes over one million high school addicts and over 600,000 college students. The sort whose addicts are 100 times as likely as the average American to commit suicide—and whose wives are 50 times as likely to do so."

Now that ole rustic voice that had influenced millions began to rise. "So it's just you you're hurtin', you say. Take a look around at the children in this room. Those boys and girls unfortunate enough to have a compulsive gambler for a parent—now or if you lay down for this—are more likely to abuse drugs, alcohol, and tobacco, to have a broken home, an unhappy childhood and teenage years, a poor self image, get into trouble with the law, regularly experience anxiety, depression, and feelings of insecurity, and perform poorly in school and employment."

Zig Ziglar's words crashed on like cracking thunder. "Demand—yes, demand!—that your elected officials say no to this poison." Then his voice dropped right down. "But most importantly, we Christians need to humble ourselves before Almighty God, and call upon Him to heal our land."

The crowd, especially Miz T and some of the other black folks, erupted, if you will, in applause, of the sort the respected writers call "sustained."

"Yes!" Miz T shouted. "That's right! Amen!" Such Presbyterian rules as might apply to this sort o' demonstratin' did not seem to be in effect that night, as I even saw Daddy let loose a holler or two.

That surprised me, 'cause he was none too pleased to be havin' this hoedown at our church, no offense to Zig Ziglar, whom he liked. He kept tryin' to ignore it and tend to his own knittin', but this pesky gamblin' deal just wouldn't seem to leave my daddy alone. Problem tonight was the other churches around town. One of the Baptist pastors was laid up a with a bad heart and another "called" to a bigger, richer church in Fort Worth. The Church of Christ minister was seventy-five-years old and had just retired. A couple the other churches seemed kind-ly shy about where they even stood on the whole issue, and most of the others were too small to hold any crowd, especially a Zig Ziglar-sized crowd.

So here my daddy was, feelin' like he had nothin' to do with what was goin' on in his own church, and big goin's-on they were, too.

It's been many and many a year now, and I don't remember exactly how he said it, but right at the end of that wonderful speechifyin', Zig Ziglar stopped and I swear he looked right at me and he said somethin' like, "You children here, if you remember anything else I say tonight, even 50 years from now, remember that it's not what's popular is right, but what's pleasin' to the Lord."

Maybe all the other children felt like he was lookin' right at them too, but anyhow, it made me realize again how smart and wise was my daddy, even though I knew that already.

*　　*　　*

I meant to tell you before about Jumpy, but I've got to now, because here is where he jumps smack into my story. I never did find out what other sorts of names he had, and I even asked Mama and Daddy and Paw Paw too. I expect somewhere along the way, I asked just about ever' grown-up I knew well enough in Cotton Patch to ask such a question. Especially after I learned the part he played in what-all happened out there durin' those days. And not a soul, leastwise that I ever talked to, knew any name for him but Jumpy. Someone said once that's all they put on his headstone in the cemetery up on Bluebonnet Hill, but I never could find where he was laid, even though I looked.

I do know that happiness in life for Jumpy was crouchin' and pickin' his wiry little body through the brush, his .22 at the ready, a pack of coyotes howling in the distance if it was late, a buzzard or crow or hawk soarin' overhead if it wasn't.

But Jumpy didn't tote that .22 for anything but squirrels. There was somethin' about squirrels that completed the happiness pitcher for Jumpy.

It was the mornin' after Daddy and I took our ride over to the Trinity Valley that Jumpy got out after the squirrels right early. I don't know if the squirrels had gotten onto Jumpy or what, but he hadn't been able to shoot anything to save his hide. I guess that's why that particular Sabbath mornin' he was out in the brush while the moon was still higher and brighter than the dawn.

"I know you out here somewhere Mr. Squirrel," he kind-ly whispered as he came to a clearin' out a ways from Cotton Patch near the Bristol Road. What he saw beyond that clearin' wasn't any squirrel, though; it was two fellas hoppin' into a pickup Jumpy figured couldn't be much greener than himself, and he was prob'ly at that point in his late 40s.

Tires screechin', off they sped—just as the Hitchin' Rail Convenience Store not far from 'em burst into flames. At that particular point in time, happiness for Jumpy had nothin' whatsoever to do with squirrels and ever'thing in the world to do with hot-footin' it back through those woods fast as only an innocent black man in the South could away from the scene of the crime.

*   *   *

Now you may know that, for better or worse, Texans love their football, and it may surprise you to know they especially love their high school football—only thing comes close to it for most folks is when the Cowboys are winnin' and winnin' big.

A Texas athlete—or his coach or parent—can be a dangerous critter to tangle with. And that includes us of the professin'-Christian sort. After all, we'll pray, and sometimes play, like we indeed have the might of the Lord on our side, ready to smite you up 'side the head—and if you get in our way, especially if you've got the audacity to consider yourself as the good guy in the battle, we're just liable to bloody your nose for you in our righteous anger!

At least the small town guv'ment schools in Texas, filled with professin' Christians, make no bones about it. Their goal is to beat the h--- out of you every year. If they can "hang a half a hunnerd on ya" as ole Coach Switzer used to tell Daddy and his teammates in college to do, they'll do it.

I guess it all helps prepare Texans to carry on our proud, hard-earned legacy of the last century-and-a-half, that of bein' the most fierce warriors—in word and deed—of any state in America whenver the country gets into another of her many wars. Yessir, whether it's Mexicans, Yankees, Indians, Germans, Japanese, Commies, or Iraqis, there is nobody more eager, or able, to kick the stuffin' out of whoever we're told needs killin' than a Texan.

So we had our placards that said "Beat Dallas" on all the store windows. And we wrote "Go Farmers!" with shoe polish on the back windshields of all our pickup trucks and cars. And we hung our banners across potholed Main Street that said "Go Farmers—Beat Wolves."

We did all that the day Dallas High School came to play Cotton Patch with that young man Jed Schumacher, and I helped, even though Mama and Daddy wouldn't let me ride the yellow school bus up Shiloh Road to the guv'ment school, but home schooled me instead.

If you thought the church was full for Zig Ziglar, you should've seen the stadium that September night when the chill hadn't come to the late evenin' air yet, even out in the country, which they built the stadium right in the middle of, east of town, and before buildin's full of people started blowin' up—at least buildin's full of our people.

Ever' seat in the stands on both sides of the field was taken, and so were all those in the portable stands they'd set up around both end zones. And the folks stood six deep on both sidelines beyond the areas reserved for the teams. Ever'body else just parked their pickups and cars outside and stood or sat on their hoods or roofs and tried to catch a glimpse of the field.

The Dallas folks filled the stands on one side, but the rest was pretty much the whole town of Cotton Patch, and the folks out around it. We knew they had a huge band, so this one time, Cotton Patch had let ever' kid in town—high school, junior high, and even grade school—that could play a note on any instrument fancier than a washboard, play in the school (or more truthfully, town) band. I think if we could've gotten a piano out there, Daddy would've let me join in too.

I kind-ly think the town fathers figured we would lose the game, but they weren't about to let some big cocky Dallas school come in and rub it in by drownin' us out in the stands while they were blowin' us out on the field. Anyhow, our "town band" made up for what it lacked in harmony by crankin' up such a volume you couldn't tell if the Dallas band (or, truth be known, our band either) was playin' the school fight song or *Waltz Across Texas.*

You could say it was the kind of game high school football and Friday nights in Texas are all about. And you could say it was one brutal spectacle of spilt blood and broken bone. Country boys and small town kids—white, brown, and black—gettin' to grips with a bunch of big city kids, many from the inner city, from two schools as different in culture and style as they were in size.

With three minutes left in the game, three players from each team had left the game for the night with injuries, one each by ambulance. And that funny ole scoreboard with the two lights that never worked where our score was said Cotton Patch 6, Visitors 19 and the Visitors had the ball at midfield. That young man Jed Schumacher, Number 33, had run for over a hundred yards and a touchdown and he'd made 15 tackles from his middle linebacker spot, but Dallas had more players, more good players, and almost all of them played either offense or defense, whereas most of Cotton Patch's best players had to go both ways.

So, they had kind-ly worn down the ole home town boys, and they had scored two touchdowns in the fourth quarter to break open a diamond-hard contest. Still, I thought Cotton Patch's cheerleaders had it all over Dallas's—and the gyrations those Dallas girls were goin' through I'm sure confirmed for more than one Cotton Patch fan that they sure as heck didn't want Dallas in Ellis County. (Maybe some of the Cotton Patch high school boys would've taken exception to that statement.)

Otis McKay was Cotton Patch's head coach, as he had been for more than a decade, since he became the first black man to hold the position. He'd surprised a lot of folks by winnin' four bi-district championships, three area ones, and two regionals during that stretch.

Of somewhat less merit, at least in the eyes of the town fathers, Coach McKay had gone about the quiet business of guidin' many a young man in more ways than how to become a good football player. That didn't grab him nearly as many headlines on the sports page as the other, and it cinched up his job security exactly nothin', but it sure made business more dull for the graveyard shift of Cotton Patch's little police department, and it hurt beer sales at Mauldin's Hop and Bop out on the river road.

Though no one prob'ly noticed, it was also the reason the grade point average of graduatin' seniors from the high school had snuck up nearly half a grade point in that ten years. With an average of 60 graduates each year, helpin' half a dozen or so of 'em make As and Bs instead of Ds and Fs, plus influencin' others not on the team to do the same'll do that after a long enough spell.

Even though they weren't of our exact theological stripe, when Daddy noticed the third one of Coach McKay's former troublemakers come back after gettin' his college degree and either help start a new church in the area or work on the staff of an existing one, why he knew for sure Coach McKay was cookin' up somethin' out of the ordinary in his stewpot. And even though Coach McKay wasn't a Christian man, at that time at least, Daddy became one of his biggest supporters, quite a bit more so than he was the Baptist deacon who was Coach McKay's head assistant. That man dumped his wife of 20 years and four kids to take a new position with a big high school in San Antone, and a new 19-year-old girlfriend too with lots of blonde hair that wasn't really blonde, and diamonds and blue eyes that weren't real either.

Three years before, they had even named Coach McKay athletic director, though more than one decent man on that school board had to fight down honest concerns in his own heart as to whether this meant Cotton Patch would have any more white boys start at quarterback. To their surprise, and relief, it didn't mean that any more after Coach McKay became A.D. than it did before. He was, after all, a partisan of the run-and-shoot and I think he had him maybe two black startin' quarterbacks the whole 27 years he coached Cotton Patch.

This particular year, Bubba Coltrane, son of Mayor Coltrane, called signals, but it had nothin' to do with politics. Bubba quarterbacked more winnin' games from 7th-12th grade than any other boy that ever went all the way through Cotton Patch schools.

And though he was a demon in the weight room and had grit enough to qualify with the armchair quarterbacks as a player with true "character," the main reason he won all those games was he had the good fortune to be in the same graduating class, and backfield, as that young man Jed Schumacher.

So there we all were, me sittin' in the stands with my friend Blanca Rodriguez, my daddy and Clay Cullum close by, and just three minutes left in the game and us down by two touchdowns. Coach McKay had his headphones on and his clipboard in hand, and he was shoutin' at coaches, runnin' players in and out, and not about to go down in this one without a whimper.

That was about as excited as I had ever seen Cotton Patch folks get at a football game, and I had seen them get pretty excited. My daddy was about the only one who wasn't. I saw him askin' Clay what time was it—my daddy couldn't keep a watch to save him—and I remembered he had come to the game from the hospital in Ennis, where Mrs. Jennings was on her last leg, and that I had heard him tell Mama he needed to go see Mr. Wright, because his wife had kicked him out of the house for comin' in late all the time.

And so, with the smell of popcorn, Ellis County pastures, and town pride fillin' the air, that young man lined up at middle linebacker for Cotton Patch and he had blood you couldn't see on his green jersey and blood on his yellow pants you could. I remember Dallas was big, big, and they were cool and calm, too. They didn't seem ever to make any mistakes, they just kept comin' right at you, and they made you pay for any little mistake you made.

The Dallas quarterback turned to hand the ball to that big bowlin' ball runnin' back of theirs, and then is when somehow, in a way I know makes no sense and prob'ly wasn't true anyway, but maybe was a little, it was like our boys on defense weren't just fightin' to hold off another football team, but they were fightin' for somethin' more; maybe we couldn't keep Dallas out of Cotton Patch, but maybe we could just a little by showin' 'em we could take the best they had to dish out and give it right back to 'em, and whether or not they took us over, we would know and they would know we would never like it or agree to it one d----- bit.

And so I saw that young man blitz right through 'em all, up the middle, shimmyin' his way between two big Dallas linemen, and they couldn't lay a hand on him, and he mauled both the quarterback and the bowlin' ball runnin' back to the ground. When the ball spurted free and Isaiah Brown, the fastest player on our team except maybe for that young man, scooped it up and started to run, I felt this deep strong desperate feelin' that I knew I shouldn't have and my daddy's teachin's had taught me I shouldn't for anything besides the things of the Lord but I couldn't help it and I was standin' up and screamin' with ever'one else and beggin' God to let Isaiah, who never had a mama or daddy that loved him but had Coach McKay that did, score a touchdown, which he did.

We were screamin' still and the band was tryin' to stop screamin' long enough to play the school fight song and the cheerleaders were all cryin' and huggin' each other still when that young man kicked the extra point and that funny ole scoreboard with the two lights that never worked where our score was said Cotton Patch 13, Visitors 19 with 2:20 remaining in the game.

But there was another dust-up goin' on that no one saw yet. That was between Blanca's daddy and Hubert Gore, a yucky fella I'd seen around town. He had a buzz-top painted yellow and tattoos on his arm. They were havin' one whale of a drunk argument down on the ground at the end of the stands off to our left.

When Dallas got the ball back, they kept runnin' their human bowlin' ball up the middle and that young man and the Cotton Patch defense kept stuffin' him and then callin' time outs.

I heard some ill-bred little girl screechin', "Go Cotton Patch— whoaa-wheee!" It was only when I caught my daddy's look that I realized it must've been me. When that young man hit the human bowlin' ball so hard on third down that it knocked his black Dallas helmet off, I guess it was me that shrieked loud enough that despite all the folks screamin' around me, Daddy kind-ly squinted his eyes at the sound of me, I was so loud. I'm sure if Mama had been there, she would've said, "Don't do that, you'll ruin your singin' voice, God only gave you one!"

I guess Dallas must've punted it back to us, because we had the ball again, way down the field. They even had great punters on that team.

"Come on Bubba, let's go, buddy!" I heard Mayor Coltrane shout.

Down on the sideline, Coach McKay shouted, "Coltrane!" and he collared Bubba and gave him orders, then slapped him on the rump as he ran back onto the field.

"Come on, Jed baby!" someone yelled.

"Let's go, Jed baby!" another one hollered.

"Come on let's go, baby Jed!" I screamed, half out of my young mind and not realizin' why my daddy let slip a bit of a grin on that one.

The Cotton Patch cheerleaders started a crowd chant and foot stomp. "Far-mers! Far-mers! Far-mers!"

It got really scary after that, because the Dallas defense was kindly stampedin' over our offensive line and Bubba nor even that young man could go anywhere, and they were knockin' Isaiah Brown flat before he could even get into his receivin' route.

Pretty soon, it was fourth down and there were almost as many yards for Cotton Patch to go for a first down as there were seconds of time left up on that funny ole scoreboard with the two lights that never worked. And we were lined up "in the shadow of our own end zone" as I used to hear the OU football radio announcers say.

I couldn't scream anymore (I think I'd already ruined my singin' voice, and time has proven that God did indeed only give me one), but ever'one else in sight was beside themselves, the Cotton Patch folk tryin' to hold it down when they saw Bubba raise his hands for quiet. Right then, that rude Dallas band in their ugly orange and black—I figured them comin' to town made for an early Halloween anyway— started playin' the craziest loudest song they had all night. If I could muster a better word than "song" I would, 'cause it sure didn't sound like any music I had ever heard before.

Just before our big center, Maria Rivera's son Tony, snapped the ball, with the clock runnin' down from 15 seconds, I saw Mr. Rodriguez and that yucky Hubert Gore layin' hands on each other, and it wasn't like that lady pastor at the pew-jumpin', aisle-sprintin' Holiness church on the farm-to-market did it to her folk, either.

When ever'body screamed, I looked back at the game. They were hittin' so hard I could hear some of it over all the crowd noise. Bubba pitched the ball to that young man, who juked one tackler way in the backfield, then Bubba cut another down at the knees.

Then is when kind of a tidal wave of noise just sorta rumbled up from the crowd as that young man outlegged two more Dallas boys to the sideline, then turned upfield and set sail right past us like Annie Lee gallopin' across the pasture on a crisp winter mornin'.

One Dallas player set right in his path and I heard Mr. Goodnight fire the shotgun that said time was out. But that young man just raised his knees and ran right over the defender. For some reason, when this happened I chanced to look over at my daddy, right when he finally stood up. I guess the sheer spectacle of it had finally gripped him, even though he just stared at what was happenin', but his face turned kindly crimson.

Then another Dallas player dived for that young man, who nearly broke the fella's neck with a stiff-arm the likes of which I never saw before or since. Two more players chased him all the way to the end zone, but they never got close. I had never seen Number 33 run like that before, and I had seen him run plenty.

As the stands and parkin' lot and ever'thing else emptied onto the field, I looked over at my daddy again. He was just starin' at the field. I think he knew he had witnessed somethin' special. I must've been jumpin' and screamin' and the like, because Blanca and I were huggin' and holdin' each other until she noticed the ruckus down at the end of the stands, where a cowboy-hatted deputy was draggin' her daddy away.

That young man kicked the winnin' point through the uprights so hard the ball hit that funny ole scoreboard with the two lights that never worked where our score was. But I noticed when the numbers changed to Cotton Patch 20, Visitors 19, those two lights startin' workin', and they have ever since.

The town had ever'one in a Cotton Patch uniform up on their shoulders and that scary-lookin' Halloween band played not a note, they just stood there with the rest of Dallas and stared like they couldn't believe Cotton Patch had the nerve to up and smite 'em down and hold 'em back at least for a night. Then I remembered Blanca and turned back to her. She just stood there, her head hangin' down. I put my arm around her as she began to cry.

Eleven

Sometimes, especially when I was a little older, in those "awkward" years, and mad at God for one reason or other, I'd look back at all those kings in Judah and Israel that started good but finished bad and I'd humor myself that it didn't much matter what you did or how hard you tried, God wasn't gonna give you what you wanted or even let you finish well anyway, so why bother?

That would satisfy me for a minute or two, then I'd be more miserable than before and with no hope at all. I just had to grow up a mite to completely understand the grace of God and His covenant with His people. Some of that I learned by how I saw Him deal with others of His sheep.

Now ole Charlie Settle had long led the "Keep Dallas Out of Ellis County" bandwagon, first as a Cotton Patch City Councilman, then when he ran twice for mayor (losin' both times), and all along as a businessman and editor and publisher of the *Cotton Patch Press*.

He stayed up half the night followin' the game so he could get the week's issue ready for delivery the next mornin', and that a day earlier than usual. Daddy saw it blazin' out at him from the newspaper racks on his way into town: "FARMERS BEAT DALLAS'S BEST."

It was the biggest, boldest, blackest headline Charlie'd run since the Feds burned down those folks in Waco. A large color photo of that young man scorin' the winnin' touchdown spread across the page just below it.

I expect Mrs. Stoerner had plenty of call to go 'round lookin' like she'd been weaned on a dill pickle, what with all her family gone—two husbands buried—her rheumatoid arthritis, the broken hip, and now losin' her best friend, Mrs. Jennings. By the time my daddy stepped out of her neat little two-room frame home, with roses windin' around the front trellises, she was smilin' her first smile in days, or maybe longer.

"God bless you for comin' to see me ever' week, Brother Ethan," she said from her wheelchair, her faded china blue eyes misty pearl centerpieces in the ancient wizened face. "No one else ever does. You good as gold."

My daddy kind-ly nodded, then just turned, put his hat back on, and stepped off the porch and toward his pickup. Just then a big, red, late-model Cadillac wheeled up and parked. Reverend Jasper stepped out of it.

"How-do, Pastor Jasper," Daddy said.

"He gone and done it this time, Ethan," Reverend Jasper said, his hazel eyes flashin'.

"Who?"

"That—that—that 'Doc-tor D'—'Whoo, baby!'" Reverend Jasper exploded with such inspired mimicry Daddy had to stifle a grin.

'What'd he do?"

"I have it on good authority—Ebenezer Dean, who supplies the good shepherd with his gin—that the man has gone and sold hisself straight to th'ole devil, Ethan," Reverend Jasper said, dramatic as though announcin' he had glimpsed the page from the Book of Life where the name of "Doc-tor D" should've been and found it absent.

"What in the wide wide world of sports are you talkin' about, George?" Daddy asked, confused as all get-out.

"Why, that slicked-back blue suede moneychanger gone and threw his hep to them bloodsuckin' gamblers," Reverend Jasper announced, straightenin' himself a bit as though concerned the one clergyman's disgrace might taint him as well.

"What? Why?"

"Hear him tell it—which I understand we will, at his own TV press conference with our good mayor and some o' them upstandin' Dallas citizens," Reverend Jasper said, "he say the casino and racetrack were bound to happen, but he wouldn't let 'em till they promised thirty-five percent of the employees to be minorities. Don't he jest love to get hisself ahead by playin' that ole race card."

"But—but he ain't just pastor of one of the biggest churches in Ellis County—he's on the council besides," Daddy stammered. "Coltrane's already for it. Two more votes and—"

"What he won't tell," Reverend Jasper cut in, "is that somebody gonna pony up to buy him his new sank-she-ary and family center he been wantin' ever since he come to Cotton Patch."

Daddy sighed, shook his head, then said, "Let's face it, George, this town's never been blessed with the smartest of God's creatures."

"Tell ya, Judas hisself'd be ashamed o' such a reprobate, Ethan," Reverend Jasper said, near tears.

"Guess I thought a lot o' things about that cagy fella, but I never thought he'd sell out his own people for somethin' the like of this," Daddy said.

"Judas, I tell ya, Ethan. Doctor Judas D. Judas," Reverend Jasper spat.

*　　*　　*

I mentioned to you a spell back about those cycles that show clearer in the country. Well, I learned early on that dogs, even puppies, are not immune to 'em. Even the times Daisy and our other female Labs had a dozen puppies, usually one or two wouldn't make it past the first few days. Those mamas only have so many teats. So when Daisy had fifteen this time, I kind-ly expected that trouble was up.

Unfortunately, I took a shine to one little fella who was all black (even though Daisy and the daddy and all the grandparents were yellow) but had little white paws. He made it past the first few days, though three others didn't, then to the end of the second week. I had picked him out as the one we were gonna keep, to give Jake and Daisy and Jeb the puppy company.

Then a little yellow (more like white) one smothered under Daisy and then we found the black one with the white paws just dead the next mornin'.

Daddy knew I was upset, seein' the little puppy and all, so he came home early from work and put him and the white one in an airtight bag. He picked up a shovel and we headed for the far corner of the south pasture. I wanted to dig the graves, so he let me try. I made it about three half-scoops, before I realized how hard was that slaty ground. I gave Daddy the shovel, and he had two pretty deep holes dug in no time. Then he laid the shovel against the corner fence post as I shoved their two little markers down into the dirt. Each had half of a paint-stirrer glued across the upper portion of a full stirrer, in the shape of a cross. I had written Mary on one and Joseph on the other. We stood there for a minute, feelin' the first stirrin's of fall on the breeze in our faces. I didn't even pay any mind to a chicken snake I saw slitherin' away under the fence just a few feet away.

"Do dogs have souls, Daddy?" I asked.

"Well, honey, not like we do."

"So Mary and Joseph won't be in heaven with us?"

"Why, I don't know how heaven could be good as God says it is 'less our dogs are there, too, little friend. Heaven's gonna be all around us after He comes back," my daddy said, sweepin' his hand across the cedars and fields, the sky and breeze, the mooin' and chirpin' and the fragrance of pines, and the redbirds and bluejays both. "The Old Book says that. God doesn't hate this world like some folks say. Oh, He hates the wicked and what they do, but He made this world and He loves it and His people in it, and He's one day gonna redeem it all and restore it to the beauty it once had, and even better, and ever' kinda creature'll be here, includin' dogs—at least dogs o' the good sort. The mean, mangy, low-down no-'count ones, why, He'll vanquish them to hell like He will bad men."

That meant only one thing just then. "And the other dogs we had that died too? Like Gipper and Judge and Travis?" I asked.

"And even all our cats and rabbits and goats, and that calf the coyotes ate, and our horses too—especially the baby ones," he said.

Now that breeze seemed to have a chill on the edge of it, which stung my eyes. That was prob'ly why they got all wet. I looked at those two little crosses risin' from the earth. "Would you say the words, Daddy?" I asked.

"Sure, sweetie." My daddy took off his hat and we bowed our heads and closed our eyes, then he spoke. "Lord, we thank You that You gave us these two little puppies. Even though we didn't have 'em long, only a few days, we thank You that You've taken 'em to a better place, to be with Yourself, Sir. We thank You You've created all things for Your own pleasure, Sir, includin' these little critters. In Christ's name, amen."

I just kind-ly stood there for a minute and stared at those little plots and I felt the breeze against my cheeks, 'cause it seemed like they were wet now too. "I do think they're in a better place now, Daddy," I said, noddin' my head.

Then he put his arm around me and I felt his soft cotton shirt and his hard-muscled body and I smelled dirt and cedar trees and his woodsy-smellin' cologne he put on days he went to the church office. "Sure they are, sweetie," he said.

And up at the house, watchin' us across the pasture out a back window, was Mama. Yep, she knew about those rhythms, those cycles of life, too, as you'll see.

❊   ❊   ❊

Only the Providence of God could allow children in our neck of the woods to grow up with any sense at all about how to behave around a baseball game, after the way most of our parents acted at our games. Even in mid-September, for a bunch of eight- and nine-year-old girl softballers, the stands were full, 'cause it was the best entertainment goin' on a Cotton Patch Saturday night.

This particular night, we were playin' one of our fellow Ellis County town's teams, with whom we had quite a rivalry, the night after that young man Jed Schumacher and Cotton Patch had hung a half-a-hunnerd on that other town's varsity football team. Plus, we had lost only one softball game all (late summer-early fall) season and it was to them and we were playin' 'em now for the county championship. So spirits were runnin' even higher than usual, in the stands and on the field.

We were behind 6–5 in the bottom of the last inning, and we had two outs left and runners on second and third when I came up to the plate to hit. If you'd had that Halloween band from Dallas High there, I do believe it would've been louder than the Cotton Patch-Dallas football game. Sure seemed like it to me, anyway, and I hadn't gotten a hit all night. I would've given anything to be anywhere but in that batter's box at that moment.

Mr. Posey, the head coach of our team, was our third base coach when we batted, and my daddy helped him as the first base coach. Sometimes, Mr. Posey, who as you have seen was normally such a nice, jolly sort, would get real red in the face, and the veins would bulge right out on his neck, but only at our softball games.

As I stepped to the plate, Mr. Posey was just yellin' up a storm from out there by third base; in fact, he was kind-ly movin' on in from the third base area toward home plate, mainly because he was shoutin' at Allison Cathcart, who was the behind-the-plate umpire. Now Allison was the sort of girl I really looked up to. For one thing, she was always sweet to us younger girls, even though you could tell she was kind-ly shy herself. For another, her own mama had died of one of those real bad kinds of cancer a while back, and ever'one felt real sorry for her. Her daddy, meanwhile, had been the pastor of the First Baptist Church of Cotton Patch for several years, but he was laid up at home now with a bad heart. He had already told his deacons to find someone to take his place. This was why he wasn't raisin' Cain over that Granger's gamblin' plans. (Fact is, Dr. Blevins warned him to turn a deaf ear even to talk of it, because just that drove his blood pressure right up.) Plus, Allison was great at ever' kind of sport, faster than most of the boys, and tall, blonde (really), and beautiful too. Finally, she always seemed to me to be a really good softball umpire, even though she had just turned eighteen years old, and she was nice to you, even when she had to call you out.

But Mr. Posey seemed to hold a slightly different view, 'cause he was like a pit bull bustin' to get off his leash at that poor girl. "Don't foul this one up, ump—remember it's the players determine who wins and loses!" he shouted, right at Allison, and her a Cotton Patch girl and a good ump too.

So I was extra nervous still, and embarrassed, for Allison and all the rest of us too, truth be known, and I was more surprised than anyone when I knocked the tar out of that first pitch and sent it out into shallow left-center field.

Ever'body in town seemed to be yellin' as I took off for first base. My daddy was there and he was jumpin' up and down and screamin' like a banshee. But Mr. Posey, clear across the infield, sounded even louder than Daddy, and Daddy was awful loud.

Ever'one was screamin' for me to make first base, Blanca to make second, and Mr. Posey's daughter Amy to make third. We all did, but then Mr. Posey waved Amy on around third towards home. My daddy shouted, "No!" when he saw this, but I guess Mr. Posey wanted to give us at least the tie, and with his own daughter to boot.

She was runnin' faster than I'd ever seen Amy run (which still wasn't very fast, as she was cartin' more than her fair share of a load), and I'd known her I guess since the week we were both born at Baylor Hospital up in, hmm, Dallas. But their left fielder made a squirrely throw that kind-ly just dribbled in from the outfield, across the pitcher's mound, up to the plate, and into the catcher's mit just in time for her to tag Amy out at home. At least, that's how Allison Cathcart called it. Me, I thought Amy, slow as she was, was safe, and so did my daddy, but I have to admit it was a close call.

But Mr. Posey, he commenced to screamin' in rage at Allison, then he just charged the plate, like somethin' sorta snapped in him. But halfway there, somethin' else snapped too. I heard a pop, even over the screamin' crowd, and Mr. Posey fell straight to the ground like a mallard who'd caught him a full pattern of .12 gauge buck shot. He was cryin' out in pain and clutchin' his hamstring. But he kept right on screamin' at Allison Cathcart, sittin' there on the ground as he was while that noisy crowd hushed and Amy stood all alone in front of everbody, cringin' in horror.

Now Amy Posey was not the sort to inspire powerful feelin's of pity in a person. She herself had never exactly shown a knack for pity or compassion or the like, and most of the time I just found her to be real work to get along with. Maybe part of that was 'cause she wasn't what you would call anything resemblin' an attractive person, and I would apply that to the inside even more than to the out, though I definitely would not overlook that part either. (I know Mama, it ain't a person's fault how they look, leastwise to some extent, but she's got to take the lion's share of the blame for the inside part; well, at least some of it, anyhow.) Oh well, I had heard all the lectures on that subject from Mama and Daddy both, and I reckon if I wasn't the best friend Amy had, 'cause I don't think she had any actual friends, I guess

I could lay some claim to bein' the least of an enemy she had. But I truly did feel sorry for her this time around.

"You blind, ignorant idiot!" I heard Mr. Posey holler at a stunned Allison. "Who the blazes hired you? You can't see anything past all that bleached blonde hair, you dizzy clutz!"

I just stood there at first base, wonderin' why Mr. Posey was so all-fired riled up when I had finally got me a good hit and we still had runners on base and one out to go. Then Daddy ran across the field, and I saw that even though he called himself a grumpy old man a lot, he was still fast as the wind.

He was still strong, too, 'cause he just kind-ly hauled Mr. Posey right up by his collar and pushed him off the field and out to where the pickups and cars were parked in the dark. When he did this, the other team's head coach, Coach Ortega, stalked after them. "Come back here, tough hombre!" Ortega shouted, but I think he meant Mr. Posey and not my daddy.

Then Clem Stephens, who owned a pest control business around Cotton Patch and was even bigger and taller than my daddy, especially with that huge ten-gallon hat he wore whenever he wasn't sprayin' your dooryard or attic or gardens or trees for yellow jackets or fire ants or field mice or brown recluse spiders or scorpions, chose to take exception to Coach Ortega's words and now he lit out after him. "You watch your mouth, you sawed-off runt!" Mr. Stephens shouted. I guess maybe he figured this all fell under the headin' of his deacon's duties at the Cotton Patch Church of Christ; you know, to look out after the folk, especially the womenfolk, and what-all.

By then, Daddy had Mr. Posey out in the dark where were the pickups and cars. The commotion back on the field mounted, and more of our fathers and uncles stepped out onto the field, and more of our mothers and aunts stood in the stands and screamed at each other and the coaches and some at Allison Cathcart, who was sobbin' now and bein' helped away by one of the Baptist deacons, but Daddy didn't pay any of it any heed. "What in the Sam Hill's wrong with you, Scott Posey?" Daddy shouted. "You know where that girl's spendin' her first year outa high school, with barely one parent still livin'? Ferryin' food and Bibles to China, where it ain't safe at all. She's sweet as they

80

come. This has been buildin' up all season, bud, but you crossed the line tonight."

Mr. Posey slouched against a nearby GMC pickup, grippin' his hamstring and hangin' his head in shame. Daddy shook his own head and paced back and forth. "I played sports my whole life," he said, "on ever' level 'cept pro, and I've never seen crazier fans anywhere than right here at these children's softball and T-ball games! And you and that smart-mouth little runt Ortega, both professin' Christians. Well, I just about had my fill o' all y'all. Leastwise the pagans admit they're pagans."

Now the racket on the field grew so loud Daddy turned thataway. Then he turned back to Mr. Posey. "So what is it, Scott?" he said. "You got a great wife and kid, you're rich, respected, you're a leader, and you got the Lord. Why do you go so ape over these little children's games?"

He saw Tater and his son Spud comin' out.

"Called it," Tater said.

"What?" Daddy said.

"Called the game when Clem Stephens lit into that cocky, struttin', shrimp of a so-called coach. Think the little peckerwood may need a mite o' sewin' up," Tater said, not brokenhearted at that part.

Daddy just kind-ly sighed at that one.

"Sorry, Ethan," Mr. Posey said, all dejected-like. "Guess I fouled this one up."

Now Mr. Goodnight, who fired the shotgun to end the Cotton Patch football games, came out. "Give it to 'em, Ethan," he said. "They just give the whole blamed thing to the rascals, and us with two on and one out still to go. It's a blasted shame."

Then the screech of burnin' tire rubber turned all their heads just in time to see a late model pickup race past on the nearby road in the dark. Somethin' flew out the nearside window and landed close to Daddy, the six-pack of empty beer bottles smashin' into a blizzard of glass shards over his feet and legs.

"What do you know," Daddy said. "Believe that was Jed Schumacher's truck."

Twelve

I think part of the reason that old rusty bell on top of the church made Daddy mad was that it just reminded him so doggone much of us, his flock of human sheep that gave him so many headaches. Maybe he saw in that bell the same hard shell that all our sin and defyin' the truth we knew had coated us with, and made us so tough to mold and conform to somethin' more tender and lovin' and usable by God.

And maybe he saw the same rust and decay that ate away at our souls and deprived them of health and growth 'cause we refused to practice the spiritual disciplines God wished for us.

Maybe, too, he saw somethin', like us, wonderfully crafted to sound a beautiful song of salvation and glory, but instead silenced by neglect, disrepair, maybe abuse, and the world so much the worse for it.

So maybe he caught a ray of hope that things might take a change for the better on that Lord's Day a couple weeks after we lost the softball championship, when lo and behold that old rusty bell began to clang and toll its song, which I had never heard it do my whole life.

Those of us that got to the church early all came outside to see, first wonderin' if maybe the Baptists or the Methodists or the Church of Christers had gotten them a bell. But no—there it was, ringin' in all its ancient glory!

And there was Clay Cullum standin' behind the church in the shadows of the alley, garbed in his white minister's robe, tuggin' the rope that rang it, a grin painted across his bronzed, square-jawed face and a cluster of young boys gathered round him, in various degrees of awe.

I looked over at Daddy, there on the yellowed church lawn he used to mow but Clay did now, in his own white robe and his green stole with the golden Celtic crosses at the ends, and reckoned he was as happy as he was surprised. That was one Lord's Day he really was happy to see all the folks; there were too many when I couldn't tell if he was or not.

But this sudden turn of events did not please one old man in the least, and he sat rockin' in his chair across the street on his front porch, cursin' grim oaths under his hard-as-kerosene breath.

*　　*　　*

There's been lots of excitement through the years in Texas, but I expect some of the best, at least around Ellis County, was back early on, when the dinosaurs had the run of the place. Leastwise, there weren't that many folks around to disrupt things for 'em, though a Christian who knows his Bible and what he should about history and archaeology knows that the two were around at the same time.

But one of 'em hasn't been for quite a spell, except that part of 'em that Jeb the now half-grown puppy had locked in his teeth as he loped across the west pasture. He loped past Daddy and me as I led along Maggie, a less game horse than Lucy and smaller by three hands than Annie Lee.

"Look at that goofy little mutt, showin' off for us," Daddy said.

"He's prancin', Daddy," I corrected him.

The sun was settin' down straight ahead of us, and it looked like God had used ever' paint on His palette to color that sky, beginnin' with fire-red for the sun and windin' up navy blue away back behind us to the east. I still see shades in a Texas sunset I never saw in a crayon box, even the ones with all sixty-four colors, and it's a long time now since that night.

"Where do they keep findin' 'em, Daddy?" I asked.

"I don't know, buddy," he said, "I've searched around, I've followed 'em, I've even tracked 'em after they've brought 'em in, but I can't find any."

"But are you sure they're dinosaur bones?" I said.

"Yep, there's no doubt about that," he said, as Maggie leaned down to take a drink from the tank as we rounded it. "The scientists over at Glen Rose and some from A & M all say so. And most the bones are lots bigger'n that one."

"Look, Daddy, he's gnawin' on it like a chew toy!" I announced.

"Jeb! Come here!" Daddy hollered.

Then Jake and Daisy galloped onto the scene, and Jeb the half-grown puppy lit out up the hill, totin' his dinosaur bone like a baton in the mile-relay run, toward the live oak, the one where Daddy carved our initials and the cross, and Molly the Hereford whiteface calf romped after them.

"Why does Molly do that, Daddy?" I asked.

"I reckon she thinks she's a dog, too."

"There's not much grass left in this pasture, is there?" I asked.

"No, it was another dry summer, despite those two days flooded the levee," he said. "Fixin' to put Molly and the rest 'em over in the east pasture."

"We're never gonna butcher any of our cows, are we Daddy," I stated more than asked. He looked sorta embarrassed at this, so I added, "That's okay by me if we don't Daddy, I like 'em too. It'd be sorta like killin' one of the dogs and eatin' him at the supper table, wouldn't it?"

He just kind-ly shook his head at the direction this conversation was takin', so I thought it best to change tack. "Daddy, do you think they burned down that Baptist church 'cause black folks went there?" I asked.

"Well, I hope not, buddy," he said. "They say the same people prob'ly burned down the Hitchin' Rail Store and no black folks were there, and the Gomez shop and that was Mexicans."

At that point, somebody else decided to get into the conversation. We heard her hooves poundin' the earth before we turned to see Annie Lee gallopin' around the tank and up the path toward us, wall-eyed and snortin'. Daddy stepped right toward her, between her and Maggie and me, and threw his arms up into the air and waved them. "Yah!" he shouted. "Git outa here you mangy nag!"

She veered away and down off the path we were on that rimmed the tank, dirt flyin' and dust billowin'. Daddy picked up a big rock and fired it at her. It struck her in the flank, and she skedaddled. "Go on, git!" he shouted some more.

For a man gentle with animals as he was, he sure lit into 'em when when they acted contrary. Another time when Amy Posey and I were takin' turns ridin' Billy the pony, Annie Lee threw a jealous tantrum like that, and Daddy threw a horse apple at her so hard I bet she felt like she'd been shot 'n the rump.

"Daddy, I wish I could ride Billy instead of Maggie," I said.

"You like ridin' ole Billy Boy, don't you, darlin'?" he said.

"I sure do!" I kind-ly shouted. "Fact, I think I'd like to ride 'im right now."

"He's sorta ornery sometimes though, idn't he?" Daddy said.

"Ah, he's not so bad, he's not really bad a'tall. I really think I'd like to ride 'im, Daddy," said I, kind-ly startin' the procedure to dismount.

"You know, Maggie's not near as ornery as ole Bill," said Daddy, ever-so-gently nudgin' me back into the saddle I'd already half-escaped. "And she's a lot more fun to ride, and easier on your hiney, too."

"Daddy!" I affected in feigned protest of his use of "hiney." Then, sighin', I got down to bidness and declared, "Daddy, I'm scared to ride Maggie by myself."

"I know, sweetie, but you handle Maggie just fine," he said.

We didn't know it, but Mama was watchin' us out one of the front windows like she often did. She would smile and fret just a bit and in this case she saw me ride Maggie a ways, then fall out the saddle.

Daddy hustled over to help me up and dust me off.

"You alright, buddy?" he asked, lookin' me over real close.

"I think so," I said, but not really sure, or sure if I wanted back on Maggie.

"Now Katie Helen, remember what I told you 'bout when a horse throws you?" he said.

"Yes sir—you have to fetch him and get right back on," I admitted.

"That's right. Think you can do that if I help you?" he said.

"Think so."

"See—ole Maggie's just standin' over there munchin' horse apples with Billy Boy," he said. "Let's go git 'er!"

"Okay!"

While Mama watched as the sun bled into the fields to the west, kind-ly holdin' her breath, we walked up on either side of Maggie the way Daddy'd taught me and we corralled her. Before I knew it, I was back on top of her, losin' all the breath in me when she broke into a full gallop toward the hill with the live oak.

I screamed so loud you'd have thought that young man Jed Schumacher had scored another touchdown, which he had scored four of a couple nights before, one on a sixty-three-yard interception runback, during Cotton Patch's sixth win without a defeat.

"Hold on with your knees and pull in the reins a shade!" Daddy hollered. "But not too hard!"

My eyes must've been big as that Doctor Carter preacher fella's when he saw the million dollar TV contract we'd heard he just got from one of those big "Christian" TV networks up in Dallas. Daddy said those folks usually charge big money to the preachers for their show to be on the network. However, the scuttlebutt was they thought they really needed a black preacher to build their ratings among black folk, and Doctor Carter had him a fat offer from some California bunch for a show if he'd move out there. So the Dallas folks shelled out the big bucks—and got a six-foot-tall former Miss Black America for his "Special Assistant and Public Relations Director."

Now Daddy wasn't the greatest preacher or the slickest talker, and he sure dressed pretty plain, 'cept when he wore the robes of his office. Still, it baffled me he could be so much worse than that Doctor Carter as to get maybe seventy five or so folks to our church on a good day, while the other fella had hundreds and hundreds and now his own satellite TV show, with (Daddy said) maybe millions of folks watchin' from their own livin' rooms. Reckon I'll ask the Lord about the math on that one, too.

I know, you're wonderin' what happened with me and ole Maggie. Well, I did what Daddy said, not necessarily because at that moment I believed him or even liked him, but because I was fresh out of other options. Maggie didn't want to slow at first, but then she kind-ly gave up the boat just a tad. When I saw that, by gobs, I realized I was a pretty fair rider after all and what was I worried about this little lightweight for anyway? I even nudged her on the sides with my boots—whilst keepin' a light hold on the reins—just to make sure she knew who was her new boss.

This time Maggie tossed her head once, but did what I said, breakin' only into a lope.

"Now don't get cocky!" Daddy hollered as I rode past him.

Mama's face broke into a grin, and she let out a relieved sigh as she watched me ride clear across the west pasture and back.

And Daddy, well, he looked as if he couldn't have been happier if I had just ridden to victory in the Kentucky Derby. When I got back to him, Maggie more winded now than me and definitely knowin' who was the boss, his cell phone rang. "Howdy, this is Ethan," I heard him say into it as I climbed down from Maggie—by myself. "Oh hi, Graciela. What? How long? Yes, I know where it is. I'll just head out there myself. No, no, I'll go, you just tuck the kids in and don't fret."

But my mind was on how good a rider I now was. I remembered Daddy recountin' somethin' he heard ole Zig Ziglar say once on a tape. Seems Zig's good buddy, the great Dallas Cowboy quarterback Roger Staubach, had told him the only difference between the big shots and the little shots was the big shots were little shots who just kept on shootin'.

I reckoned I was well on my way to big shot status.

*　　*　　*

Daddy said the Yellow Rose Bar, like countless others of the type, was a phony church of sorts. It was where folks came for fellowship and buckin' up, where they feasted on wine (and more), where music to roll the roof back was heard and often sung, and where they received the good news of the Gospel of Inebriation—that they were, after all, entitled to their sins, forgiven of them, and free to commit more of them, even tonight, and even with that pretty painted lady at the bar, or against that down-in-the-mouth workman or cowboy drownin' his sorrows.

The Yellow Rose was all fancied up for that great American holiday, Halloween, when my daddy got out of his pickup and walked across the gravel parkin' lot. Just as he saw a heapin' gold harvest moon hangin' low in the eastern sky over the Rose, he heard glass smashin' and he turned to see a fistfight break out to one side of the buildin'.

When he got inside, his ears rang from the honky-tonk music and his eyes burned from the smoke that hung thick as steamin' gravy over chicken fry. Among the drunken company, he spotted Eduardo Rodriguez, then found himself a seat at a small table next to Rodriguez's, which was the only one in the place where no one sat. Daddy chalked that up to one of those small Providences of God's that were big a miracles as the partin' of seas and creation of woman and such. A waitress of faded beauty, a short skirt, and open-toed high heels, and with red hair piled high and brown and gray peekin' out, was with him in an instant. "What'll it be, sugar?" she said with a familiarity stoked by the potential of a profitable evenin'.

"Just start me with a Dr. Pepper," my daddy said. When it looked like she might laugh right in his face, he slid her two ten dollar bills. "One of those is for DPs and the other is for you to keep 'em comin'."

The royal blue paint on her eyelids kind-ly hovered over her grayish, would-be blue eyes. "DPs," she said.

"Yes ma'am," Daddy said.

"Alright, sugar," she said, with a smile and a wink I reckon she figured she could include for the $20 she took as she walked away.

Daddy saw Rodriguez had noticed him. The man sat there like he'd just seen snow in July in Cotton Patch, or any other time for that matter, perhaps at least partly because he had his arm around a cute young woman who was not Graciela. Daddy pushed his hat back a bit and nodded. Rodriguez did not return the courtesy, since it would have been hard to do both that and swear the oath he was now cursing in Spanish.

The waitress had Daddy's DP back out to him in a jiffy, with another smile and wink to boot. As he sipped it, he received a visitor, a smelly, unshaven fella who had the blue eyes the waitress wished she had and who did not appreciate her flirtations toward Daddy.

"What kinda id-jut come in here and suck on a bottle o' pop?" Blue Eyes slurred, unable to keep down a belch that could've claimed the lake of fire itself, or a near environ, as its origin.

"Never cottoned to the harder stuff, friend," Daddy said with a smile.

"I ain't your friend and see if you cotton to this," Blue Eyes scowled as he smashed a beer bottle over Daddy's head, knockin' him bleedin' out of his chair and onto the floor. Daddy was stunned, but when Blue Eyes pulled him up, he gathered his senses about him and shoved him away.

Blue Eyes scowled some more, then fumbled out a knife and came for Daddy. Quicker'n you could say a fifth o' Black Jack with a Jim Beam chaser, Daddy broke the man's arm for him, the knife clatterin' to the floor, then slammed him over a collapsin' table and to the ground, glass smashin' and people tumblin' out of their chairs. Before Blue Eyes knew what happened, Daddy had a chunk of broken glass at his throat.

"Keep it up and I'll splitcha ear to ear, bub," Daddy allowed, sorta matter-of-fact-like.

As my daddy's blood dripped into Blue Eyes' face, the drunk's eyes grew wide as a full moon over the Trinity.

"Don't do it!" the bartender pled with Daddy. "I saw the whole thing. I'll call the deputy on 'im, just don't hurt 'im worse."

Daddy dropped the glass, shot a glance over at Rodriguez, for whom this evenin' was chockful of surprises, then walked out of the room, which was now quiet as a cemetery.

Outside, he put his hand to his bleedin' head gash and grimaced. It was just beginnin' to throb and hurt somethin' fierce. Then Rodriguez appeared. "Pastor Ethan!" he said, with a sight more concern than he'd shown for anyone else, includin' his wife, in a long time. "That needs doctorin'. Let me take you to the hospital."

"Don't think you'd pass any breathalyzers right now, Eduardo," Daddy said. "You can ride with me though, if you've a mind."

Rodriguez nodded. "Alright—just no God talk, alright?"

"Fair enough," Daddy said, wincin' in pain as he fished for his keys and turned toward his truck.

The last thing he saw as he pulled out the gravel parkin' lot was that waitress, standin' outside the front door of the Yellow Rose watchin' him leave, the gray in her hair showin' a lot clearer in the tacky neon and Halloween lights.

Thirteen

D r. Blevins told Daddy to take a few days off from pastorin', a week in fact. A slice of that beer bottle had clipped some sort of nerve or other, and he was supposed to come back at the end of that time, or if the pain got too bad. Meanwhile, Cotton Patch clinched the district title, mainly because that young man Jed Schumacher ran for over 350 yards, which we weren't quite sure if anyone had ever done in Ellis County, or even all of Texas.

But Daddy wasn't allowed to go to that either, and he couldn't even read because that gave him a headache. A movie he went to see did, too, and he didn't fancy TV at all, so that about left fishin'. And since Clay Cullum had more'n he could say grace over, in more ways than one, fillin' in for Daddy at the church, Daddy took him fishin' at Dr. Blevins's old stock tank over toward Palmer, more to coach him along a bit than to go fishin'. The good news was, you could catch a passel of fish there; the bad news was you had to throw 'em back.

So they had their lines in the water, and Daddy had a bandage drapin' part of his head and a headache poundin' it all. But it was altogether a fall day of the caliber that reminded you a great and a good Creator must've made ever' bit of it Even the cottonwoods clustered to one side the tank loomed majestically, branches and limbs appearing stalwart as so many royal sceptres.

"And Rodriguez said nothing at all in the truck?" Clay was askin'.

"Fact he was in the truck I assayed as a breakthrough," Daddy said.

"Well, it's the least he could do, watching you take sixteen stitches because of him," Clay said.

"I've had worse," said Daddy. "Say, gimme another lure."

"And that's another thing. Does anyone in this whole town even know you played college football, much less who for and what all you did?" Clay asked.

"I'm their pastor, not their coach," Daddy said, flickin' his line back out into the water. "How'd you know?"

"You kiddin'?" Clay said, incredulous. "Growin' up in Mom's house? Why we—" Then he caught himself right quick and turned back toward the water.

"Aw, go on, I know who your mom is," Daddy said, pullin' his line in some. "You look just like her, and you're as contrary."

Clay just kind-ly fished there for a minute, then when he spoke his voice was a couple notches quieter and slower. "I heard about Ethan Shanahan and Barry Switzer and Heisman Trophies and National Championships from the cradle," he said. Then he seemed to turn a corner of some sort, and he lit up. "Why, Mom used to tell about that big Texas game where both y'all were undefeated and somehow she got the crimson scarf she won for being Miss O.U. to you in the locker room to let you know she was sorry for—"

"Got me one, Clay!" Daddy said, reelin' it in. He had him a four-pound bass and a cluster of golden maple leaves droppin' about his shoulders and a long road he'd traveled I didn't know much of but that he never got all the way behind him.

*　　*　　*

Daddy and the Session were havin' 'em a short meeting that turned out not to be so short, to discuss the annual church hayride that was comin' up. The meeting was the day after Cotton Patch played their bi-district championship game in the first round of the playoffs. They beat some poor bunch 51-7 which had lost only one game all year. But those boys hadn't seen anyone like that young man who ran over 'em for 200 yards and six touchdowns.

Mr. Posey had the words "Farmers All the Way to State" scrawled in shoe polish across the side of his brand-spankin' new Toyota pickup, though it was Mrs. Posey that took Amy, Blanca, and me to the church. Part of why the meeting went so long was they had to figure some things out on their own that only Mr. Posey, who was head of the Hayride Committee, knew, and no one could reach him.

Right when we got out of the truck, we saw Jose pedal past on his old bicycle. He looked sober but tired. When he was sober, that old bicycle of his just sorta shimmied a bit, side to side. When he was three sheets to the wind, it'd weave all over the road, so you learned to appreciate Jose when he was sober, because he was a much harder target to miss when he wasn't.

When the meeting finally ended, we were still playin' on the church lawn with a few other children. Daddy saw Old Man Taggart rockin' on his front porch across chugholed old Church Street. "Wait here for me," he said.

But I didn't need any such encouragement. I had already been thinkin' on how I might squeeze a few more minutes of playtime out of Daddy, if not a few more hours. I was in no hurry to get home, because I knew that even though my dogs and Maggie were there, so were more homework and that beastly piano.

A few minutes later, I could see my daddy standin' before Old Man Taggart like a defense lawyer pleadin' a case before a hangin' judge. "But Mr. Taggart," Daddy said, tryin' to keep the scarlet wave comin' over his face at bay. "All I'm askin' for is five minutes each Sunday mornin'. That can't be so bad, can it? 'Specially when you consider how many people love hearin' that ole bell ring again."

But Old Man Taggart just kept right on rockin', starin' at nothin'.

"Tell you what, sir," Daddy said. "I'll even buy you some ear plugs for those five minutes each week."

Old Man Taggart's face twisted up in confusion. He turned toward my daddy. "Huh?" the old coot bellowed, cuppin' his hand to the side of his head. "Corn in the ear this late?" Then he kind-ly squinted even more than he already was and said, "What in tarnation happened to yo' head, boy?"

Dr. Blevins had taken the bandage off a couple days before and the side of my daddy's head was not a pretty sight.

I reckon, lookin' back, there's a sense in which a country preacher pastors the whole town, not just his own church. Like as not, though, he'll find the town's not any more cooperative than the church.

* * *

That night, Mama and Daddy sat on the front porch watchin' another one of those golden harvest sunsets, just the memory of which can lighten a pitch black room for me in the dead of night.

"That bell doesn't hurt Mr. Taggart's ears," Mama said, kind-ly sighin'. "The poor old fellow is legally deaf. He hasn't set foot in a church in forty years. Keep bein' nice to him and prayin' for him."

Daddy just sorta frowned and tried to assay which dog had dropped the latest dinosaur bone, the size of a baseball bat, on the porch. He turned it over in his hands as he sat in his rockin' chair.

I'm sure they had a passel of those types of talks when I wasn't around. After all, turns out bein' a pastor's wife was no more of a picnic than bein' a pastor, and in some cases come to find out, even less.

* * *

The next week, after we'd won the area football title in another rout, two mules pulled Tater Tatum, his boy Spud, and their straw-filled wagon up in front of the church for the hayride. Amy, Blanca, several other children, and I had been waitin' all week for this moment and we outdid ourselves seein' who could squeal the loudest (despite Mama's many previous admonitions to the contrary).

I'm sure the four or five teenagers would've traded us for more grasshoppers in August, but the half-dozen or so adults seemed amused.

As we piled onto the wagon, Daddy saw Reverend Jasper step out the door of the pastor's office, which lay around the side of the church. He walked over thataway.

"Why, George, you don't look as though you're walkin' in too high a cotton today," Daddy said to him.

"Can't get anybody to church," Reverend Jasper said. "They come and then they stray away. Some of' em won't come at all as long as we're—we're holdin' services in your church."

Daddy sighed, then said, "George, have you ever thought to ask Miz T and her friends to throw in with you? Y'all believe all the same things."

"I expect they some strong women, Ethan," he said, cantin' his head. "'Sides, we have different ways o' lookin' at some things."

Then he just kind-ly walked past my daddy, real slow-like, his shoulders stooped and his head bowed down low.

*   *   *

I don't reckon I mentioned to you that down Shiloh Road maybe a quarter-mile from the front gate to our place was a tiny, paintless, one-room frame structure beloved by the wood ants and termites. It was younger than the nearby Trinity, but older than just about anything else around those parts.

The folks at the First Baptist Tabernacle of God in Christ didn't have 'em any hayrides that year, but, as I have previously alluded to, my, could they speak to one another in psalms and hymns and spiritual songs, and could they ever sing and make melody in their hearts to the Lord.

And when they did, a harmony sweeter'n the first fragrance of bluebonnets or honeysuckle on the spring breeze, and as pure-soundin', carried out of that little place and across the gentle cedar-dappled hills 'round where we lived.

Inside, Miz T and maybe fifteen other black folks, mostly old and mostly female, would lift their voices in joy to their Creator. Many and many is the night those thrillin' heralds of assurance and hope found their way to me in the pastures, at the tanks, inside the stables and barns, or tucked under the covers. Those folks sang many of the same songs we did at our church, but their singing' seemed a blamed sight more "anointed," if the Lord wouldn't be upset at me borrowin' that term.

I reckon, like as not, when the end of the pilgrim way comes for me, it'll be *In the Sweet Bye and Bye* that is echoin' through my head, just as they were singin' it that night when Tater and Spud and their two mules took us past 'em on the haytruck.

*   *   *

95

The Cotton Patch Press sittin' in the newsrack the next week at the Ennis Auction Barn had two main headlines. One was "Farmers, Unbeaten El Paso Team Headed for Showdown?" and the other was "Concealed Carry Applications Highest Ever for Ellis County." And that didn't count all the folks just carried without botherin' to get a bunch of suits' permission in Austin.

Mama wasn't feelin' well that day, and Daddy had been chewin' over addin' a calf to his "beef herd," so we suspended the Shanahan Classical Christian School for the day and Daddy and I headed out in the Shivy for the auction.

When he opened the door to let me climb into the cab seat, Jake leaped past me into the front seat, and Daisy did the same into the cab. You might've thought Jeb the three-quarter-grown puppy would've had the inside track for the third position, but you'd be wrong. Molly the whitefaced Hereford shouldered her way right past him, even rudely steppin' on one of his paws and drawin' a loud yap, and had herself halfway into the truck before Daddy wrapped his arms around her neck and shoved her out. "I expect you'll be layin' down on your back soon an' wantin' us to scratch your tummy for ya too, ye big lug," Daddy "scolded" her. When she bowed her head down and sorta shrunk away, it got him. "Well alright," he said, fishin' a range cube out of a box in the truck bed and lettin' Molly gobble it out of his hand just as smooth as Maggie now took carrots and horse apples out of mine.

Plus, that got the dogs out of the truck, jockeyin' for their own bovine range cubes. Jake stole one from Jeb, the three-quarter-grown puppy, but then Jeb stole one from Molly and lit out like a bat out of Hades through the hole Paw Paw had cut under the hogwire fence into the east pasture.

Later, at the weekly auction in Ennis, a steer came burstin' out the chute from the pen area into the auction ring. I kept glancin' over at Daddy each time a calf'd charge out, to see if he'd spotted himself a winner, but nothin' seemed to strike his fancy. Once again, the auctioneer, ole Fred Miller from out near Gun Barrel City, barked out the particulars, to a crowd of a hundred folks or so.

Daddy just kind-ly sat there with his hat, a straw one, tilted back on his head and his arms folded, a toothpick from Bubba's Barbeque, where we'd eaten lunch, juttin' out one side his mouth, then he scratched his chin. Me, I just kind-ly sat there with my hat, a straw one, tilted back on my head and my arms folded, a toothpick from Bubba's Barbeque, where we'd eaten lunch, juttin' out one side of my mouth, then I scratched my chin.

I expect he was awaitin' another good baby Hereford whiteface, 'cause I knew he'd grown more partial to Molly than he let on.

Then Clay appeared at the door, spotted us, and made his way over. "Ethan, got some tough news," he said right out of the chute.

"What now?" Daddy said.

"Maria Rivera's brother-in-law told everybody in Dee's Cafe at lunch today that she's gonna vote for the gamblers to come on," Clay said.

I'd seen that billboard I saw on the way home a hundred times if I'd seen it once. It featured a big ole bull and it said "Honey, Slap Me, We Missed Bubba's."

Well, we didn't miss Bubba's, but we didn't find us a baby Hereford that day, or anything else, either.

✻   ✻   ✻

Lotta times the sky out in the Texas cotton patch will look mean enough to scare you right down to the ground, even if it ain't that time. Trouble is, you never know for sure when it's gonna be tame as a declawed tabby cat and when it's gonna turn you ever' which way but loose.

I saw three horses flung from one end of a pasture to th'other by a tornada, while the dog standin' next to 'em remained in a composed squat and completed his business. I found a city limits sign to Ferris—over ten miles away—stuck six inches into the ground outside our main barn after one twister, and I saw one of my friends' double-wide trailer homes wrapped up like one of those curly-que french fries at the Arby's used to be in Ennis, the trailer two down from it thrown a quarter-mile, and the one between them untouched, while the family inside slept through the whole deal.

Why, I saw five hundred acres of County Commissioner Stanton's maize fields sheared clean by locusts durin' a drought, all the stalks and the woods surroundin' 'em scalded out by a brush fire the next week, then the whole kit n' caboodle washed into the Trinity by a flood spawned by a hurricane come up from the Gulf two weeks after that.

One night I heard—and felt—a twister settin' down on our home. It sucked ever' knothole out of the framed construction of an addition we put on on a few years before and it blew 78 window panes out of our house, includin' several that were spread in pieces across the top of my bed blankets when I came back up after duckin' under 'em.

But the day of the great Ellis County storm when I was young looked too dark even to be day. As I was runnin' back to the house from the stable after givin' the animals their afternoon feedin', Mama hollerin' out the window at me, I shot a glance back over my shoulder to the north. I caught my breath at seein' a gigantic black wall of thunderheads stretchin' clean across the horizon, from the ground up, high as the eye could follow.

*　　*　　*

More than one storm was in the works that day. If I'd have been out on Shiloh Road frontin' the Rodriguezes', which I was not, I would've heard the sounds of another big argument driftin' out, even over the sound of the rain beginnin' to pour in sheets.

Inside, Graciela was readin' the riot act to her husband, who was sorta cowerin' like he just lost the fight for he-bull. She pointed to a spot on the shirt of his she held. Lipstick smeared the collar, and not of a variety she carried in her purse.

She was way past screamin' at him in anything but the mother tongue, but what she was hollerin' was, "I should not scream at you; a man is worth screaming at, but you are not even a man, you are a weak, cowardly animal!"

The audience for this tussle was the same as usual, Blanca and three of her four siblings, who stood in a corner and watched. The ten-month-old was, mercifully, asleep in his cradle.

Blanca and the others jumped at the sound of their mother's closed fist smacking their father's face. They jumped the more when thunder crashed outside, thunder the likes of which Blanca couldn't ever remember hearin' before.

Before long, though, she couldn't even hear the thunder because the hail was hammerin' the house so hard, and ever'thing around it, includin' her daddy's pickup. Then darkness black as midnight came down like a canopy.

Somethin' had just kind-ly snapped in Graciela, and she just kept sluggin' her husband over and over and he just kept cowerin'. Finally, as the lights started flickerin' off and on, he supposed he'd had enough of that so he did some snappin' too, straightened up, grabbed her wrist, and raised his own fist to strike her.

"No, Papa!" Blanca shrieked.

Before his fist could come down the lights went out, an explosion that sounded like it came from one of those old 12-pound cannon with Hood's Brigade or Gano's horse soldiers at the reenactments rocked the house, and screams and smashin' sounds filled the darkness.

✻   ✻   ✻

That tornada, actually that set of tornadas, just tore up a chunk of Ellis County. You didn't have to be Sherlock Carter, or ole Rip Ford, to see where they went. You could just follow the path of dead livestock, cleared-out woods, mangled trailers, flattened houses—and the whole block of the old Cotton Patch town square, includin' Dee's Cafe, that lay in rubble.

Daddy had the radio on KBEC as he headed out our gravel path and onto Shiloh Road. He silently thanked God that the twisters had skirted our property. We just lost a few trees. That and, well, one of our cows we never saw again, even though no fence was torn.

"That brings the unconfirmed death toll of yesterday's tornado to five, with thirteen injured," the radio announcer was sayin'. "Stay tuned to Classic Country 1390, KBEC Waxahachie, Ellis County's only radio station, for continuous updates and information."

Daddy saw a shumard red oak tree trunk across Shiloh Road stickin' through a window of the Curtises' house, which had an exterior of peelin' sheetrock, but it was that way before the storm

99

too—the outside of the house that is, not the shumard tree trunk through the window.

"Joltin' Jed Schumacher and the still-undefeated Cotton Patch Farmers play for the regional championship this weekend . . ." the announcer was sayin' as Daddy gasped at the sight of the Rodriguezes' ravaged little home.

Fourteen

The Rodriguez place was still standin', but just barely. The tornada had swept out about ever'thing that was not a wall or roof. Graciela stood in the yard holdin' her baby, Blanca and the other three children not far away. It was a warm, steamy day for that time of year, not like the storm had freshened things up any, and Graciela was wearin' only one of those little tube tops that looked like it would've fit on Blanca a mite more accurately, and some shorts that, tiny as she was, were tinier still. Even her sandals were skimpy.

One of these days we women'll figure out the effect those sorta things have on the male of the species. Well alright, I guess we already know it plenty well, and that's just the problem, 'specially when we go to whinin' about what a low-life that handsome gentleman turned out to be, the one whose gaze we grabbed by flashin' him a little more skin than we should've, the one who wasn't interested in our brilliant mind, charm, or fascinatin' personality after all.

So my daddy shifted his dusty Shivy out of gear, parked, and walked toward Graciela Rodriguez. Top of ever'thing else, she had been cryin' and after givin' Daddy a brief brave smile, she began to do so again. "Thank God none of us was even hurt," she sobbed, "but we have no insurance, no money to repair any of this. And Eduardo went off angry and to drink, and we have not seen him since."

Helpless, abandoned, beautiful, vulnerable, and half-clad.

When a couple of the younger children clutched Graciela, sobs racked her.

"Graciela—has Eduardo ever struck you?" my daddy inquired.

She shook her head no, sobbin' harder. Daddy patted her on the shoulder in a pastoral sorta way, whereupon she buried her head in his chest, in an unpastoral sorta way, causin' him to embrace her in a hug. Now this disturbed my daddy, not because he wasn't a man and hadn't noticed all those things about Graciela I just mentioned, but because he was and had.

That, and he noticed the Rodriguezes' water service must've been knocked out by the storm, because it smelled like Graciela had taken a bath in some kind-ly sweet-smellin' perfume he had never before smelled on her, leastways in that dosage.

He pulled back so she would raise her head off him, which she did, the sobs slowin'. But when she looked up at him, her almond eyes shimmered and her tear-streaked face shone radiant and invitin' and deadly. You might say caution was thrown to last night's winds and this mornin's abandonment.

That may've been Daddy's first blush that went clean from head to toe. When her lips parted, he saw they had turned out in all their glory, too, in a shade akin to one of his old Sooner football jerseys, and with enough paint heaped on 'em to last maybe till the next twister. Her eyes just kind-ly searched his face and he stood there, like the ole deer in the headlight.

Right when she started her face toward his, my friend Blanca said, "Mama."

Daddy snapped out of whatever that ancient spell was and pulled away. He walked, faster than he usually did, to his truck and came back with a jacket, which he wrapped around Graciela's bare shoulders, and a large picnic basket, which he handed her. But he would not look her in the eye any more. When he spoke, he was starin' at the ground. "The basket is full of food my wife put together for you."

Graciela sorta blinked like she'd been smacked in the face, which in reality she had been more than once by her lovin' husband.

"Sara Lee Blevins will be by any minute to pick y'all up. They want you to stay with 'em till the men of the church get your house fixed up. Well, alright."

Head bowed, he turned and headed toward his truck.

"Pastor Ethan?" Graciela said, her voice sorta quaverin'. He stopped, but he did not turn back. "You—you are a good man. Please thank Lorena for her thoughtfulness and love."

Never showin' her more than his back, he nodded, then climbed back into the Shivy and pulled out, quick-like.

*   *   *

If you had a notion the storms were far from over for Cotton Patch in that eventful season, you would be right. And isn't that the hurt of it all, that the messes we see with our eyes are nothin' compared to the messes we can't see?

Daddy figured he didn't need any coffee that mornin', and besides the Hitchin' Rail was already burned down, and that was where he would usually get him a cup, in the special 24-ounce size they kept on hand for him.

He went on to the church, where he picked up Clay. "Anyone around?" Daddy asked him.

"Just Mrs. Posey, dropping off a bunch of food for folks. Say, Scott hasn't been around much lately, has he?"

"Sure he's got his hands full like ever'one else in this one-horse town," Daddy said like a man who maybe did need some coffee after all.

"You know, I can't much figure out what you think of this place," Clay said.

"Well don't go losin' any sleep over it, alrighty?" Daddy sorta snipped at him. "You'll be outa here soon enough and off to start some fancy new church up around Dallas."

This caught Clay flat-footed, not that it wasn't true, but that it was and Daddy had nailed it right on the head. *Right on the head indeed*, Clay thought to himself as he saw Jefe jog past in his usual fashionable get-up. But what he said was, "What happened with you and my Mom?"

Daddy glanced kind-ly sideways at him, which was somethin' he did even less than he blushed, which he had already done today too. "Was her sent you down here wadn't it?" he said.

"Uh—no, Presbytery sent me down here," Clay said, feelin' like those old Nebraska quarterbacks must've felt when Daddy blitzed them.

"I know your Mama. And I knew what Cullums you were from right when I saw you."

"She's not a Cullum anymore."

"Heard as much." Then, under his breath, "she's still half-Cortez, though."

"What?" Clay said.

"Nothin'," Daddy said, cursin' to himself, at least in spirit, when he saw what was left of Dee's and realizin' that was the only place on the square that brewed half-decent bean.

"She's on her third go-round," Clay said. "But she's at least content with this fellow. They've been married ten years."

Then my daddy's jaw set sorta tight, and Clay saw one of those veins in his neck that only showed up when there was no room inside for all the churnin'. After a few seconds, Daddy kind-ly relaxed and his jaw and neck resumed normal operation and he even sorta nodded. "That's good," he said, noddin' some more, almost like to convince himself. "That's real good."

"But Ethan?" Clay said, lookin' around like somebody might be eavesdroppin', even though they were on I-45 now, though back before it was all clean and widened out from old Supercollider tax funds, and headed south toward Ennis. "I wouldn't say this to anyone else—but I don't think she ever forgot about you, even through all the marriages and all the years."

Daddy just looked out where the winter wheat was already planted, but he didn't see any of that, nor the herds of grazin' cattle, nor Palmer nor the Garrett landfill as they passed them, nor even that tornadas had lit down hither and yon around there too. "Strange the ignorant contempt with which a boy holds things that when he's a man he wouldn't take a million dollars for—if he could put 'em back into a jar to keep on his shelf and pull out when he was of a mind to," he said.

Clay looked at him, then out his own window, thinkin' that might've been the most words he'd ever heard my daddy say at one time, preachin' aside. Thinkin', too, that though the people up in Dallas had their own problems, he was about ready to start hearin' some of those instead of all the goofy stuff kept presentin' itself to him uninvited from Cotton Patch folks.

They both sat quiet for a minute, until Daddy flipped on KBEC.

"That's Willie Nelson and his classic, *You Were Always on My Mind,*" the announcer said.

"Does anyone besides him work at that station?" Clay said. "Every time you turn that on, he's the D.J., and the news and weather guy, and he does that auction thingee—"

"The on-air flea market?" Daddy cut in.

"Yeh, that—" Clay said.

"Hey, I got me a good Remington off that," Daddy said, "and a bicycle for Katie, too—"

"—and I heard somebody say he announces the Waxahachie football games too," Clay kept on.

"Basketball and baseball, too," Daddy said. Clay stared at him like an armadilla had just lighted on his head. For his part, Daddy realized Clay could only have "heard somebody say" about the Waxahachie football games, because you couldn't get KBEC north of downtown Dallas, and you couldn't have pinched together enough quarters for a cup of coffee, even at the Hitchin' Rail before they burned it down, if you counted one for ever' night Clay Cullum had been south of downtown Dallas by the time of evenin' high school football kicked off.

"Clay, do you entertain any notions of rentin' you somethin' down here, at least temporarily, before you get you that church in Dallas?"

"Well now—"

"I understand our place is a little far off the highway for you to take that extra bedroom we offered," my daddy said, "and I know your mama's cookin'—or that of whoever she hires to do the cookin'—is mighty fine, but did you ever think of actually livin' in the same county where your people are?"

Course he thought of it, all the time, 'cause his people were in Dallas.

"Well Ethan," Clay sputtered, tryin' in his educated manner to decide which point to tackle first, "seems to me livin' right near the folks hasn't exactly endeared them to you."

"Son, lemme tell ya somethin'," Daddy plowed on. "I'd say a man needs five good years away from the cemeteries (which was his word for seminaries) after he graduates just to get his wits back enough to have somethin' to say to folks out there in the real world that'll help 'em."

"Well, Ethan, with respect, I'd expect that from someone who plans to spend his life in Cotton Patch, America, mowin' his own church lawn and workin' hard to keep his congregation under a hundred," Clay offered.

It was prob'ly good that a third man entered the conversation at this point, 'cause things were rapidly headin' in the direction of no return between those two.

From the direction of the radio came a familiar smooth Texas drawl. "Howdy friends, this is Garth Chisholm. As a lifelong resident of Ellis County, I've had the privilege to know many of y'all."

Daddy and Clay stared at each other, and Clay turned up the volume.

"And you know what you've been tellin' me?" Chisholm continued. "Especially after those awful tornadoes cut through the county last night? You want the jobs and business the new family fun and gamin' complex on the outskirts of Cotton Patch would bring."

Daddy switched off the radio in fury. "How'd he get in there to get that commercial done so quick? And who had time to tell him anything since last night? Some of his high-steppin' bank board buddies?" he said. "'Sides, last time he promoted a good jobs project was when he sold WorldMart the land to build their new superstore and put a couple dozen more little guys outa business."

"I don't believe it," Clay said—about Chisholm's two-step on the "family fun and gamin' complex." He had no doubt about the WorldMart deal.

*　　*　　*

Now you may know there are few things Texans prize more highly than good barbeque, or "barbechew" as Paw Paw preferred. Even more than chili, I'd say, and I'm a chili fiend of the Terlingua-inspired, four-to-five-alarm variety. And the barbechew Paw Paw spoke of, and himself excelled at makin', usually on a spit over a big fire of mesquite kindlin' out in the dooryard, away from the big barn, was real barbechew, not that fraudulent piggy fare of the Tennessee sort. Real live beef barbechew from real live Texas cows, which most folks grew for other reasons than for pets.

But no offense to Paw Paw, around our part of Ellis County, if you wanted the best sit-down, store-bought barbechew, hands down you went to Bubba's, already mentioned, on I-45 at the east end of Ennis. My heart always skipped a note when I'd see that big ole he-bull model loomin' massive in the front parkin' lot, out front of a smoker so big and with so much smoke pourin' out of it, I was several grades through the Shanahan Classical Christian School before I realized it was not a locomotive engine. When I was little, that bull looked big to me as Big Tex the giant fifty-foot cowboy at the State Fair. When I got bigger, he got smaller, but the barbechew inside still had my mouth waterin' so that I'd be needin' paper towels while I was still out in the parkin' lot.

If they didn't agree on anything else, pretty much ever'body agreed about Bubba's. That's prob'ly why they were all there that day when my daddy and Clay pulled in for lunch. The only other thing needed was Merle Haggard's *Walkin' on the Fightin' Side of Me* to be playin' on the speaker, which it was.

Right outa the chute, Daddy and Clay saw that Clint Granger holdin' forth at a table of men which included Mayor Coltrane.

"How much you think ole Shorty's got?" Granger asked the table.

"Always a few dollars less'n he'd like," Mayor Coltrane said, which the table appreciated. "'Sides, I think for him this as much 'bout keepin' the Mess-kins off that land as it is the dollars. The guv'ment was fixin' to stick Section Eight housin' in there till you boys and your Austin and outa-state buddies got 'n the loop."

Course, Daddy and Clay did not hear any of this, nor even see that Granger and the others till they were next to the table, en route to the food line. Then one of the table, his back to 'em, turned around and they saw it was Will Hankins.

"Ethan," said Mayor Coltrane with a nod.

But my daddy just kind-ly stood there like someone had clubbed him 'cross the head with a two-by-four chunk of cedar. And he was starin' right at Will Hankins, even after that fella turned away, which was pretty quick.

Then Daddy managed a nod to the table, gave 'em that short stiff underhanded wave from the hip with the palm down in the Texas fashion, and walked away, decidin' after all that he had no stomach for barbechew today, even if it was Bubba's.

Fifteen

Prob'ly the only reason I spent even as much time with Amy Posey as I did, which was as little as I could manage, was that we got thrown together because our daddies were together a lot on church business. Leastwise they had been in the past, though not so much it seemed of late.

Summer kept tryin' to grab back the reins from fall as it will do in Texas, even after that young man ran for one touchdown, caught another, and threw for a third in a 35-14 state quarterfinals victory. Many has been the time when summer battled fall right through to the next spring, never lettin' winter get so much as a toe in the water. Why, I've seen July, August, and September scorch townfolks' lawns yellow, then they've looked lush and green as one of those North Dallas golf courses at Christmas time.

Only reason I believed snow had ever come to Cotton Patch was we had a video my daddy shot of the pint-sized snowman he built for me outside my window. It was good he shot that video when he did, 'cause that little fella had melted plum away within 24 hours. But even with that video, and me in it, I thought it might have been one of those dubbing jobs; you know, where they shoot one scene, then splice in another from a totally different time and place, but like it fits all together when it really doesn't? Folks like Hollywood-types and New York TV networks and guv'ment agencies are good at that sorta thing.

However, my daddy wasn't, which was why I finally figured snow really had come to Cotton Patch when I was three years old, though it hadn't yet returned by the time Amy and I were out prowlin' through that quiet, dark hideaway tucked along the south boundary line of our west pasture. There the world was how you wanted it, or if not, you could just conjure another of your own makin'. Either way, the chocolate cobwebbed canopy covered you from sun, moon, and other elements alike. Once when the sun shone out of a sky still half azure and cloudless, but a gullywasher unleashed on me from the other half while I hunkered down in there, it seemed like a half hour before a drop got down to the ground and me and the squirrels and the dogs who provided my swirlin' sniffin' escort.

With the passin' of the seasons, as those rhythms and cycles grew me up, I would less and less go there as going toward things, and more and more as creeping away from them. And I wouldn't make new worlds as much as just have no worlds a'tall.

"Daddy named this Katie's Woods," I explained to Amy, not for the first time, as our little boots crunched twigs and sticks and crisped leaves and we ducked limbs and heard those nasty, thorny briars lashin' our jeans. "No one ever comes back here but me—'cept when I bring you."

I figured if I had to take care of Amy while Mrs. Posey was up at the house visitin' with Mama, I might as well teach her some things that might help her as she went along in life, even if she didn't see the need; in fact, especially if she didn't see the need.

Sometime later, after Dallas came to Ellis County, but never got near Katie's Woods, I recalled what a shelter it had been against more than rain. Seemed as though whenever I took Amy out there, away from things, she blossomed lovely inside and out. How much of that was me and how much her I cannot say, but I know that some of both was mixed in there.

Pushin' a post oak bough back, I pointed to some twisted bob-warr fencin' I had led us to. "Look at the double-bobbed ties on this wire," I said. "My daddy says they haven't made that kind of bob-warr since before the War."

"Really?" Amy said. "World War II was a long time ago, wadn't it?"

"No, silly," said I, but not agitated like I would've been outside the chocolate cobwebbed canopy, "the *War*—the War Between the States."

"Oh, yeh," she said, noddin' and steppin' over a viney stump toward bob-wire. "Wow—this fence has been here that long?"

"I reckon it has." I said. "Or at least since maybe right after the War, anyhow." Then I heard a crackle and somethin' smacked her right in the face and her head shot back.

"Ah!" she blurted.

Now I giggled again. "'At's just an acorn poppin' loose," I said. Then she began to giggle, and actually laugh, which she hardly ever did out there. And she never ever laughed like she did when, like God was givin' me a humbleness check, another one shot loose and smacked me right on the nose.

"Ow!" I said.

Then we both just laughed for quite a long time, as loud as I can remember ever laughin'. Finally I pointed through the undergrowth and said, "See over yonder? That's where Daddy and me built us a campfire one night. Well, he did most of it, but I helped."

"Wow, you built a campfire way out here?"

"Sure did," I said expertly. "Course, just once."

"Why only once?" she said. "If my daddy would ever do anything like that with me, I'd make him come back all the time."

"Well, we would've," I said, "but Mama wouldn't have it, 'cause some sparks caught our brush pile on fire and we nearly burned the whole woods down."

She affected the beginnings of astonishment, then she remembered we were inside the chocolate cobwebbed canopy and she started to giggle instead, which to my surprise I did too, till I remembered it had only happened 'cause Daddy's mind was on some bad doin's at church, and how bad Mama yelled at him after it happened, the hurtin' sorta yellin' that doesn't just wash out in the shower or the creek.

Then I saw one of the few folks you'd ever run across out there. "Hey, Mr. Jumpy!" I hollered.

He was movin' along the path down at the end of the bob-wire and Katie's Woods, which, alas, was not far away.

"Afternoon, ladies," he said with a smile, tippin' his old slouch hat.

"Hey, Mr. Jumpy, what'chu have in that sack you're carryin'?" I said. "You been poppin' squirrels again?

"Oh yes, I have, and they sure good for meat and soup!" he fairly beamed.

"But Mr. Jumpy, my Paw Paw says it's not good to go around shootin' squirrels 'cause if you kill the mommas, all the babies will die too," I said.

Guilt covered his face.

Then I heard Jeb, the now three-quarter-grown Lab puppy, whimperin' from out there. "Jeb!" I said, runnin' out of Katie's Woods and not carin' that the limbs were slashin' me, and in the face, too. He was close by, near the tank. He was kind-ly stumblin' along, then he fell over right under that stand of cottonwoods and I saw blood on his mouth.

I think Daddy was soapin' his saddle over in the stable when he heard me screamin', from way over there.

*　　*　　*

Daddy had Doc Gibbs out there within two hours. Didn't take him long to get around to the tank, where my whole life I had watched our animals frolic when it was full, and where we put the pumpkins I learned how to shoot on when it was dry, and around whose path up around it the bluebonnets spread like a royal carpet ever' spring.

Doc Gibbs had already looked at Jeb, my beloved puppy, and he felt pretty sure he had a general idea of what had happened. He and Daddy were walkin' the ground where Jeb had been, a ways off from the tank, when Daddy stopped and bent over a few feet from one of those nasty locust trees he must've missed cuttin' down. He stared at a patch of dirt.

"What is it, Ethan?" Doc Gibbs asked.

Daddy shook his head once and clicked his tongue. "That's cougar tracks, Doc."

"Why, it's been years since I heard of a cougar around here," Doc Gibbs said.

"Tater Tatum shot one up on Sugar Ridge ten years ago that had torn into his herd," Daddy said.

"Fella shot one other side of Bardwell Lake last week," Doc Gibbs said.

Daddy took off his hat and ran his fingers through his short brown hair, sighin', "Thought I had this whole place fenced proper."

But it was no cougar that messed with Jeb, my dead puppy.

Just then a noise north across the pasture, other side of the hill with the live oak, drew their attention. Then Paw Paw came chuggin' over the rise on his bush hog.

"Swear, Doc, don't know which is older, Pop Gremillion or that ole contraption he's drivin'—or that's drivin' him, I'm not sure which," Daddy said.

Smoke filled the air as he came down the hill.

"He billows up like a volcano 'cause his knees got the rheumatiz and won't let him work a twelve-hour day anymore," Daddy said.

"But didn't he catch that gimp when his horse fell on him?" Doc Gibbs asked.

"Tryin' to bring back a stray calf down in the bottoms, and that was no more than three, four years back," Daddy said.

"He's a tough ole bull," Doc Gibbs said.

Daddy stood up and nodded and said, "Guess I'm proud the old boy'd rather be on his bush hog, even when the grass doesn't need cuttin' and he's hurtin' all over, than sittin' in front of the TV all day like most folks his age."

Doc Gibbs stepped to the tank and stuck some sorta tube in there. Then he pulled it out and squeezed a couple drops of somethin' else into it and stared at it. Then he sniffed the water and tasted a mite of it.

After that he turned to my daddy and said, "Ethan, this tank's poisoned."

* * *

Daddy picked up Jeb, my puppy, in his own arms and carried him to his truck. I was already cryin' like a banshee, but when I saw he wasn't goin' to bury him out by Mary and Joseph, nor even anywhere on our spread, I broke away from Mama and ran screamin' out of the house and commenced to tryin' to pull Jeb away from him and when I couldn't do that, I just startin' sluggin' my daddy hard as I could, cause I wanted bad to hurt the whole world and I knew I wouldn't hurt him no matter how hard I hit him, but I thought if I hit him hard enough, I might indeed hurt the rest of the world.

By then, he wasn't in a mood for socializin', nor father-daughter talks, nor "teachable times," neither. He told me to get back in the house, but when I just stood there in the dooryard cryin' the more, he put Jeb my puppy down and came over and knelt down and held me and told me he loved me while I heaved and wailed.

After a couple minutes, he picked me up, then turned and started to carry me back into the house, but Paw Paw was standin' there. "What the h--- you think you're doin' boy, makin' my baby girl cry like that?" Paw Paw was crazy mad; he must've dug into a gallon of that Decadent Devil's Chocolate Swirl or whatever Blue Bell after he got off his bush hog. Then he wound up his fist and took a half-step toward us. "Put her down, you d----- fool!"

"Paw Paw?" I cried out, though I could hardly see him I had so many tears comin' out. "What are you doin'?"

"I said put her down!" Paw Paw bellowed. "You crazy d----- fool, tryin' to save the whole world and you with plenty of your own problems and now look what you done, you --- d----- fool—you brought 'em onto your own land and your own family ain't safe—my baby girl ain't safe!"

"Paw Paw!" I screamed, feelin' Daddy tense up, and fearin' what he might do, 'cause he-bull or not, he'd have torn Paw Paw in two if he put his mind to it once he had his Irish up, even in Paw Paw's prime. "You shall not take the name of the Lord your God in vain, for the Lord will not hold him guiltless who takes His name in vain!"

The only person more surprised than me all that catechism seemed to have actually took, was Daddy, judgin' from the goofy way he looked at me.

Somehow it even shut Paw Paw up—sorta shamed him, I 'spect—although it was way too late already, but it did let Daddy make his way to the front door, where he sat me down just as Mama appeared.

Her face was whiter'n dogwood blooms flutterin' through the air at spring plowin' time. I figured she must be plenty riled at her father, with whom she'd had many a tangle through the years. But I figured wrong. "You cruel, inconsiderate—man," she growled, the words crawlin' out slow and heartless like from some dark, scary place. "How dare you bring this horror into our lives—how dare you endanger the only child you ever gave me!"

That was my daddy she said that to.

Now she was screamin' and pullin' me to herself. "Go on—take the dog you killed with ever'thing else you've killed and get the h--- out of here! And don't mind comin' back!"

I put an exclamation mark at the end of her sentence in the recountin' of this nightmare for you, but Mama's exclamation mark was slammin' the front door so hard in Daddy's face that it shattered the storm door into pieces. You figure that one out.

*   *   *

It wasn't like when Zig Ziglar came to speak. Though the whole community was again invited, maybe forty people came to Cotton Patch Presbyterian this time. Mama wasn't among 'em, but I was. I had broken loose from her and run all the way down the gravel path and Shiloh Road to the Rodriguezes and caught me a ride with Miz Graciela. Right then, I was thinkin' Mama could go straight to that place down under, and I'm fair certain I voiced that sentiment to her right before *I* slammed the front door shut.

The whole ride into town, my daddy'd been frettin' how it could've come to this pretty pass. A fight that should've been no fight a'tall was lookin' now to be a losin' fight, and he who had no desire even to be in it was the one standin' before the forty, on the floor, not up in the pulpit.

There were no other leaders now, just some of us Presbyterian folks; some of those Baptist and Church of Christers who didn't have preachers now, except for Reverend Jasper's little group; a couple of Methodists; and some of the holy rollers who had that lady pastor. But she was outa town preachin' somewhere at a healin' and deliverance conference.

Word was gettin' around some of the pastors were steerin' clear of the gamblin' issue 'cause it was fixin' to cost 'em some of their biggest donors if they spoke out any more.

"Well, it all seems to be turnin' against us, friends," my daddy said, feelin' almost bad as ever'one there felt for him. One thing hadn't yet turned against us; Cotton Patch had blitzed its state semifinal foe and now had its first shot ever at a state championship. In fact, while the forty gathered at our little church, where I noticed a couple of the ole-timey ceilin' lights had burned out, ten times that many cheered the football team, not at a game, but at a pep rally in the high school gym.

"Anyone else have anything to add?" Daddy asked.

I was glad to see Mr. Posey rise from his seat near the back. I hadn't seen him around church lately, and when he wasn't there, Amy bugged me to death. He had been the most fired-up one in our church from the start about the whole gamblin' deal. "This is a hard thing for me to say, Ethan," he said in sort of a quaverin' drawl. "But I need to say it, because I've got to put what is best for all the folks in this community ahead of what people might think about me. I—I'm gonna vote in favor of the family entertainment complex."

A collective gasp rose from the sparse gatherin'.

You could hear Miz T, a few folks down from me on the first row, kind-ly under her breath and kind-ly over it, but disgusted as if she'd just sipped ice cold but rotten buttermilk, "Family enter . . . "

Stung, and prob'ly other things too, Mr. Posey grew a little bolder: "This town—'specially since the tornada—well, it's dyin', Ethan. We got to get us some help."

Only then did I notice neither Mrs. Posey nor Amy were there, which was the first time I ever remembered them bein' absent from anything at church unless they were near death with sickness.

A couple of people nodded their agreement with Mr. Posey.

My Daddy couldn't believe what he was hearin'. "But Scott, you of all people, my—our—only rulin' elder, you're the one's led the way all along for us on this deal. How could you do this?"

"Ethan, you said yourself we're not even gonna be able to worship in this buildin' if things don't pick up," Mr. Posey said, talkin' a lot faster now, his face beet red. "Presbytery's gonna shut us down."

Sayin' this in public about knocked my daddy over.

"That's why they sent Clay here to help you," Mr. Posey went on. "I'm tired of shoulderin' your—the finances—on my own. I can't keep it up. Maybe it's time we rethought a bunch o' things."

With that, he fairly stomped right out of the building. I couldn't tell if he was mad or embarrassed or what. But I know this—you could've heard a turkey feather land on the worn-out red carpet in that sanctuary just then.

Miz T lowered her head, her hair now seemin' much whiter than I remembered it bein', and shook it.

I felt like cryin' all over again, this time for my daddy instead of at him. He didn't know what to say. He looked lost as a lone goose flyin' north at harvest time. I reckon he felt like his last friend in the world had just up and skedaddled on him. Well, I knew better'n that, he had him at least one left, so I started to stand up, but before I could, the door at the back of the sanctuary—the one our rulin' elder Mr. Posey had just left through—opened up and Mrs. Blevins pushed Mama down the aisle—in her wheelchair.

Well, no, I didn't tell of that ole wheelchair, did I?

They stopped near the front row. Daddy looked over at her, wonderin' if he was fixin' to catch one more lick. She stared at him a minute, then gave him the prettiest smile I ever saw her give anyone, and she had a beautiful smile. That's when the tears just kind-ly bubbled up and out of his blue eyes, which were now more red I think than blue, and so did they with quite a few other eyes in the group.

"God has a way of knowin' when we've gone just about as far as we can go, doesn't he?" my daddy said, his voice tighter'n the bark on a tree. For just a minute there, I wasn't sure what sound, if any, was gonna come out of his throat next. Then he got out, "In the seven years since—the accident—she ain't complained once, even though it changed ever'thing in her life and left her, 'cause she won't lean on painkillers, hurtin' all the time."

That was all he could say, and when she saw the feelin' overcomin' him, Mama wheeled herself right up to him. He knelt down, embraced her, and began to sob. I saw her lips movin', sayin', "I'm so sorry for what I said. I love you."

Then Miz T came forward to pat him on the back, then someone else did the same, then someone else, until the whole shootin' match was clustered around us, the Shanahans, 'cause to my surprise I found myself somehow right'n the middle of 'em all, holdin' Mama and Daddy and bein' held, some of 'em cryin' softly, some prayin'.

That is one of the times I saw what Christ's Church really is, more'n anyone, even my daddy, could've told me or preached to me. And that is why when the hard times, the real hard ones, soon came, and when they come again, I shall always know that what he preached is real and they can't move me with ten thousand times ten thousand.

Sixteen

One of the best things about Texas sunsets, especially in autumn and winter, is if you're sittin' on the porch with someone and there's hard things to say, or there's nothin' at all to say, well, that painted sky kind-ly takes away the need to flap your gums if you don't want to.

For instance, Mama and Daddy were out there the next evenin' and that rainbow-lookin' sunset came in mighty handy.

Finally, Daddy said, "Why I am even worried about it? What kind of people want their vices so badly they would kill animals, break the hearts of children, and put their own greed ahead of the good of the community?"

He made a face and swatted his neck. "Why in the world do we have buffalo gnats this time of year?" he said. He glanced at his hand, which was now smeared with the enormous insect and its blood. "Well, if they don't offer me that P.R. job with the country club up in Oklahoma City next week, I may resign anyhow."

"You can't make these folks do right, Ethan," she said wearily. "You can only encourage them along the way. Whatever our own ancient distresses, you need to do that."

"You know I've been fed up with 'em for a good spell now," he said, brushin' off the buffalo gnat's remnants with dirt from a nearby potted plant. "Lookee at what my one elder went and did."

When his voice trailed off in dejection, Mama said, "Luke Blevins is ready, he knows the Westminster Confession, he even passed examination at presbytery. Why can't you get him on?"

"Him and his painkillers?" Daddy said. "His nurse caught him first, we found out about it next after he swore he'd quit, then the medical examiners got on to him—only last Christmas, remember—after he'd sworn to us all over again. I still can't believe they only gave him probation, but that was only 'cause ever'one, includin' Sheriff Lookabaugh, liked him so much, else he wouldn't even still be in practice. That plus the fact he's the best family doctor Cotton Patch ever saw and we need him so bad." He shook his head. "No wonder Sara Lee lives by that Prozac, example her own husband sets."

Mama started to speak again, but she knew Daddy well enough to tell he already had his mind on what he was gonna say next and wouldn't hear a word she said anyhow.

"A pastor may not love his folks or he may not be much of a preacher, but he better not be both and I am," was what he said, noticin' one of the dogs had deposited another dinosaur bone under his rocker, even bigger than the last.

"You give your life for these people, week in and month out, year after year. I know because we have to give ours with you," Mama said.

"Clay's leavin'," he said.

"What?"

"Well, since he got ordained a while back, and he's got a group up north of Dallas—a group with more money than our whole town has—that want him to start a church for them. Guess it was too much to hope that he'd stay here long with us little people," Daddy said.

"Well, the little people have you; I expect they mustn't be greedy," she said. She eyed him as he stared at the ground. "You really like him, don't you?"

"Yeh, guess I do," he said. "He's young and full of himself and wrongheaded too much, but—well, I thought it'd leave the church in good hands if I take the Oklahoma job." Now he looked at her. "You don't want to go to Oklahoma, do you?"

"Ever'body and ever'thing means anything to me in the world is out here," she said. "But I'll go wherever. I just want to make sure we're runnin' to somethin' and not from it."

He thought about that for a minute as a hawk called from the cobalt sky overhead and the cool of the autumn evenin' fields curled around them. He thought, too, on how he would've jumped the tracks and crashed headfirst into the ditch long ago without Mama's often painful but rarely unwise counsel. He took her hand in his, then leaned over and kissed it. "I'm pastorin' the town, or at least one little chunk of it, and you're pastorin' me, Loree," he said, his eyes shiny in the dusk. "Even after all the hurt I've brought you."

She held his hand too and smiled a little smile. "You're just a man," she said.

Just that helped him some and he stood, sayin', "Guess I better go tuck in our little bird. She's still frettin' about Jeb."

*　　*　　*

That evenin' I lay under the covers, replayin' all of what I had seen in recent days. Even in the country and even when they're homeschooled, kids fret about things. I don't think most folks understand that. When a child is sad, she's just as sad as a grown-up. When she's mad, same thing. And when she's afraid, well that can be even worse, 'cause she hasn't lived enough to know how to deal with some things.

Plus, a child doesn't know how to tell it to you like a grown-up, or she's afraid to, or grown-ups don't give 'er a chance. So nobody thinks she has such thoughts and worries, which like much else we think is wrong.

I was mostly, above all else, hopin' Mama and Daddy'd be nice to each other like at the church the night before and since. Then I heard the coyote chorus, like ever' night if I was still awake. And like the other nights, I sorta frowned, then got out of bed and crossed my pink carpet to the window. I pulled up the blinds and the sight of a magnificent golden harvest moon hit me right in the face so that I gasped. How beautiful it was, and I thanked God He had those old coyotes howl just then, 'cause those moons don't last more than a few minutes.

I looked up through the darkened appendages of the pine tree that stood outside my window. My eyes tracked across the searchless sky, its starry host aglitter. Far to the east, beyond the invisible Trinity Valley, I saw Scurry and Rosser a'twinklin'.

The coyotes simmered down, then one of the Labs barked, prob'ly at that moon. But I knew which Lab it wadn't, and tears filled my eyes and I felt my chin start to quiver. Then I heard somethin' else off in the distance, right faint at first. I threw open the window and the chill night braced me. At first I only heard a whippoorwill. I drank in the fragrant cool aroma of Texas like it was ice cold buttermilk from a pottery crock in high summer.

Then, carried along on the breeze, came the melodious harmony of singin' voices across the cedar trees and the rollin' pastures.

"Hmm . . ." I said aloud. (You talk aloud to yourself a lot when you're an only child in the country.) "Never heard y'all this late of an evenin' before."

I listened to 'em for a minute, then returned to my bed, but I left the blinds and window open both. I nestled down under covers radiant golden from the moon and a smile covered my face as I closed my eyes. Driftin' off, their voices in my ears and heart, I whispered, *"When We Cross . . . Over Jordan."*

✳   ✳   ✳

Next mornin', I rode Maggie down the gravel path and out onto Shiloh Road while Paw Paw bush hogged the Johnson grass both sides of it. He had apologized in his own way for his outburst the other day against Daddy. He'd thrown away all the ice cream, pie, cake, and candy in his double-wide, sworn—to himself and God—never to eat any of them again, and fixed us up a series of meals so scrumptious a dead man would've heard the dinner bell for 'em, or at least wished he had.

We knew all we had to do was let him know how good it was and he would keep it comin', leastways for a while. I will say I never had better dirty rice from him nor anyone else than that batch he brought us.

When I looked down Shiloh Road and saw the little wooden church burned down, kind-ly of a gray cloud still shroudin' the blackened rubble, I motioned to Paw Paw and galloped thataway.

Miz T, alone, cane in hand and tremblin', was walkin' a jagged path among the spare, still-smokin' ashes. Here and there, embers still glowed orange and yellow. Maggie snorted and shook her head as I rode up to Miz T and opened my mouth, but no words would come out. I do not know if that is because that nasty greasy air had clogged up my throat or because my brain couldn't muster anything to say, though both of these were sure enough true.

"Folks burned down the church, honey," Miz T said.

Several more seconds passed before I squeezed out, "But—not again. How—could—they?"

"'Cause some folks hates other folks, and some folks hates God worse," she said, without malice.

I got off Maggie, who was fussin' 'cause of the air, pulled the reins over her head, and walked to Miz T. I held the reins in one hand and put my other arm around that lady. Then I wept many bitter tears into her breast and she was cryin' just as hard, which I had never seen her do before and I had known her since I was born.

*   *   *

Normie had his mandolin with him rather than his guitar that afternoon at the Cotton Patch General Store, and he was strummin' the old gospel standard *Farther Along*. He, Huey, Newy, and Scooter held their usual spots around the domino table, and the Duke stood his ground too. Those boys reminded me of that old post card where the cigar-smokin' dogs are at the poker table and one is passin' another a card under the table with one of his hind paws. Once again, Arvel sat on a packin' crate, this time guzzlin' a Mountain Dew, and Tater whittled a cedar stick atop a pile of oat sacks. Red-headed Hank from the post office was there too, puffin' on a cigar; Wednesdays were his day off.

"Dag nabbit, Scooter, you done it to me again," Huey announced, assessin' the shape he was in on the domino table.

Newy rang home his agreement with a brown bullet to the spittoon.

"Anyhows, it's over," said Scooter. "Why, I bet they ain't a one 'o them council folk but what'll vote agin' it."

"Ah, some o' them preacher-types will, sure," said Huey.

"Shoot, that Doctor D or whatever, he tole the whole world he's fer it. Fixin' to put him up all kind-ly buildin's fuh that pew-jumpin holy fire church o' his," Scooter dissented, eyein' Newy. "I 'spect that man's suits cost more'n an acre o' yore land'd bring, New."

"Reckon some o' them boys gittin' they skids greased by them Dallas yahoos?" Tater said.

"Know fer a fact they bought that ole Ford dealer lot Garth Chisholm and his bank been settin' on last three years," Scooter said.

"How the Sam Hill you know that?" Huey said, and even though he clearly meant business with that domino he held in his leathery hand, he stopped right where he was.

"Got me an in-law works there saw the paperwork," said Scooter. "They forked over a perdy penny too."

Tater whistled, Newy spat, Hank from the post office blew rings with his cigar, and Arvel cackled.

"Heck, Charlie over at the newspaper tole me other day Shorty's a'gonna use that Mary Ann Riviera to hannel the sale of his land," Tater said, squeezin' him off a pinch of Copenhagen. "And—he said Shorty may not be finished sellin' land to them dandies."

"I'm thinkin' you boys more full o' hooey'n the Christmas turkey," Newy sounded off.

"I'm thinkin' evah-buddy on that council cuttin' theirselves best deal they kin," said Huey.

"Reckon only two ain't saluted yet's Scott Posey 'n that Pastor Jasper," said Arvel, maybe 'cause his Mountain Dew was empty.

"I hear tell ole Scottie fancies takin' a turn at the wheel hisself now and again over to Shreveport," Scooter said, layin' down two more dominos.

"I got twenty bucks says Cotton Patch takes the state champeenship this weekend," said Tater. "Who'll take a turn at the wheel on that?"

*   *   *

Couple days later, Mr. Posey was out of town on business again and Mrs. Posey came over to visit with Mama on somethin', I don't know what. Since she was workin' durin' the day now, leastways till

4 o'clock or so, by the time she came over, Amy was out of school, so she brought her along.

I had had fun with Amy that day at Katie's Woods, but the next day I found out she was tellin' other kids that my family must be really "weird" and "gross" to have such things happen as poisoned tanks and killed dogs. I knew Amy had said things about me before, but when she started runnin' down my family, that pretty well tore it far as I was concerned.

Me, I had had my fill of all the Poseys.

When they got there, I disappeared into my room and shut the door, then I hollered at Mama that Amy could go jump in the lake and she could tell her I said so, in those words.

Daddy was next, but he used a different tack. He said let's go shoot some pumpkins down at the old tank, the one with the dogwood tree turned purple in spring and that was always dry, not just usually, and which had not been poisoned by somebody. I said fine if Amy didn't come. Then he said he was gonna use me instead of pumpkins if I didn't get a move on.

So there we were, me, my daddy, and that nasty little viper I couldn't shake to save me. Daddy was usin' his Sergeant's Special Colt .45 and the viper and I were rotatin' on the scoped .22 and the Ruger .243 rifle. He didn't bring any of the bigger rifles or the shotguns that day; maybe he figured the viper didn't have sense enough to be trusted around such firearms.

You couldn't miss with that .22, but I liked that Ruger too. It had a rubber stock and the shiniest stainless steel barrel you ever saw, 'specially clean as my daddy kept it. Like he said, it was "light and smooth and perfect for kids." These sorts of convictions were among the many reasons my cousins Heather and Ashley up in Plano—which could as easily have been a suburb of Chicago or Seattle as Dallas— thought I was "uncouth" and "a boor." They'd never know how many times I heard my daddy say things like, "If you walk through that door and that breech ain't exposed, I'm gonna assume it's loaded and you're through shootin' for the month."

Course I guess I sort of understand. Lot of city folks never get the chance to learn how to use a gun the right way, nor a horse or barn or bush hog or a lot of other of life's useful tools.

After we'd shot maybe 35–40 rounds 'tween the three of us, and knocked around a few pumpkins and chunks of firewood, Jumpy showed up, squirrel gun in one hand, a burlap sack slung over his other shoulder. My long face must've spoken plenty.

"Now hold on, Katie," he protested, "I don't shoot squirrel no mo'—these be jack rabbits, big ole honkin' jacks! They runnin' wile all over out hea'. I'm just doin' folks all a service by shootin' 'em! Even got me an armadiller in hea', been diggin' up half your pasture."

Somehow, the wind had sorta just gone out of my sails. I said, "Daddy, I'm tired of shootin'. Can we go back in the woods and play?"

"Well alright," he said, "but don't go off."

I emptied the bullets out of the .22, then handed it to Daddy, and Amy emptied the Ruger's magazine. Then she and I, squealin' in delight I expect, ran off toward Katie's Woods, a hundred yards or so from the dry unpoisoned tank with the purple dogwood tree.

Daddy opened up a new cartridge box, of hollow points, then reloaded several clips, eyein' Jumpy as he did.

"Usin' the good stuff on these punkins, are you, Ethan?" Jumpy said.

"Reckon my mood's a shade on the foul side today, Jump," Daddy said. Then he glanced closer at Jumpy. "Why, you look plum spooked. You're whiter'n me."

"Oh, Pastor Ethan," Jumpy said, layin' down the burlap sack. "I's out a'huntin' yest-dee afternoon—rabbits, not squirrels—and I happened onto yo' friend Mr. Posey and one o' them city slickers while they's a'fishin'. I's afraid if I kept walkin' and they saw me, they'd think I's eavesdroppin', so I had to jist stand they, be quiet, an' listen."

"Uh-huh," Daddy said, snappin' a clip up into the .45.

"And Pastor Ethan, you ain't never gonna believe what I heard," Jumpy said, his eyes like moons. "Why that fancy Dallas man askin' yo' friend Mr. Posey if three hundred be enough to pay off what he owe."

"What?"

"And Mr. Posey, he be drinkin' lot of them nasty cheap Lone Star beers he like, an' he laugh and say fifty thousand be more'n 'nuff, and to git him a line of credit at the new place 'sides. Fifty *thousand*, Pastor Ethan. That mean what I think it do?"

Seventeen

The next night, Doc Gibbs was back over, this time on livin', not dyin' business—or so we hoped. The vet had lost his partner to a heart attack a few weeks back and he was wearin' himself to a frazzle tryin' to take care of what seemed like all the animals in our part of Ellis County.

"You need you some sleep, Doc, or you won't be much good to anybody," Daddy said as Doc Gibbs tended to our pregnant gray, Esther.

"Easy to say, Ethan," Doc Gibbs said, "till you got a case like this one; either I'm there or she dies. And that's goin' on all the time."

"Yeh, I sure don't want to lose another one," Daddy said. "Last time nearly killed Katie."

"Some kinda run you've had with your animals here of late," said Doc Gibbs. And when folks start throwin' poison around, you don't know who it's gonna hurt. This mare's goin' to foal a full month ahead o' time. Anything else happen out here of late, Ethan? Any signs o' that cougar?"

"Saw more prints yesterday, out on our far west pasture," Daddy said.

"Yeh? Toward the McCains?" Doc Gibbs said, lookin' up. "Why that's in the direction toward 'civilization.'"

"And found some more fence cut the other night," Daddy added.

"I'm sure sorry to hear all that," Doc Gibbs said, his face drawin' tighter'n it was. "Say Ethan, I'm gonna stay here—like I said, I don't expect either of 'em, especially the little one when it comes, can last long. You go catch you a wink."

Daddy shook his head, figurin' if looks measured how a person felt, he must look worse off than Doc Gibbs. "Believe I'll just lay down in the truck and flip on the game," he said.

"Plum forgot about the game," Doc Gibbs said. "I been out on calls since 3:30 this mornin'."

"Thanks, Doc," Daddy said, pattin' his slumped back. "Sorry we been such a nuisance to you of late." He walked out of the stable to his pickup, which he had parked outside, followed by Jake and Daisy. A light feather of clouds blurred some of the stars overhead, but most winked at him like little shiny diamonds God had flung into the sky and that stuck up there.

He got in and turned on the radio. As usual, hay and dog hair garnished the Shivy's seat. One of my many hairbrushes lay on the floorboard, and one of those little "scrunchies" girls gather our hair with to keep it out of our eyes when we're ridin' or playin' ball and such. Fishin' for the kleenex box, Daddy flipped on the overhead lamp and discovered a trail of cat tracks clear across the front seat, from one window to the other. But they weren't cougar prints, they belonged to Puffy our fat family cat.

"It looks as though Cotton Patch's long, undefeated march may come to an end tonight on the very brink of the school's first-ever state football championship," the KBEC announcer said.

Daddy frowned, or more liked groaned, then lay across the front seat.

"Jed Schumacher has two touchdowns and a hundred fifty-seven yards rushing," the announcer went on, as though he knew my daddy had just sat in and he was givin' him a recap of the evenin's action, "but this tough El Paso team, defending state champions and undefeated in twenty-six straight games, is much better-balanced."

Daddy shook his head and guessed he might as well admit this whole day had gone south. Then he pulled his hat down over his eyes.

"Under a minute to play with the defending champs holding a 24-21 lead and the ball on the Cotton Patch three yard line. It's fourth down. Quarterback Russ Madden takes the snap and rolls to his right. Oh—he's got a receiver open in the end zone. He cocks and fires and it's—intercepted at the goal line by Schumacher! He scoots out of a crowd and heads down the sideline."

Why, don't you know Daddy came right up off that seat, his eyes shootin' wide open. He was nearly as excited as that KBEC announcer—and yes, it was the same fella Clay'd been pickin' on.

"Schumacher races to the forty, the forty-five, across midfield!" the announcer shouted. "It's gonna be a foot race. Only one man can catch him now and that's Tyrone Washington, two-time state hundred-meter dash champion!"

Daddy swung his legs off the seat onto the floor and cranked up the volume. That ole announcer sounded as though he was the one hot-footin' down the field tryin' for a state championship.

"Washington has the angle and he's closin' on Schumacher—oh go, Jed, go!" the announcer shouted.

Daddy leaned forward and pounded the steerin' wheel, tears in his eyes. "Go, Jed, go!" he shouted.

"Oh no, he's gonna catch him—" the announcer choked, as though struck.

"No!" Daddy cried out to God.

Then a loud thud 'bout jolted him out of his jeans. He turned and saw Jake, standin' on his hind legs lookin' sorta worried-like at Daddy, lookin' him eye-to-eye through the window.

"They're both staggering now," the announcer breathed. "Washington reaches for him—oh—Jed won't stop. He's to the twenty, the fifteen—oh no Washington collars him—the ten . . . Jed's draggin' him on his back, Washington's hammerin' him, hittin', sluggin' him to bring him down . . . oh—TOUCHDOWN!"

"Ya-hoo!!" Daddy screamed. He vaulted from the truck, shoutin' at the stars, the feathery clouds gone now. Jake and Daisy and two new puppies, Luke and Old Jack, reckoned that was plenty good excuse to join in howlin'. "Yi-ahhh! Yi-ahhhhh!" Daddy went on, takin' a minute to notice Doc Gibbs callin' from inside the stable.

"Ethan! She's comin'! Help me!"

Daddy rushed back in there to Doc Gibbs's side.

"Mama didn't make it, Ethan," the vet said, sweat streakin' his tired face.

Daddy's glee turned straightaway sorrowful as he spied a scrawny little colt, barely breathin'.

"Why look at that big splash o' white on 'er neck, Doc," Daddy said.

*   *   *

Couple more hours went by and the old owl started his hootin' up in one of the cedars. The mare lay on hay on one side of the stable, a blanket over her, the skinny wet little colt with a big splash of white on her neck on the other. Doc Gibbs and Daddy could hardly hold their eyes open. "Don't think the baby's gonna make it, either," said Doc Gibbs.

Daddy was just then frettin' that he had once again broken his vow to God, for the hundredth or more time, never to pray for one team over another in a game. *Why is it I can't get as excited about church matters?* he fretted himself. *What could I do if I had an inklin' of the passion for Jesus and His Church that I had when ole Jed was gallopin' down that field?*

He had started wonderin' if it was right to pray that way in wars either, since the more history he read, the fewer wars seemed righteous on either, or any, side, especially once you got past the whitewashed fiction of the court historians. They had their own campaigns to wage, he now realized, for fame and fortune and college chairs, and Pulitzers and Nobels and even Newberys. And they knew those who dispensed the baubles required you to tow the party line, whatever it might be that year.

When he looked up, I was standin' in the doorway. I must've looked awful. "I'm sorry, bunny," he started, "looks like—"

I went to the newborn, sat down, laid her head in my lap, and began to stroke it. "It's alright, little friend, ever'thing's gonna be alright," I said, eyein' that patch of white on her chestnut neck. "I'm gonna name you Splash."

That was one of the only times I prayed from all the way down at the bottom that if there was a God in heaven, He would show Himself strong, for that little colt, but I now realize, especially for me.

*   *   *

That sunrise looked like the Lord had mixed together V-8 juice with propane from our 500-gallon tank, then lit 'em on fire. But I never saw it.

My daddy was stretched out on a stack of hay bales and first light woke him up, which was still way late for him. Doc Gibbs, his face bleak, was already lookin' over the colt. Poor little fella's head was in my lap, like it had been all night, and I was sleepin' sound.

A queer sorta look came across Doc Gibbs's face as he pulled off his stethoscope and clicked off his little flashlight he looked close at horses with. "Don't know if I'm more surprised this little baby's still alive or that we won the state championship, Ethan. To tell the truth, I can't believe either one."

*   *   *

The trees were sure enough turnin' in Ellis County by the beginnin' of December, blanketing the hollows and woods with a bed of leaves.

Daddy thought he caught him a glimpse of a deer takin' a drink from Possum Creek just after he'd turned off Shiloh Road onto the farm-to-market that led into "Metropolitan Cotton Patch" as he favored callin' it. As he approached town he dialed a number on the cell phone. "Clay—can you head up the work on the Rodriguez house today?"

"Sure," said Clay. "Any sign yet of Eduardo?"

"No. Neither Graciela, nor anyone else, has seen him since the tornada."

"Where are you?" Clay asked.

"Headin' to the hospital in Ennis," Daddy said. "We heard Jose got really lit up last night. He fell face down into a fire ant mound and passed out."

Daddy smiled and waved at Jefe as he jogged past just east of the railroad tracks.

"Good grief," Clay said. "That—is that life-threatening?"

"For anyone but Jose," Daddy said. "He's had his skull broken with a baseball bat, he's been shot, and he got run over by a train once. Most of those, he was on his bicycle, too."

Clay couldn't muster up anything to send back on that one, so he turned course and said, "Any word on the little church burned down out by you?"

Daddy could not even give voice to his thoughts for a minute, which may have been a good thing, considerin' he was a pastor. Finally he growled, "Town's raised $5,000 reward money so far if someone leads us to the—culprit."

"Looks like it must be somebody hates black people," Clay said.

"Yeh, Lorena wondered if the Macedonia Church was 'cause of black folks too. But the other fires haven't been, so I don't know."

Soon, Daddy wheeled up onto I-45 headin' south and fifteen minutes later he hustled through the front doors of the hospital in Ennis. He had run extra hard on his joggin' circuit around the east pasture the day before and he felt his left hamstring tug on him a trifle. But he was in a hurry, so he just kind-ly reached down and squeezed it, then hurried on through a corridor toward the emergency area.

When he got to the waitin' room, he spotted Coach McKay, coach of the state champion Cotton Patch High School Farmers, lookin' worse than he did the time Ferris scored two touchdowns in the last minute to beat the Farmers by one point.

"Coach McKay, what happened?" Daddy asked right off.

"My baby, my precious beautiful baby Vanessa," Coach McKay choked out, rills of tears racin' down where others already had, "she was nearly killed ridin' with that slimy TV preacher."

"What?" Daddy said.

"That Reverend D-man or whatever they call him," Coach McKay spat. "Guess that hypocrite been messin' with my precious daughter, and he and—and—two drunk drivers, Ethan, and one of 'em—" Coach McKay's throat caught him again just then. After a minute, he straightened up and looked my daddy in the eye. "Now the hypocrite walk away alright and my beautiful baby, if she live, in a wheel chair rest her life. Yo' God, Shanahan—yo' lousy God did this!"

Course, the way Coach McKay had long assayed it was you couldn't swing a dead cat by his tail in Cotton Patch without splattin' against at least a couple of money-grubbin' preacher-types. Me, I never could square, if a man wanted to get rich in the preachin' bidness, why on earth would he come to poor ole Cotton Patch, when there were so many places you could go that actually had folks with the money to make you rich? But maybe Coach McKay would've said Doctor Carter put the lie to that theory.

He collapsed onto his chair, shakin' and in tears. Daddy, shaken up plenty himself, turned away to find his own seat and nearly ran into a tall, attractive black woman with a countenance fallen lower'n the catfish in Lake Bardwell. "Hello, Mrs. McKay," he said.

He stepped aside as Coach McKay and his wife fell into one another's arms cryin'. Then he saw Dr. Blevins, pale as the white coat he wore, and walked over to him.

"Oh, Ethan," Dr. Blevins said.

"But who was in the other car, Luke?" Daddy pressed.

*   *   *

Charlie Settle stopped the presses that day at the *Cotton Patch Press*—to lay over a whole new front page for the next afternoon's weekly distribution. Good and bad, the eventful happenin's of that fall were in the process of savin' his newspaper, which three months ago was ready to go belly-up.

In bold black letters matched only by the football team's wins over Dallas and in the state championship, the main header read, "STAR ATHLETE, PROM QUEEN CRITICALLY INJURED IN AUTO CRASH." A secondary header read, "Prominent Pastor Driving Car, Uninjured."

Large photographs of that young man Jed Schumacher and Vanessa McKay spread across the front page. A smaller one of Dr. Xavier D. Carter appeared down within the body of the story.

133

Eighteen

Tall and impressive as the massive stadium scoreboard was, the humdinger was on its back side, not its front. The back read:

"UNIVERSITY OF OKLAHOMA
NATIONAL FOOTBALL CHAMPIONS
1950 1955 1956 1974 1975 1985."

Later it would read 2000, and maybe some other years too.

But Daddy was on the other side of it, down on the field, walkin' 'longside his old roommate Matt Cutter, who had quarterbacked the Sooners their junior and senior years. "Here's where you threw that pass against Nebraska," Daddy said as he moved toward the left hash mark at about the 40-yard-line on the south side of the field, the late-afternoon sun peekin' over the west upper deck and splashin' gold on his face.

"Your best play didn't happen here," Cutter said.

"What do you mean?" Daddy asked.

Cutter's handsome, barely-lined middle-40s features crinkled up. "You kiddin'? When you stuffed that ole what's-his-face Texas hoss on the goal line down in the Cotton Bowl? Holy moly, what a hit. And him with twenty-five pounds on you."

"I can still feel that hit," Daddy said.

That might be 'cause it broke his helmet and knocked out both him and the Texas hoss.

"Saved the game for us," Cutter said. What he didn't say, but what they both remembered, was that no one gave them a chance to win.

I still love those shiny crimson helmets, and I get excited even though I try not to when I see 'em movin' up and down the field.

Sometimes I pull the old one Daddy practiced in down out of the closet and look at it, even though some of the paddin' inside drops out and I have to stick it back in.

If some of my Texas friends don't like that, I reckon I've listened to 'em grumble all my life and it doesn't faze me any more now than it ever did.

Daddy and Matt Cutter made their way over to the South Oval of the Oklahoma campus and wound through a verdant green so lush it brought thoughts of Eden to Daddy's mind.

"So I don't know what I'm gonna do," Cutter said. "I like sportscasting, I get to go all over, doin' the best college games in the country. And runnin' for lieutenant governor of the whole state— figure I'd have to sell my soul to do that."

"No, you wouldn't," my daddy protested. "Not you. With your name, you could be yourself and win. 'Sides, you're just the sort we need in public office."

"So you gonna accept our obscenely high offer to come schmooze the high rollers at the club?" Cutter said, with no variation in his voice.

Daddy nodded and said, "Prob'ly. Just don't think I'm makin' any headway down there. There's so few folks to begin with and who's there could care less. Those we have are poor, poor. Lorena's doctor bills are mountin' up and Katie needs braces. And this race track mess has me ready to quit."

"Now, you know I'd never fault a man for not fightin' the chance to get him a race track," Cutter said, tickled with himself. "Other hand, never saw you quit a fight. Why, I seem to remember you already had a broken thumb and a broken wrist *before* you busted your bonnet on that Texas hoss."

Daddy's voice was dog-tired as he walked. "Matt, I just hardly think I care enough for those folks anymore to be their pastor," he said.

Just then, a series of wild, loud horn honks startled them. Several cars flew by, decorated with red and white streamers and shoe polish, college boys and girls hangin' out the windows, laughin' and shoutin'. One horn blared the distinctive school fight song *Boomer Sooner* over and over.

"Frat boys," Cutter said with a smirk. "Some things never change."

"You joined one o' them frats didn't you, Matthew?" Daddy said, the blue eyes twinklin'. "Till they tried to show ya which end of a mop to use."

Cutter shot him a go-to-heck look and a wry smile.

Then my daddy found himself at an old wooden bench, now ensconced in a deep dark arbor. He stood starin' at it, his back to Cutter. His buddy remembered the night, the mornin' I guess, after his own pass beat undefeated and top-ranked Nebraska for the conference title and another trip to the Orange Bowl. Daddy came back to their dorm room and woke him up and told him he'd spent the last six hours sittin' on that bench talkin' with a girl like none he'd ever met, and he'd met all sorts and all sorts had thrown themselves at him, especially when he got famous.

He'd only walked her home when a peach-colored sunrise blossomed over east Norman and fear gripped him of what gettin' her back to the Pi Phi house in daylight might do to her reputation, especially with those sorority "sisters" who were jealous of her, her looks, her smarts, her dazzlin' black eyes and wild hair—he thought she was Comanche or Apache when first he saw her that night—the spell she seemed to cast over ever'body in her path.

It was the same girls who sniped behind her back with low talk that shoulda shamed 'em, such as about her mother. Not her White stepmom, but her Mexican mother who bore her with her Scots-Irish father that owned the little hardware store in the dusty Southwest Oklahoma cross-in-the-roads where she grew up. The mother who word had was crazy, though none of 'em ever met her.

"Funny how time slips away, ain't it?" Daddy said.

"You seen her lately, Ethan?" Cutter asked.

"Not 'n a long time," Daddy said. "Years and years. Saw her right there on the sidewalk in downtown Dallas once, but didn't let on. Her boy's workin' with me now."

"What?"

"Well, lookee here," Daddy said.

The one and still only Barry Switzer himself churned past amidst a throng of well-heeled sorts. "Well, I be hanged," Switzer said. "Matt Cutter and Ethan Shanahan."

They may have called him a riverboat gambler and a bootlegger's boy—and other things not so nice—but Daddy thought Cutter summed it up best when he said once Barry Switzer had qualities, of the heart that is, none of the rest of them had. And the notion impressed my daddy that Barry Switzer, winner of one Super Bowl at Dallas and three national championships at OU, could still whip nearly any man his own age or anywhere near it.

His square tanned face beamin', Switzer couldn't get a hand out fast enough to shake with Daddy and Cutter. "Heard a bad rumor 'boutchu, Shanahan," he said. "Heard you a preacher boy!" Ever'one in sight, especially Daddy and Cutter, laughed at that. "Come on up and join me for a free steak tonight at my new restaurant. Matt knows where it is."

"Which one, Coach?" Cutter jibed him. "You got a whole fleet of 'em."

"Then take your pick, boys," Switzer said with a laugh to Daddy, even as he popped Cutter so hard in the upper arm it nearly knocked him down.

"Good seein' ya, coach," Daddy said, meanin' it.

Switzer wheeled and charged off, head forward and shoulders bowed in that determined way he had had all the way back to Crossett, Arkansas, where the bad guys thought he was a blonde square jock and the good folks looked down on him 'cause his daddy ran moonshine. Then he stopped and turned back, his entourage doin' the same. But now his face was right solemn and he was lookin' straight at my daddy. "When you broke your hat on that big Texas son-of-a-b-----'s numbers—bravest hit I ever saw," he said.

Then, he was gone. Daddy swelled with pride, of the good sort, for he knew such a statement from Barry Switzer carried much weight. He would think about these words, and others spoken during these days, as well as remembrances from days gone by, and who he was and had been, as he returned to Texas.

*   *   *

Next week, my daddy was mendin' bob-wire fence out along Shiloh Road, fence cut by somebody like fence around our spread was bein' cut each week. They wouldn't cut a lot each time, which was part of the spookiness of it all, that someone would come all the way out there, cut just a little, then keep comin' back, cuttin' just a little each time.

Wearin' his thick work gloves, Daddy wrapped the supplemental wire he had brought around the five strands of wire on one side of the cuts, then connected it, twisted it, and tightened it around the strands on the other side of the cuts, and pulled that section of the fence back up.

Then Jose wobbled up on his bicycle. He was drunk and his face was still blistered from more fire ant scars than Carter had oats.

"Now, Jose, I told you not to come around here when you been drinkin'," Daddy said, standin' up.

Then, to Daddy's surprise, Jose commenced to cryin', then gesturin' and speakin' in broken English. "Store burn," he said. "I in store, Ethan."

Daddy stared at him a couple of counts before sayin', "You were in the store when it burned?"

Jose shook his head like a wild man.

"The—Hitchin' Rail Store?" Daddy asked.

Now Jose nodded and said, the stench of the breath comin' out his mouth lost in the weight of the words comin' out, "Sleep there. Almost burn up. Run for life."

Nineteen

Our church bell was not ringin' that next Lord's Day. My daddy stood at the door in his preacher get-up, welcomin' folks. Graciela, Blanca, and the other Rodriguez children came up. Graciela was carryin' the little one. "Thank you for all the work you and the other men have done to rebuild our house," she said to Daddy, keepin' a rein best as she could on her feelin's.

Daddy gave her a nod, then said, "Heard anything yet from . . ."

Tears filled her eyes and she shook her head before he got the name out. Daddy breathed a little easier just havin' her pass on into the buildin'. As she did, he saw Blanca look up at him like she had a question but didn't know how to ask it. That is the kind of thing that kind-ly tears a pastor, a real true one of the shepherd sort, apart.

A little while later, Daddy stood before the congregation at the altar, where lay the brass dishes containing the elements for the Lord's Supper. He admired how Graciela had stuck it out and stayed faithful to the church and the other spiritual pursuits in her life, includin' raisin' her kids up the right way. Even now, though, he could see the pain and sadness tryin' to make their way in and disrupt her pretty face.

"Each week in the Lord's Supper," he declared, "we look back in remembrance of the perfect life and atoning death Christ died for us who are His redeemed."

Then he spotted Eduardo Rodriguez, dirty and disheveled, comin' through the back door of the sanctuary. It was the first time he had ever seen the man set foot in the buildin'. Daddy's eyes widened and his voice lifted a shade, the more when he saw another first-timer half a dozen rows from the front: Tater Tatum, along with his wife and younger son Homer.

"But He also meets with us in an unusually direct way in the here and now," Daddy said. "He is spiritually present with us even more than normal, as a means of grace as we receive these elements, and through them He gives us strength and confidence."

Rodriguez spotted his family and shuffled toward them.

"And too, the bread and wine are a sign and seal of our union and communion with Him, and a promise to us of that glorious future day of Christ's final return, wherein our fellowship with Him will be consummated," Daddy proclaimed, with more conviction.

When Graciela saw her husband, she leapt into his arms, right there in front of God and ever'body. And the folks, all 40 or so of 'em (it had come down some durin' the gamblin' set-to, with the Poseys and a few other families leavin' the church), why they stood up and applauded, and with gusto too.

His face breakin' into one of the bigger smiles he had ever sported, leastways around church, my daddy fairly shouted, "Come forth, taste the Lord, and see that He is good!"

*   *   *

Couple nights later, Daddy had a late meetin' with Dr. Blevins and his two other deacons to discuss a purchase offer from The Way Out, one of the new aisle-runnin', pew-leapin' holy roller bunches that wanted to move from the livin' room of their four-times-married pastor and his thrice-hitched wife—to our church buildin'. And they had some cash to do it, leastways to ante up a good down payment.

Daddy winced at the wide-open look Dr. Blevins's eyes had, where they never seemed to blink. And the thumpin' of his fingers on the table, and the light tappin' of his foot on the floor. It was that general sense of nervous energy hangin' about the person of Dr. Blevins which my daddy used to see, but hadn't since about—the Christmas before.

He made himself a mental note to speak with his friend about that, tomorrow. Then he said, "I need to tell you men that Presbytery's got us—me—on a short leash right about now. They may say get that money while the gettin's good, what with us losin' these other folks, and what Scott said about me in that letter of his to 'em . . ."

Daddy just kind-ly looked down then, bowed under by the weight of the worst betrayal he could recollect. Seemed to me Mr. Posey had pretty much tried to blow up my daddy and our church, what with accusin' him to his bosses of incompetence and narrow-mindedness and mean-spiritedness and other things that I guess still come with the territory when you're a faithful Presbyterian of the Old School variety, especially when viewed by men of low and cunning natures.

None of the other men said much till Dr. Blevins said, the words comin' out rat-a-tat-tat, "Ethan, seems to me we're doin' what we're supposed to here, maybe stumblin' some as we go, but you can't deny good things are happenin'. Why, look at Eduardo Rodriguez comin' back and dryin' out. Garth Chisholm just hired him on as cleanup man for the bank buildin' and I'm doin' the same at my offices. Look at how the Decker boys' lives have turned around. Some of these older folks, the shut-ins and what-not, well, they swear by you. And I know we all hate to see Clay Cullum go, but you've developed him into a right fine preacher boy."

"God's developed him," Daddy mumbled, his voice hollow.

"Ethan, you can't force folks to do right," Dr. Blevins persisted, now soundin' like someone else Daddy had heard of late; Daddy prayed these were words from Dr. Blevins's heart, and not from somethin' else. "If the town lets this thing in here, well, one day soon our church'll be more needed than ever. Us losin' folks now of all times, and the reason for it, is a shame, but not on you or our church. When doin' right ain't popular, that doesn't make it less important; it makes it more important than ever."

Here, Dr. Blevins looked down, and Daddy thought he had run his course. But when Daddy started to say somethin', his friend looked back up, the thumpin' and tappin' stopped, and his eyes were red now and tired lookin'. He said, "Ethan, you stood by me when my hand was flush and when it was thin. And I'll stand by you whatever you say."

"Seems like lotta the folks you help aren't the sort rich enough to build buildings or fancy enough to where other folks wanna go where they go just to say they do," said Carlos Romero, who used to sell marijuana, but now was the best carpenter in Cotton Patch and had a wife and four young'uns.

"And whoever saw Tater Tatum inside any church 'cept for weddin's or funerals, and he was here Sunday," said Jim Langtry.

Seemed nobody had anything else to say after that. Pretty soon, the other men all just kind-ly nodded that they were with him and my daddy knew what they meant. "Far as I'm concerned," he said, "we're not for sale—at any price. We'll see what Presbytery says."

After the others left, Daddy stayed in his office at the rear of the church to put his thoughts on paper for Presbytery while they were fresh on his mind. However, his thoughts may have been fresh, but his mind wasn't, and wasn't long before he was face down asleep on his desk, still wonderin' about Dr. Blevins, the little lamp that looked like it'd been in that office since the church was built glowin' amber.

It took awhile before he heard the knockin' on the battered, chipped door leadin' outside from his office. After a good thirty seconds, he came to and sorta stumbled over and opened it. Jefe stood there, sweatin', in his usual get-up. He pointed out, toward the front of the building, and made the motion of lightin' a match and throwin' it.

The thought struck Daddy he had never heard Jefe say a word, and he wondered if he could talk, in any language. Then my daddy hustled out the door and down the half-dozen steps to the ground. He spotted two shadowy figures fifty or sixty feet away. One was pourin' gasoline on the ground along the wall of the church, the other lightin' a match.

"Hey!" Daddy shouted.

He charged them, but halfway there his left hamstring blew out; he cried in pain and slowed down. But then he reached back, grabbed the torn muscle, and charged on.

He piled into the arsonists, knockin' both to the ground, the five-gallon gasoline can bangin' against the hundred-year-old pecan tree nearby. Daddy was swingin' his fists like a triphammer before either man could rise. He knocked one senseless. He recognized him as Hubert Gore, the local ne'er-do-well who fought Rodriguez at the Cotton Patch-Dallas football game. Then he pummeled the other man. A clear bag of white powder fell out of one of the man's pockets.

After a moment, Hubert gathered his wits and smashed the still-nearly-full gas can over Daddy's head, knocking him flat. As Daddy shook his head, Hubert raised the can again, his eyes glowin' from somethin' more than anger. Suddenly, another body flew into him, sendin' the gas can flyin' again and Hubert crashin' into the brick wall of the church. It was Rodriguez, cleaned up and cold sober. He jerked the arsonist up and slammed his head against the wall. "Hubert Gore!" Rodriguez screamed, saliva spewin' like cottage cheese out his mouth into Hubert's face. "You and your brother Hector there, you the scum burnin' down churches? You better tell me, punk! Tell me!"

Over and over, Rodriguez banged the man's head against the wall.

"Yes, yes!" Gore finally shrieked.

"Why you burnin' this one?" Rodriguez hollered. "Ain't no black folks here. Why?"

"Yes, they are, this a n----r church now, too," Gore said, hate refuelin' his voice.

"Pastor Jasper . . ." Daddy said, stunned.

Then Hubert Gore looked Rodriguez in the eyes, his own glowin' red from somethin' illegal, and said, with a voice low and full of murder, "And Mess-kins like you."

"And Jose in the Hitchin' Rail," Daddy breathed.

"And Pepe Gomez's store," Rodriguez said, horror fillin' his face. Plus, he could feel loathin' for himself and venom comin' out of Gore no less than if someone shot him with a syringeful of it. He stared at the arsonist, the hater, the murderer, searchin' for some other explanation, any other at all; but like so many before him in the long sad journey of this ole world—of America—he found none.

So he loosened his grip on the man, then turned away and began to weep. Daddy, his knee on Hector's throat, lowered his head as the first Cotton Patch police car pulled up.

*　　*　　*

She had been with him from the start, from the time they picked cotton together at ancient old Colonel Slade's, over near Waxahachie. Reverend Jasper marveled as he realized that not only did William Barret Travis Slade, whom he remembered, with his snow-white flowin' beard and empty sleeve, earn his colonelcy for a country that had not existed for over a century, but the man owned Reverend Jasper's own grandmother and grandfather till they heard they were free that June day in 1865.

But they had gotten married and stayed on with the "Kunnel" as free workers till both died in the 1920s. And the pallbearers at the Kunnel's funeral were Amos Obadiah Jasper and five white men. Folks said the Kunnel himself had been a pallbearer at General Hood's funeral.

Reverend Jasper and his Hannah were six years old when they picked that first cotton together, rags tied 'round each other's bleedin' little hands 'cause they all had to work day and night to get it in before that awful plague o' grasshoppers wiped it out. And she was with him still. You could tell it by the collection of pitchers of them together that covered the whole sideboard in his livin' room, and the table next to it, and the wall on the other side, too.

And you could tell it by how he was himself, now that he was alone.

"What my little vote anyways?" he asked aloud of one of her many likenesses, all of which preserved the beauty folks still talked about. "Fifty thousand dollars lotta money. It finish us out a church right nice and hep us send that fine Jackson boy to seminary."

A noise sounded outside, and it wasn't a mockingbird nor a coyote neither. He peaked out the window blinds and saw my daddy's Shivy pull up. Daddy got out, pulled some buckets out the bed, brought them up to Reverend Jasper's front porch, and left them.

Givin' us more paint for our new church—if them state folks don't condemn it 'cause that lead they say's still there in the old paint we used in the cellar. My, that boy look like he been through the mill today, Reverend Jasper thought to himself, seein' bruises on daddy's face in the dim light from the Shivy and the house. Then he shut the blinds and closed the curtains. And if he'd had more blinds or curtains or another wall he could've thrown up, he'd have done that, too.

He turned back to an old framed weddin' portrait of Hannah and himself. "Oh, don't look at me thataway baby; we gonna lose anyhow," he pled. "Ain't been same since Lawd took you home, Mrs. Jasper, ain't been same a'tall."

Then, unable to meet her gaze any longer, he turned the lights out on it and went to bed, though bein' a good and Godly man, that didn' mean he slept.

* * *

One other fella still up so late was that Granger, in his highfalutin' highrise North Dallas office. He sat in his Jacuzzi, talkin' on the cell phone, hot water swirlin' and bubblin' around him, a long fat unlit Havana cigar hangin' out his mouth. "Reckon we got us one more to go," he said into the phone. "He ain't got a vote, but I know this one's special to you, so I'm throwin' it in—on the house you might say."

He listened for a minute to the voice on the other end, as his blue-eyed "secretary"—or as we say in Texas, "seckaterry"—in the tub with him, wrapped her arms around his neck. Now, she was even prettier than Doctor Carter's former Miss Black U.S.A. "executive assistant," almost as tall, and had even more blonde hair, though not any more that was really blonde.

"Yeah, money wouldn't faze him," that Granger said into the phone, not payin' near as much attention to the seckaterry as she was to him, "but ever'body's got their soft spot, and thanks to you, we know what his is. Alright, Shorty, talk to you tomorrow."

Then he clicked off the phone, laid down the cigar, and turned his attention to matters much closer at hand. "Let's get this meeting started, darlin'. I told my wife it would be done by ten."

* * *

It was "SHANAHAN" sewed in white 'cross the back of the crimson jersey. Shoulder pads bulged out on both sides atop it, and the bushy brown hair of the back of the player's head above that. A shiny helmet with the logo "OU" sat in the locker fronting him.

The thunderin' roar of the massed hosts outside sounded like a battering ram gettin' ready to bust in the door to the locker room. A public address announcer said, "And head coach for the University of Oklahoma Sooners is Barry Switzer." Somewhere out there you could hear a band playin' *The Eyes of Texas*. "Shanahan" pulled a crimson scarf from his locker and stared at it.

Then my daddy woke up to a familiar voice on his radio alarm clock. It was the all-purpose KBEC announcer so revered and admired by Clay. And Daddy wasn't in the locker room gettin' ready to head down the Cotton Bowl ramp (or rampart, as a later coach of dubious distinction misspoke, the whiskey still perhaps on his breath) to do battle with the Texas Longhorns, and he wasn't holdin' any red scarf either. He hadn't done any of that in twenty years.

He looked over at Mama, still asleep in her separate queen-sized bed. Leastways her restless hurtin' hadn't driven him out the room through the night this time.

"Well, tonight's the night of the big city council gamblin' vote over in Cotton Patch," the announcer said. "And I'll be reportin' the proceedin's live to you from the Cotton Patch City Hall, till the issue is decided or KBEC goes off the air for the night, whichever comes first."

Daddy sorta smiled at that. He was beginnin' to think that, on this subject at least, maybe Clay had a point.

*   *   *

It would wind up bein' one of the most unforgettable of a whole passel of unforgettable days. After Daddy led the weekly early-mornin' men's prayer meetin' at the church, which that day drew a record eight men besides himself, includin' Eduardo Rodriguez, he drove to the hospital in Ennis.

There he sat at the bedside of Miz T, unconscious and with more tubes snakin' into her than she had breath comin' out. After a couple minutes, Clay came into the room. Daddy got up and followed him outside.

"How's Miz T?" Clay asked.

"Not good," Daddy said. "She had her stroke week after those curs burned her church. She's hardly been conscious since. Why, you're really gettin' after this hospital visitation. Was like pullin' teeth to get you to do it at first. Believe this the third time I've run into you here in the last week."

But Clay wasn't feelin' prideful today. "I've got some real hard news, Ethan," he said. "Hard even to say." He looked down at the linoleum floor, embarrassed, which wasn't usual for him. "Seems Mr. Granger and his friends have more land up their sleeves than just their casino and track."

"What?" Daddy said.

"Looks like there's room enough for a so-called 'adult entertainment complex' to open up just down the road," Clay said. "Something for the entire family, I guess they say."

"But—there's been no other land transactions out there, Clay," Daddy said. "We been watchin'—"

"They bought it two years ago, Ethan," Clay said. "It would open a year after the casino. And Ethan? The money that bought it was Chicago money—not-so-nice Chicago money if you know what I mean."

"Lord in heaven," Daddy said, not feelin' his lips move nor hearin' his own words. "How can you know all this?"

"Er . . . well . . . it was Mom," Clay said, blushin'. "She hired the best team of private investigators in Dallas, and they spent three months diggin'."

"But—why?"

"'Cause she knew what you're trying to do and what all they're comin' at you with," Clay said.

"Angelina Cortez McCullough . . . Cullum . . . and whatever," Daddy mumbled, starin' into space.

"The P.I.s know who the Chicago group is," said Clay. "They told her you're probably gettin' threat letters by now, too."

Daddy colored and looked down. "First one came yesterday," he said. "Thank God I got to the mail box before Loree."

"But Ethan, they can't prove any of this," Clay said. "They said it happens over and over again when the—mob—moves into an area with gambling and pornography and the like. They probably won't hurt anybody, but they'll scare you plenty. Most folks just back right off 'cause they don't want their kids in danger."

Then he kind-ly shifted a bit, from foot to foot. "But, Ethan?" he said. "For some reason, they want this one real bad."

Twenty

He was lookin' out the upstairs window of the ancient two-story coffee-colored building. As usual, the blinds were pulled and smoked roiled out the slightly open window.

When a knock came from the door inside, he said a flat, "It's open."

Then my daddy stepped into the plain, smoke-choked old office. Whatever life and noble doin's had come from there—and there were glimmers here and there if you could've seen into the shadows—were now manteled with dust like that which covered the physical surfaces and dueled with cigar smoke for control o' the stale air.

The only light was an ancient green-shaded lamp on the desk which Shorty Anderson sat behind in the shadows, thick long Havana aglow, though I guess in a larger sense the haunted little hideaway no longer had any light at all.

"Ain't no chair 'cause I don't take no visitors," Shorty announced. "And you ain't gonna be here long enough to set. I just wanted the satisfaction o' seein' ye crawl then tellin' ye to git the h--- outa my sight."

"I know we've had our differences—" Daddy started.

"Hah!" Shorty blurted, the Havana clenched in his teeth.

"—and I've long since apologized for my part," Daddy said.

"Gotta admit I'm a might befuddled at why ye so all-fired worked up 'bout all this, preacher boy," Shorty said. "See I know ye fer what ye are. You're no d-----good as a preacher and ye ain't never even liked the folks since ye moved out to ye daddy-in-law's land."

"I won't deny that, Shorty," Daddy said.

Shorty's eyebrows kind-ly arched up at that one.

"Up to now that is, about the folks," Daddy said. "But Shorty, you gotta know this track and casino—this 'adult entertainment complex'—"

Shorty's eyebrows climbed a little higher.

"—it's poison for all of us," Daddy said.

"The h--- you say, boy. Why, it's jobs and money and a new chance for a h--- of a lotta folk," Shorty said. "It's you and your narrow hypocrite ways what's poison to the folks."

"I'm beggin' ya, Shorty—"

"Beg?" Shorty exploded, surgin' forward in his chair. "Didn't I beg you to let me hep you git that d----- ole church goin'? Didn't I beg you to let me have a chance to do somethin' fer good? All you did was throw your cocky jock strut 'n your high-handed preacher-boy ways back in my face. No!"

Then he leaned so far forward it looked to my Daddy like he'd fall out of his chair and hit the floor, if all that dust and smoke didn't catch him. Chompin' down on that ole Havana like he'd bite it plum in half, he growled, "I tell ye, if ye got down own ye knees and crawled beggin' 'crost the floor to me an' licked my boots I wouldn't listen. Now take ye Mess-kins and ye n-----rs and git the h--- out!"

Daddy's head dropped right down and he turned and walked out like he'd just heard a death sentence passed on himself—or on his town. He didn't hear, but from out of those grainy shadows he'd just left came the sound of ice cubes clinkin' into a glass, then a bottle openin' and liquid gushin' from it into the glass, nothin' at all to mix with it.

"D--- 'im, d--- 'im to h---," Shorty Anderson said as he rushed the glass to his lips, but they weren't hardly words he spoke, don't you see, they were more like just sounds, comin' from away down some deep bad place.

* * *

A shingle with the words "Ellis County Social Club" now hung proudly over the entrance to the back room of the Cotton Patch General Store. Beyond it, the domino game was in session, Arvel and

Tater at their posts, and Normie strummin' *Cotton-Eyed Joe,* this time on his banjo.

"Reckon we got us a track and casino comin', eh boys?" Huey said as he made a count.Newy launched an usually pregnant wad into the spittoon.

"They say Miz T didn't stroke 'cause o' the church burnin' after all, but fer frettin' o'er the track and what-not," said Tater, eyein' the reddish piece of wood he was whittlin' in his thick tanned hand.

"Ye been thinkin' own such matters since ye started churchifyin', Tater," Newy declared.

"My ole daddy, he picked cotton with Miz T," said Arvel.

"My granddaddy picked onions with her and the Mexicans in the summer when school let out, then culled 'em with her in the sheds," said Tater. "He wadn't over twelve when he started."

"I remember them ole sheds," said the usually-taciturn Arvel. "They used to set along the railroad tracks, from downtown Ferris clear out to the ole cotton gin." Ever'body in the room stared at him when they realized he wasn't finished. They had never heard him say this much in the same day. "Them Mess-kins come in ever' year on the side frames o' them bob-tails, whole families of 'em. Go farm to farm, plant 'em some onions, then harvest 'em. Maybe plant 'em some cotton a spell later."

"Onions mostly gone down to the Valley and out to the Panhandle now, I expect," said Newy.

"More Mexicans out there," said Huey.

"Things change," said Arvel, risin' to leave. "They shore change."

"I 'spect they fixin' to change some more," said Scooter.

Newy spit again, but this time it was no ringer. It was not even close.

*   *   *

Well, I've told you some about our sunrises and sunsets too, especially when it got cold and clear. But that evenin' the Lord just kind-ly lit the ole heavens up with His own glory so nobody'd forget, regardless what happened at the City Council meetin', Whose the world was, and the fullness thereof.

I watched through a window as that sunset burst into flame and color; the farther down the sun went, the more magic gushed out of it, spreadin' and streamin' clear across the western horizon. I was reminded of Merle Haggard's *Rainbow Stew*, but I reckoned this was more like a big ole bucket of rainbow paint.

Silhouetted against it was a man ridin' his horse along the summit of the west pasture. Mama wheeled up next to me.

"Mama, why isn't Daddy gettin' ready?" I asked.

"He is," she said.

He was on Annie Lee, but he had a train followin' him—Jake, Daisy, and the half-grown puppies Luke and Old Jack. I found I was takin' quite a shine to Luke, but I was careful not to take too much of one, at least not yet, 'cause I was scared that'd be dishonorin' to Jeb my puppy.

And speakin' o' shines, not far away, on still-spindly legs, young Splash struggled to keep up with the pack. Daddy smiled at her, then turned into the sunset and sucked in the sweet air. Then Jake scared up a small covey of quail and it was time to go.

*   *   *

While supper was cookin', Mama had on KCBI, 90.9 FM, one of the Dallas-Fort Worth Christian radio stations we could get even out where we were. Course, KCBI, 90.9 FM was a 100,000 watt station and you could get it all the way south to Waco and north up into Okieland. Speakin' of Oklahoma, KCBI, 90.9 FM was one of the many legacies of a native of El Dorado, Oklahoma, Dr. W. A. Criswell, whom God had used to help build the First Baptist Church of Dallas, which at one time had the most members of any church in the whole world.

Daddy loved to tell of goin' down one time to "First Dallas" and meetin' that great old lion in person after listenin' to one of his sermons. When Criswell found out Daddy went to OU, and figured out he played football there, he placed a hand on his shoulder and said, in that benedictory voice of his, "God *bless* you, son. First church I ever had was in Chickasha."

Which was right down windin', bumpy ole two-lane (back then) Highway 9 from Norman.

Even though Criswell was a Baptist, Daddy heard a sermon tape once where he called himself a Calvinist, which I've since learned to my pleasure many Baptists do. And on other tapes Daddy heard, Criswell would tell of the mighty works of creation and providence and heaven and judgment and hell and the like, and then he would slam his fist to the pulpit and thunder, "And *God* did it!"

Criswell could preach like Daddy used to could play football, and then some, and like Daddy would like to have been able to preach, but never quite could. Mama told me one time after he was gone that he said even though he didn't sound out loud like W. A. Criswell when he preached, he could hear himself inside and there he sounded just like him.

My daddy loved that man, even though he only ever met him one time, for just a minute.

But on this night, the night of the long-awaited vote, Daddy had already left for the meetin' and he wouldn't let me go, and Mama was hurtin' too much in her legs to go. KCBI, 90.9 FM, had a lot of fine announcers, but two of my favorites were Ron Harris, who was also the top hand of the whole station, and Johanna Fisher, who hosted a popular daytime talk show.

Here was this tall, attractive single black lady from up north somewhere, with a voice that could nearly melt the microphone it was so pleasin', and this good ole Fort Worth boy who proudly claimed the Christian General Stonewall Jackson as an ancestor. And I know from listenin' to 'em through the years they didn't see eye-to-eye on ever'thing. Yet they worked together smoother'n a fresh-waxed pine floor and helped make KCBI, 90.9 FM, one of the best stations around, at least in my opinion.

I always thought Ron Harris and Johanna Fisher workin' together was not just about Christianity, but a mighty fine demonstration *of* it.

Now they were talkin' right there on the air about us.

"Well, tonight is the big city council vote down in Cotton Patch," said Johanna.

"You know, Johanna," said Ron, "it's turned into quite a nasty fight, too, with rumors of pastors being threatened, business and political leaders bribed, and at least some of the churches supporting the gambling interests."

"We're even hearing now that more may be in the offing with this project than gambling," said Johanna.

I figured it might've been the first time a lot of KCBI, 90.9 FM listeners had ever heard of Cotton Patch. And lookee how they were hearin' about us.

✳   ✳   ✳

There was only one *Cotton Patch Press* left in the newsrack outside City Hall. The newest big, bold headline read, "EX-CON BROTHERS CHARGED WITH ARSONS."

Inside, the main chamber was again packed, but this time with TV camera crews ringin' the room. I'm not sure a TV camera had ever before penetrated the city limits of metropolitan Cotton Patch. The city council members again sat up front. As you might remember, they were Mr. Posey, Reverend Jasper, Will Hankins, Mayor Coltrane, Garth Chisholm, Maria Rivera, and that TV preacher, Doctor Xavier D. Carter.

Doctor Carter had now brought him in a preacher boy flunky from Louisiana or somewhere to do the preachin' and pastorin' at his church. This was because he himself was on TV or "guest preachin'" in much bigger churches around the country, sometimes on their own TV shows, and since the heat was a little less on him for his after-hours exploits the farther away he got from Cotton Patch.

I was amazed to see how many of the folks in his own church, not to mention his TV audience, actually believed his cockeyed story about the Vanessa McKay affair, all evidence—and even his own *nolo contendre* plea to reduced charges—to the contrary.

He explained all that, while ignorin' the five years probation they slapped him with, at a press conference, which some of the Dallas-

Fort Worth news media stars lapped right up like Puffy our cat drainin' a tipped-over quart o' warm milk: "I have indeed registered this plea, which is no admission of guilt, so that the demonic hosts of the Satanic power may be thwarted in their devious machinations to expunge me from my ever-burgeoning ministry to the poor, oppressed, and put-upon underclass of this land. And besides, whenever a strong black man get up, the white man and his racist media and po-lice try to slap him down! But we just gonna forgive—though we certainly shall not forget—and we gonna love 'em and pray for 'em. And if they don't straighten up then, we gonna pray the Holy Spirit machine gun will shoot 'em all down!"

That last part, of course, was kind-ly drowned out by cheerin', and the sound of a not-inconsiderable number of the young ladies of Doctor Carter's ever-growin' "congregation" hittin' the deck after bein' "slain in the spirit."

A couple of 'em, I regret to say, hit the deck again later that evenin' with Doctor Carter. And both times they hit it, they hit it on their backs.

Now, if you suspected by now I couldn't come up with all the hifalutin' words of that press conference on my own, you'd be right. I copied 'em right outa the pages of the *Cotton Patch Press*, where ole Charlie Settle posted him an editorial callin' on folks to ride Doctor Carter outa town on a rail. Charlie did a special word count on his new computer and made sure his editorial was bigger'n the story itself. He wadn't about to let Doctor Carter get the last word on him, leastways in his own newspaper. Why, he couldn't of looked ole Bedford Forrest in the eye, as the Wizard of the Saddle stared down at him from the original oil paintin' up there on the wall of Charlie's office.

The problem, you see, was that Doctor Carter had a similar paintin' in his own office, but his was of W. E. B. DuBois.

Now he was speechifyin' again, at the City Council showdown, with a power no one else in town could touch. Why, the glint in his hazel eyes or the hands he waved in the air either one gave more gusto than anyone else's words. He was like a buckin' bronc you could barely keep in the chute till the gate opened, and if you didn't watch out, you'd find yourself believin' some of what he said.

"This family entertainment complex will not only be the most fun, clean endeavor around," he announced, "but it will bring jobs and revenue to Ellis County we desperately need, especially after the recent tornado."

Some female, sounding as though she was in the process of bein' slain in the spirit again, shrieked, " Ooh—Doctor D, baby!"

Now Mayor Coltrane may've been sidin' with Doctor Carter on the proposed family entertainment complex, but he was still workin' behind the scenes to find a way to hang the good reverend for the Vanessa McKay deal, and a lotta other things that riled him.

I expect I can tell you now, he later on kind-ly helped set up Doctor Carter on a "date" with somebody just a few years older than me, but with more interestin' drugs than were in my family's medicine cabinet, somebody that proved to be good fun for one hour, but very bad for TV ratings.

More importantly, to Mayor Coltrane, it spurred some of the other black leaders of Cotton Patch to inform Doctor Carter that if they ever so much as saw his smilin' face within the metropolitan limits again, they would see to it he wouldn't be quite as pretty next time he smiled for his TV cameras.

For now, though, Mayor Coltrane didn't want his plans for the meetin' gettin' sidetracked, so he just rapped his gavel, which didn't amount to much, because Doctor Carter went right on. "And," he said, "as you may know, certain of us on the council have employed what humble influence God has given us toward attaining our partners'—and isn't that what they are, after all, partners with our town and county—our partners' agreement to pledge ten cents of every dollar they make the first year to Ellis County charities!"

They were partners alrighty, with some in the town and county.

Then things kind-ly stirred up at the back of the room and everone saw Miz T, awake now but on her hospital bed, gettin' wheeled all the way up to the council tables, intervanous tubes and all, even those black sunglasses you couldn't see through. "How can *you* be talkin', foo'?" she bellowed right into the for-once ruffled face of Doctor Carter. "After what-all you done, you got no shame at all, boy?"

Daddy couldn't help but thinkin' this was the first on-earth resurrection he himself had ever witnessed.

Mayor Coltrane slammed down his gavel. "Miz T—er, Mrs. Tollett—you will refrain," he sputtered, "or I'll have you wheeled back out just the way you were wheeled in."

Doctor Carter went on, but he was more rattled than a treed coon. "So for these and so many other reasons, I shall vote for Cotton Patch, I shall vote for you, I shall vote for our precious children—" (Mrs. McKay just did manage to keep Coach McKay from doin' one of them red dog blitzes on Doctor Carter like he used to do on the quarterbacks in his college days at Texas A & I.) "—I shall vote for the family fun complex," Doctor Carter proclaimed.

Miz T provided what I thought was a fitting Texas benediction: "You all hat and no cattle, pervert-man!"

My daddy's jaw set harder'n the smell of an acre o' garlic as applause swept the room, includin', but sure not limited to, Doctor Carter's faithful followers. Clay, Dr. and Mrs. Blevins, Tater and Spud Tatum, Carlos Romero, Jim Langtry, and Graciela and a still-cleaned-up Rodriguez sat along the same row as Daddy.

Ever'body on the council except Mayor Coltrane and Doctor Carter appeared quite bowed down. That Granger and a nest of his buddies looked smug as you please, and Shorty Anderson sat in a back corner poker-faced.

Mayor Coltrane rapped his gavel some more and said, "The speakers bein' concluded and this bein' a public vote, I'll ask for a show of hands of all those in favor of the proposed family fun complex."

One by one the elected representatives of our little town, almost all of 'em professin' believers in the risen Christ, raised their hands—Doctor Carter, Garth Chisholm, Maria Rivera, Mayor Coltrane, Will Hankins, then Mr. Posey. None of 'em but Doctor Carter and Mayor Coltrane would even look at the audience.

Daddy saw that only his old friend Reverend Jasper had not raised his hand. Finally ever'body started lookin' right at him. Just when Mayor Coltrane was fixin' to ask him was anything wrong, he lifted one hand, just a few inches, just enough to be counted. The whole anti-gamblin' section, which was definitely now outnumbered, kind-ly let out a group gasp. Daddy just blinked, and he felt like his blood froze up on him.

"I reckon Dr. Tollett was just pretty near right about you, wadn't he?" Miz T said from the back of the room. Ever'body in the place knew who was she talkin' to and about.

Reverend Jasper hunkered down farther than he already was.

But the room burst into cheers.

"By unanimous vote the motion carries," Mayor Coltrane said, rappin' his gavel some more and you could only see his lips movin', which they seemed always to be doin', you couldn't hear any of his words, which hardly ever were worth hearin' anyhow. "This meeting is adjourned!"

That Granger, Mayor Coltrane, and others threw a flurry of "high fives." Shorty sat there in his own little world, his face blank as a Llano Estacado flat at noonday. Mr. Posey, Will Hankins, and others just filed out, like they hadn't done anything to be proud of, which they hadn't. Reverend Jasper, well, he just stayed sittin' and lookin' down.

Daddy and his friends couldn't believe it. His eyes scanned the room, fillin' with tears as they did. Then he went ahead and rose to his feet, and he and his torn hamstring limped out, his friends followin', including Miz T, still wheeled on her bed. Daddy gathered 'em in the hallway while the celebration continued in the main chamber.

Doctor Carter, well, he waved too, hugged, and high-fived, his own mob of supporters, and he kissed some select ones from the group, too, of the younger female variety.

"Ooh—Doctor D! Doctor D! Ooh, baby!" they shouted like he had just scored the winnin' touchdown, which he had and much more.

Then came singin' from out in the hallway that most of those hoo-rahin' never heard. "Praise God from whom all blessings flow, Praise Him all creatures here below."

Shorty heard, still stone-faced in his corner, folks shyin' away from him now. They were singin' to the tune of the *Old Hundredth*.

"Praise Him above ye heavenly host, Praise Father, Son, and Ho-ly Ghost. Ahh-men."

Mayor Coltrane came over to Shorty from that Granger and the others, still carryin' that gavel he like to rap with. "Shorty ole boy, we did it—you did it!" he said.

"Get the *h*--- away from me," said Shorty.

Twenty-One

N ext evenin' toward dusk, Puffy our cat was sittin' like he was the Queen's Guard or the like on our front porch. Then here came ole Jake, the Lab, aimin' to find himself a spot there.

Now Jake could lick any dog from one end of Shiloh Road to the other, which was several miles, and had licked most of 'em, even though that meant one time he had half o' one ear kind-ly hangin' off for a spell. However, when Puffy our cat billowed up like a blowfish, hissin' like a bull snake, you'd have thought Jake was the mangiest, scroungiest yard dog in Cotton Patch, way he slunk away.

But Jake was smart, in season and out, and he did about the smartest thing he could've done—he went and got Daisy and brought her back with him. When she showed up and Puffy our cat commenced to billowin' and hissin', Daisy just gave him one of those good ole don't-touch-any-of-my-babies-or-I'll-tear-your-throat-out, mama growls, even though she sure wadn't Jake's mama. But Puffy our cat wadn't frettin' over any such minor distinctions at that point, he was holdin' the hand he was dealt, which wadn't much, and watchin' as Jake plopped himself down on that prized spot of real estate at my daddy's feet as he rocked next to Mama.

So we had Puffy our cat actin' like a dog, Jake actin' like I don't what, and when Daddy glanced over near the main barn, he saw Barney the angus calf and Molly the whitefaced Hereford followin' Luke and Old Jack around, actin' like they were puppies, too. Only when Old Jack commenced to lickin' Barney's face like Jeb my puppy used to do did Barney break momentarily into the role of a cow and try to gore Old Jack. But even then it looked like that must've been Barney's way of playin' too, 'cause next thing you know, there he was, rollin' on the ground like Luke and Old Jack, and they were both tryin' to gore him, to the extent Labrador puppies can gore a cow with their wet black noses.

163

Seemed like ever'body was somethin' different than folks thought they were, and what they were supposed to be.

"You did your best, darlin'," Mama said. "Now you can go to Oklahoma with a clear conscience."

"Our poor little town," said Daddy. "We have gone and sold our soul."

"But not you, dear," said Mama. "No one can ever accuse you of not standin' in the gap even when you stood alone."

Daddy shook his head, starin' at the last flickerin's of daylight. "I was never faithful. I tried ever'thing I could to stay out of that gamblin' fight, till there just wadn't anyone else. I never even loved my own flock like I should've, much less the town."

"Then why are you cryin'?" she said.

"It was when I looked around the room, Loree, when most of 'em were happy and celebratin'," he said. "I felt such sorrow for 'em in their blindness I thought my heart would burst."

"Oh, Ethan. And now we're leavin'," she said.

For a minute, just the breeze, pregnant with winter, sounded.

"No," he finally said.

"What?"

"I called Matt Cutter back today and told him I changed my mind," my daddy said.

Mama sat up a little straighter in her wheelchair. "Oh Ethan—is it so? I prayed for it, I truly did."

"'Sides, with Clay leavin' to start his new church, who'd pastor ours—Rodriguez?" Daddy said, the lines around his eyes Mama hadn't noticed before crinklin' up just a shade. She let out a giggle, which he hadn't heard her do much in a long, long time, not much in fact since before the accident.

"I don't know, darlin', at the rate he's goin', maybe some day he will!" she said, claspin' Daddy's hand.

Then he started gnawin' on his lip, like she knew he did sometimes when he was antsy. "What is it, Ethan?"

"It's what I felt when I was lookin' at all the folks," he said.

"Love?" Mama said.

"Hate," he said. "'Cause their ignorance and sloth was like a mirror on my own. I hated 'em more than ever because they hadn't listened to what all I said and most of all 'cause that reminded me I hadn't listened either. I wanted God to d--- 'em all to hell, forever. But most of all, I wanted Him to d--- me there, 'cause however bad they are, I'm worse, 'cause I know more and I been given more and—and how I pushed you away when you needed me worst, 'cause my twisted ways convinced me you didn't have what I needed anymore."

Then he just bowed right down and started cryin' like Mama'd never seen him cry before. Normally that would've made her sad, but this time she was thankin' Almighty God on His throne in heaven 'cause she had cried to Him for years, prayed to Him, complained to Him, begged Him, and said many other things she was not now proud of, 'cause she could not understand why He had let her husband, at the exact time she needed him most, after she had lost her walkin', her confidence, most of her looks, and about anything and ever'thing else a woman can fall back on—why, it was right then when she kindly lost Daddy too. At first she just thought he felt put-upon. Then resentment came in there on him, and when this resurrected old ghosts from his misty famous past, why, contempt set in on him, grew roots, and blossomed into a long bitter harvest that was so very different than she had always thought it would be.

For she knew he did love the folks, once, a long time ago, before the accident. And she was beautiful and confident then, too. But now there was hate in her and ugliness in him. Finally, last night, whilst she was prayin' during the council meetin', it was like God just kindly parted the thunderheads and let in the light and grabbed her up as His own again, and she knew if she never got love from Daddy or anything else she needed from him again, she was Christ's and she would carry her cross, and even with joy like those saints did which she could never understand, how you could have sufferin' obedience and joy both and not just one or th'other.

She had had her own cry last night after the thunderheads parted, when she figured out God had given her just as long to make Him and not Daddy her idol as he had given Daddy to get his act squared away. For once, she'd given in and told the Lord to have it His way, but she knew even that was His doin', not hers, 'cause she'd said no to that way just as long as she had any strength to do so and when she didn't have any more strength, she said yes.

Now, less than twenty-four hours later, she was watchin' repentance overwhelm her husband in a flood tide of tears and she was holdin' him like she hadn't in a long time and later on that evenin' they would do a whole lot of other things they hadn't done in a long time. "We're forgiven', Ethan," she said, soft as an eiderdown quilt, takin' his hat off him and strokin' his short thick hair. "Even for those things we did long time ago, honey." His sobs relented for a moment and somehow he understood what it was a long time ago that she meant. Then he cried a lot harder than before, realizin' for the first time she knew.

And she smiled knowin' that she did still love my daddy and within a few hours she would know he still loved her, too, and there wouldn't be, so far as I know, any more harshness or suspicion or hatred.

I reckon that would all go under the headin' of much, much better late than never, and that I truly mean.

*　　*　　*

Strangest thing is, you couldn't have convinced those folks in a hundred years my daddy didn't love ever' one of 'em like his own. And I think that's 'cause he truly did love 'em. But he grew up wrong in some ways and made some wrong choices after that and after while that'll kind-ly put a smudge on even the good things in your life, maybe make 'em seem not as good even when they are.

But if he did always love 'em, which I think he did, once God squared him up to some bidness needed takin' care of, why that really cut him loose to show folks what a shepherd is and what a real man is besides.

It pains me to say the front page headline of Charlie Settle's next *Cotton Patch Press* just read "R.I.P." It was more big and bold letters and they spread across the page, but they were halfway down, 'cause a huge photograph they had gotten hold of covered most of the top half of the page.

It was a pitcher of Miz T. Now, I kind-ly get all choked up even now 'cause I miss that great lady still. But then I make sure to remember to cry my tears for the livin', 'cause there's nothin' but praise and thanksgivin' to offer up for where she is now. She's gone home, to her true home and her true Father, not the one what did awful things to her when she was little, things we don't speak of.

Which all makes that wonderful smile of hers so much the more amazin' to me, that God could heal her up enough that she could smile and praise Him and love and help so many other folks.

Includin' me, 'cause I'm one of those that shoots off my mouth when I have nothin' helpful to say, then I sit there quiet when ever'thing important needs sayin'. But she, she was the kindliest lady I ever saw, and gentle too, especially with the children and the old folks and the others that had nothin' to give back for kindness. Yet she was the Lord's own warrior against the evil and wickedness that was so strong no one could seem to stand against it.

She would not lay down even if it killed her, which it finally did.

But that is some of the power of bein' part of God's covenant family, don't you see? You don't just have the folks that are with you today to learn from; you don't want to learn what most of them have to teach you anyway. What's great is you got this "great cloud of witnesses" to draw from, kind-ly like they're right here with you today, which in a way they are.

And so as I mosey along my way, even now, many and many a year since happened all of what I am tellin' you, I have Mama and Daddy and Miz T and some of the others to kind-ly guide me right along the way, and to help me guide the young ones along. What a genius the Lord is, and how comforting to know that our efforts, the things we try to do that are good and true, why, they don't die with us.

From lookin' at some of their lives, it's beginnin' to dawn on me that in fact, some of our greatest deeds, our real contributions, don't even happen till after we're gone, which should give us some hope in the midst of our disappointment and frettin'.

Leastways I can't deny that is the case with some of these folks I'm tellin' you about, because I'm writin' their story and that is sure how it seems to have turned out for them.

*   *   *

It was nothin' fancy like you get in Dallas and other places, with wide emerald lawns and lakes and water fountains and statues of angels and the like. It was just a simple old country cemetery in winter with a few hackberries and post oaks to one side without leaves, a chain link fence that cows had leaned into in some spots runnin' 'round it, and more than a hundred years of plain markers and a few headstones laid out amidst the crisp yellowed grass.

But on that slate gray December day, hundreds of folks—black, white, brown, old, young, and in-between, includin' Daddy, me, and even Mama—surrounded the open grave of Miz T. Standin' before us all was Reverend Jasper, in his fanciest preachin' get-up, Bible in hand

"We all here today to honor the memory of one of God's choice servants, Mrs. Charles Tollett, Sr.," Reverend Jasper said. "We outside 'cause they ain't many churches 'round these parts left to hatch, match or dispatch in."

Then he turned a hard gaze on some of his fellow blacks and said, "And those they is ain't good 'nuff for some folks."

Hardly anyone noticed a black stretch limousine with an engine quiet as leaves hittin' the ground pull to a stop on the asphalt road behind the gatherin'.

"Anyhow, preachers must be in short supply too, else wouldn't be me standin' afore ye today. I sure ain't worthy of her," Reverend Jasper said. Then his voice kind-ly caught and he looked down at the cold ground. No one saw a near-side rear window of the limo lower a shade and smoke curl out of it. "What few days that grand old woman had remaining she ended by goin' out sick into the cold to fight the scourge that is about to beset us," he continued, his voice still pretty choked up. "And while she fought the wrong with her last breaths in this world, *we*'uns took what-all we could to support it. I took *this!*"

A murmur rolled through the whole gatherin' as he raised a wisp of paper into the air and announced, "That's right, peoples, I took this fifty thousand dollar check for my support."

He didn't need any outdoor speaker system like these fancy-talkin' preachers now that have internet church names and sanctuaries that look like basketball arenas. "Oh, it's all legal, they're right careful about that," he said. "I took mine for a new church and to hep some boys needed heppin'. Told myself—told my dear departed Hannah—it was my due! Rich folks gettin' richer, white folks gettin' mo', burnin' down other folks' churches, too. Time—way past time—for the po' man, the honest man, the black man to get some o' his due. Now we gonna get our due, alright, honeylambs."

I looked up at my daddy, and looked like nothin' since all this craziness begun surprised him more'n what he's hearin' right now. Then it occurred to me to look around, and I saw Mr. Posey, Will Hankins, and Garth Chisholm hangin' their heads.

It was too bad Doctor Carter had to be in California that day to film a scene where he was appearin' in one of those "Christian rock" singers' new movies. One of those "Christian TV networks" was producin' the film, and promotin' it 'round the clock on their own station. The last movie they'd produced had been about the end of the world, which was due any day (but hasn't happened yet, decades since the movie was made); honest critics, secular and Christian alike, panned it as the worst theater-intended motion picture made in America that year, and one of the worst any year, but it still netted a couple million dollars—all tax-free of course, since it, the network owners' private jet, the film stars' beach homes, and ever'thing else concerned were part of the "ministry."

Course, Doctor Carter had sent a typewritten note, written by his "executive assistant," for Reverend Jasper to read aloud. But I kind-ly suspect Reverend Jasper might've mistook that note for the newspaper he was linin' his canary's birdcage with that mornin'.

Speakin' of Reverend Jasper, he was just now hittin' his preachin' stride, in a way none of those present, even his own congregation, had ever quite heard before. "We all dirty, we all covered up in it, ain't none of us 'ceptin' a few like Miz T and Pastor Ethan there ain't greedy," he boomed. "And we ain't trustworthy and that's why the Lord ain't a'givin' us nothin'."

I was afraid he was addin' fuel to the fire with all this, and that folks were gonna get riled up with him sayin' it when he was supposed to be given' the eulogy, or "urology" as I called it at the time, for Miz T. So I was surprised to see, peekin' as I was out the corner of my eyes, faces all over the crowd were droppin', tears runnin' down their cheeks, and Coach and Mrs. McKay, too, and heads shakin' and noddin' all over the place. I looked up at my daddy and I couldn't any more make out what he was thinkin' than you could figure gray clouds to the north in spring before you knew what direction they were movin'.

But Reverend Jasper didn't seem first concerned with what folks thought about his words; fact is, he didn't even seem to be speakin' first to the folks. For now he was lookin' up to that low steely sky, tears streakin' his face too, and sayin', "Well, I can't change my vote, Miz T, but I can sure send this back to the devil whence it come."

Then he tore that check right up. Some of the folks nodded, but nobody made a peep, not even any amens.

And no one at all saw that limousine in back pull away, the window closed, only a whiff of cigar smoke stayin' behind a minute before it, too, was gone.

Twenty-Two

The sun rose blood red next mornin' from the cedars over toward the valley, like a ball squirtin' loose up out the fires of perdition, but still bringin' some of 'em with it.

I was helpin' my daddy with chores that mornin', and we were carryin' buckets of oats from the stable to the horses. But we weren't speakin' a word.

Daddy opened the gate to the west pasture, where were all our horses. We walked through it, then to a pair of feedin' racks hangin' on top the metal rail of the gate. The half dozen horses stood there, jockeyin' for breakfast position. We poured the oats into the racks and they gobbled it up—except for still-spindly Splash, whom the others forced away from the troughs. I kept aside a half a bucket for her, for when the others finished.

Daddy began to curry and comb Annie Lee. I did the same to Splash.

"You're quieter'n a wolf on the prowl," he said to me.

My mouth might've been quiet, but my mind wasn't. After a minute, I said, "What's it like to die, Daddy?"

"Been thinkin' on Miz T, have you?" he said.

"Yes, sir."

He worked on Annie Lee for a spell, then said, "'Member that day you finally rode ole Maggie girl here?"

"Yes, sir."

"'Member how tired you were?"

"I thought I was gonna die," I said, eyein' Billy to make sure he didn't spot Splash's half a bucket.

"You conked right out on the front porch swing after supper," Daddy went on. "Didn't even wake up when Daisy 'bout licked your whole face off."

I giggled at that one, in spite of myself.

"Know what happened then?" Daddy asked.

"No, sir."

"Why, I picked you right up, carried you to your room, and put you in your bed. 'Member how surprised you were when you woke up next mornin'?" he said.

"Yes! But I still don't understand, Daddy."

"Well, dyin's like that, sweetie. A famous Presbyterian pastor long time ago, Peter Marshall, preached such. He said one mornin' we just wake up in th'other room—in our own true happy room the Lord Jesus prepared for us 'cause He loved us and we loved Him," my daddy said.

I thought about that as I scooped a handful of oats from that half a bucket and fed Splash out of my little hand and petted her.

"Won't that be some fine mornin', Daddy?" I said, smilin' at the thought of it.

*   *   *

Well, I didn't know it, but certain folks weren't exactly enjoyin' the fruits of their victory like they'd expected. Ain't it like that in life, 'specially when it's gilded gain?

You take ole Mayor Coltrane, for instance. Why, there he was later that same mornin', havin' him what he expected was a carefree day at the golf course, hannelin' by cell phone the little bit of bidness he hadn't dumped onto his underlings, and lookin' forward to spendin' the holidays in the Caribbean, courtesy of his recent labors in behalf of the new "family entertainment complex."

So it must've come as quite a surprise to the mayor to find himself frantic, sweatin', and scarlet-faced while sittin' in his cart, nine-iron in hand after a smokin' drive from the fifth tee box, and screamin' into that cell phone. "You better track that lyin' skunk down, and quick!" he was hollerin', not seemin' to care who heard. "I want some answers! Me and Chisholm—and others—are knee deep in this—legal, financial, reputations—and I'm hearin' that stogie-suckin' old sidewinder has pulled outa the whole deal!"

With that, Mayor Coltrane spiked his phone to the ground so hard one of those plastic pieces popped right off it.

* * *

Meanwhile, that Granger, why, he wadn't in any better frame of mind a'tall, sittin' in his highfalutin' highrise North Dallas office. Fact is, he appeared a might fevered, shoutin' into that speaker phone as he was. That flashy seckaterry stood in the doorway.

"Then you better *find* Mr. Anderson before these Chicago goombahs catch wind what's up!" that Granger hollered at his speaker phone.

"Uh, Mr. Granger?" said the seckaterry. "It's that Texas Ranger again."

Now, the Rangers had kind-ly forgot to tell the F.B.I. about this deal, 'cause last time they let the Feds in on bidness with that Granger, the Feds and their politickin' and bure'crats and Yankee lawyers screwed it up so bad, that Granger wound up suin' the state of Texas for a few million dollars, and nearly collectin'.

"Tell 'im I'm still away on bidness and take his number again," that Granger snapped.

"But sir, he's here this time and he won't leave," the seckaterry said, fumblin' with her hands, which she needed to be careful of, 'cause the nail job that Granger paid for her to have each week came out to roughly the same as our monthly family grocery bill.

For once in his life, that Granger couldn't think of a thing to say, especially when the Ranger stepped right into the room, boots, Stetson, .45, and all. You'd have thought he looked the spittin' image of ole Rip Ford, if you had any idea what ole Rip looked like, or even who he was.

* * *

My daddy didn't know any these happenin's; he was just drivin' his ole Shivy, which looked like it hadn't been washed since seedtime, down the farm-to-market from Cotton Patch toward home, the pretty strains of the Statlers' *Elizabeth* on the radio. As I think back, it seems those pretty, sad songs were the ones Daddy liked best, though I didn't know at the time.

Some of 'em he'd stay in the Shivy for if they were still playin' when he got where he was goin', and he'd wait till they were over 'fore he'd get out. He'd do that for *Elizabeth* and some of the Statlers' other songs, like *Silver Medals and Sweet Memories,* and Don Williams' *I'm Just a Country Boy* and even ole Kris Kristofferson's *Why Me, Lord?*

Me, I was in the back seat, which was the only place he'd let me sit in any vehicle. My, how Daddy used to rant when he'd see other daddies speedin' down Shiloh Road in their pickups, their kids bouncin' 'round back in the bed. Or mamas speedin' to or from Dallas in their big ole vans and Suburbans and the like, with their kids bouncin' 'round in the front seat, with no seat belts. "There's a heap o' stupid to go around out here," he'd say, and other things of a less-complimentary nature.

"Look, Daddy!" I shouted. Up ahead, proud as could be, stood a big chestnut-coated mama cow, suckling her calf smack out in the middle of the farm-to-market. I had lots of times seen cows and all manner of other critters near the road, on the road, and smooshed *into* the road. But I hadn't exactly ever seen this. And that mama cow had no intention of movin' off that road.

"Looks like Tessie busted through ole Tater's fence again," Daddy said, his eyes twinklin', as he slowed way down then pulled around the pair. Tessie stared a hole through us the whole time, so I reckon the little one saw no reason to interrupt supper, since mama obviously had ever'thing well in hand. "Hafta call 'im so he can coax 'er home with some oats."

Down the road a piece, I saw Daddy kind-ly blink when he noticed Mr. Green had let 'em put up a for sale sign on his acreage, which always brought in a good crop of cotton or sunflowers or at least alfalfa. But Mr. Green couldn't pay his dead wife's medical bills, or his own health insurance any more, or for the big John Deere the gov'ment got him good terms to buy and the salesman talked him into gettin'. "That ain't even a Texas area code on that sign," Daddy said, cut to the quick, shakin' his head and sippin' his A & W Root Beer.

He was never a farmer, though he grew up on the land, hauled him a lot o' hay in the summers when he was young, rode nearly from the crib, and worked plenty of cattle. But somethin' about those men who worked the land had coiled itself about his heart and never let go. Like ole Hank the post office man—who wadn't always the post office man, you see—and the years he spent gettin' him that bleedin' ulcer and divorce from workin' the land he loved, then waitin' in line at the gin to see how much they'd give 'em for his cotton, or even if they'd give him anything.

Or Billy Don Coldwater, Lord rest his soul, for whom cattle and maize prices both went down once too often for a man with seven mouths to feed and a weakness for Wild Turkey, but who had dreams when he was young and dreams still when he died—not old—and a wife who loved him from third grade on and never loved another.

Maybe it was 'cause my daddy, a big man and a strong man, never could shake loose o' those that were small and weak; he never could move too far on lessin' they could come too, no matter how much they riled him. Lot of folks he'd known, mostly of the college-educated variety, felt so sorry for him that he never did move too far on.

Maybe, too, it was 'cause those men brought forth the bounty o' that creation he loved so true, helped it be more beautiful even than before, helped God's plans for it work the way they should. And I always thought when Daddy thought God was happiest, that was when he was happiest himself.

Whatever the reasons, even when most of 'em never came to his church, at least regular, those men never had a truer friend than my daddy, to the end.

Then we saw someone tall walkin' along side the road, sportin' a slight gimp.

"Daddy, that's Jed Schumacher," I said.

Daddy pulled the Shivy over and rolled down the passenger side window. "Hop in, Jed," he said.

Without sayin' anything or without even an expression, that young man opened the door and slid in. I sorta hunkered down in the back, hopin' he wouldn't see me, but at the same time hopin' he somehow knew I was back there. We drove a ways before Daddy spoke.

"Long walk to your place," he said.

"Doesn't matter. No one there anyhow," that young man said.

"Why not?" said my daddy.

"Mom's latest boyfriend moved out, and she's been off somewhere drownin' her sorrows the last two days."

I think right about then my mouth just kind-ly dropped open, but I covered it up quick with my hand, so as not to draw any attention at all to myself in the back seat. I was tryin' to be so invisible that no one would know I was even there, and they'd keep talkin' like they were of such grown-up things. I was wonderin' what the other girls would think if they knew what I was gettin' to hear and who was in the Shivy with me.

"Oh," Daddy said. He took another sip of his root beer before sayin', "Heard about your knee."

"More great news," that young man said, lookin' out the other window. "Coulda played at OU like you, Mr. Shanahan—or UT or A & M or Nebraska."

"Or anywhere," my daddy said, real serious-like. "Jed, I want you to listen to me, buddy. I been playin' or watchin' football all my life. And you're the best high school football player I ever saw. And that includes at least three Heisman Trophy winners."

That young man's head dropped right down to his chest. I didn't know whether to look or hide, so I kind-ly did both. Then I saw tears fallin' down into his lap and I don't know why, but this powerful need came over me to cry too, so much that I had to put my hand over my mouth again, and this time I wasn't foolin' in any way.

"Son, I know you feel extra bad 'cause o' how it happened," my daddy said. "But I've watched the way you have with the children. And I know you make good grades. Can you still play golf?"

"Yes sir. Went to the course just the other day. 'long as I wrap my knee and ride 'n the cart, it's just fine."

"How'd you do?" my daddy asked.

That young man just looked down again.

"Aw, I know how you did," my daddy said. "Coach McKay told me he's only ever seen two other people hit the green off that eighteenth tee box, and they were both PGA players."

Then I saw my daddy bite his lip, which as you know meant he was a little nervous for some reason. He turned to that young man and said, "Son, the golf coach at OU is an old teammate o' mine. You could go there on a full ride, get your degree, then coach the young people—not just how to play ball, but about what's right and true. They hear the other from so many places. That way, what the Lord gave you doesn't die with that knee."

That young man stared at him. "Reverend Shanahan," he said, "you're the first person 'sides Coach McKay give me the time o' day since the accident. I can't understand why a preacher'd care 'bout someone like me's wasted so much and I sure don't know why Coach—after what I did to Vanessa . . ."

My daddy laid a hand on his shoulder. "Son, it was Coach McKay told me how good a golfer you were," my daddy said.

"Daddy, looks like Mr. Rodriguez has a problem," I said, noticin' him up ahead on the patch of land he had started sharecroppin' from Will Hankins.

Daddy pulled the Shivy over where Rodriguez was leanin' sad-faced against a beat-up old tractor, at the edge of a partially-plowed field. "Tractor problems, Ed?" Daddy said.

"This tractor's got a problem, alright," Rodriguez said. "It's got a man still pickled who can't stay on it long enough to get his winter wheat fertilized."

"Jed, can you take Katie home, then take the truck to your place? I'll be by for it later," Daddy said.

"Sure, Mr. Shanahan," said that young man.

"Katie Bird, do your piano and be in bed by eight-thirty. I've got a meeting back at the church after this and I'll be late," Daddy said. Then he leaned over and kissed me, and we hugged each other across the seat. I could smell that woodsy cologne and our land on him.

"I love you, Daddy," I said.

"I love you too, little friend," he said.

He got out and walked around the truck to Rodriguez. A redbird soared by just then and landed not far away. My daddy look kind-ly surprised, then he smiled and drank in the air. "Spring's comin', Ed," he said. Then he turned back to me with another smile, just for me, and he said, "I'll see you in the mornin', darlin'."

We waved at him and that young man drove us away.

*   *   *

Mama and her wheelchair were parked in the middle of the family room later that evenin', surrounded by baskets. "Katie Helen Shanahan, I'm waitin' on those ribbons for the care packages," she called to me. I rushed into the room, my hands full of ribbons. I wasn't that excited about this project, especially when I knew all there was at the end of it was piano.

"Hope folks in Peru are more thankful for all we do than folks around here," I said. (I had been watching the video of another Katie, Katie Scarlett O'Hara in *Gone With the Wind*, for the umpteenth time.)

"Shame on you, Katie Helen. We don't give to get thanks, we give to give," Mama scolded me.

"Ye-es ma-am," I said, the knowin' I was wrong not makin' it any happier a confession.

It was the last time that doorbell ever rang, 'cause I made Mama take it out after. I answered it and let in Rodriguez, who was plenty shook up.

"Oh, hello, Mr. Rodriguez. What's wrong?" I said. I knew somethin' was mighty wrong when I saw the look on Mama's face, before he said a word.

"It's—oh, Mrs. Shanahan," he said, the words gushin' like a broken faucet from a windmill. "Pastor Ethan was fertilizing for me on a hill and he come across a hurt 'possum. A stupid, da—he pulled around it and—the tractor—it just rolled over on him."

I still remember how Mama looked down like somebody'd hit her and stunned her, but she made no sound. Rodriguez, though, fell down on his knees wailin'.

Me, I mainly remember windin' up back in the little closet
he called his office and sittin' in his chair, which I still kind-ly
disappeared into it was so big, wonderin' what he'd tell me to do now.
I looked up and saw that old pitcher of his daddy, that he never knew,
'cause he died just two years after my daddy had been born in Baylor
Hospital like me, and like his daddy before him. Mama said Daddy
woke up when he heard his daddy fall in the bathroom early one
mornin', and he walked in and saw him dyin' in Grandma Shanahan's
arms.

He never did talk about him, but Mama said he was a brave man
and he kept volunteerin' to go to that other war, World War II, even
though he had only one eye worked proper and he couldn't hear out
of one ear at all. She said he went back again to the medical board
and switched from his bad to his good eye on the test and the doctor
prob'ly saw it but he let him by 'cause they needed ever'body by then
'cause we were gettin' beat bad for awhile.

I remembered another doctor later on told Grandma Shanahan
part of why a barrel-chested man of 35 years had dropped dead of a
heart attack was because of a delayed stress somethin' or other and
that it was happenin' all the time in the '50s and '60s to our fathers
who went off and spilled their blood and gave away their futures and
left their families without daddies to win World War II.

I also remembered Mama sayin' my daddy's daddy went off to the
Pacific with the thickest, curliest head of yellow hair you ever saw,
just like in some other old pitchers we have of him, but when he came
back three years later, after New Guinea and Leyte and what-all, top
of his head was smooth and shiny as a cue ball.

For the first time ever, it occurred to me that Mama nor Daddy nor
any of my other grandparents had yellow hair like I did. But I could
see it was no secret at all whence it came.

So I kept lookin' up at Sergeant Patrick Ethan Shanahan, whom I
never knew, in his uniform and his cap with the eagle and that hard
level stare my daddy got from him. Mama said he had been busted
back to private twice, once for cold-cockin' one of those "Jerks and
Jersey Bums" he wrote home to his own daddy about, this one a
lieutenant who kept mockin' him 'cause he talked like a Texas hillbilly
and was stupid as an Irish potato farmer, and he guessed he was both.

That fella may have kept mockin', but he didn't do it around my daddy's daddy anymore.

Now I started to figure out for the first time why my daddy would just kind-ly sit and stare at that pitcher when he didn't know I was watchin', and I began to wonder if he might've needed his own daddy growin' up, maybe even needed him real bad.

And I wondered if those old men who get the young men into fights by doin' things like our old men did when they drygulched the Japs on their oil and ore and what-not, then didn't let on we knew they were comin' after us at Pearl Harbor, even though we did, well, I wondered if those old men ever took account o' just how many folks their wars hurt and how long that hurt keeps on, even after folks are dead and new ones are born and here I was lookin' at Sergeant Shanahan's pitcher and wonderin' all this.

Finally I realized how important havin' a good daddy was, that it didn't come automatic, and how fortunate (us Calvinists don't consider it luck) was I to have had my daddy even long as I did. And a thought struck me that is with me to this day, how the real countries are not what those old men lead, nor places on a map, nor what they tell us in their New York books we belong to.

The real countries are us, you and me, and if my daddy was a hero and he was, and no one ever knows it like they think that Granger was who built an arena in Dallas or Doctor Carter who was on TV, or even Mayor Coltrane, who they named the new bypass after, why if I know it, then he's a hero in a whole big wide land full of heart and color and grandness and beauty, and that country'll grow even larger when I pass it down to my children, and they to theirs.

My daddy taught me to think for myself, though with respect, before God (*Coram Deo* we Latin experts call that), and I commenced to prayin' that God would give me half a man as him for my husband some day. For I remembered after General Lee died, his daughter Mildred told her Mama, "To me he seems a hero—and all other men small in comparison."

Mildred was good to her word. Neither she, nor any of her three sisters, married—even till the day they died.

Twenty-Three

Lots of things happened durin' those times, alright. Charlie Settle had him a spankin' new headline in the newsracks that very day. It said, "COTTON PATCH COUNCILMAN POSEY INDICTED." The subhead read, "Fraud, Racketeering, Forgery Among 16 Counts."

Seems the man who first fired us up against gamblin' comin' in had lost his own battle with the habit, and it wound up landin' him in more trouble than he could ever have imagined. Like ole Solomon said, "the foxes, the little foxes, that spoil the vines . . . " He found out what those pesky foxes could do, and Mr. Posey did too.

I don't remember much about the funeral couple days later, except they couldn't fit all the people in the Cotton Patch Presbyterian Church, even includin' the balcony, which surprised me, and they said lots of nice words about my daddy.

I remember plenty about after, though. Some folks were leavin' the church, dressed formal, so far as country folk dress formal. Inside, the chancel area at the front of the sanctuary was covered with flowers. A line of other folks formed up in front of Mama, whose wheelchair was parked near the altar. This line stretched across to one aisle and up the length of it to the foyer.

Dr. Blevins stood at the head of the line. He was talkin' real low to Mama, but since I was standin' next to her, and eavesdroppin' best as I could, I heard ever' word he said, which was, "Lorena, I—I received an anonymous money order to pay your medical expenses."

"What medical expenses?" said Mama.

"All of 'em," he said. "That is, it's enough money—it's an incredibly large sum. And Loree? I've already sent a check to Dr. Campbell, the orthodontist I told you about in Ennis. It'll handle Katie's braces."

It sounded good to me 'til that last part.

"But who, Luke?" Mama pressed him. Mama liked givin' charity, but she hated takin' it, and I figured we must be hurtin' if she was even participatin' in this conversation.

"I don't know, but I have an idea," said Dr. Blevins.

Mama straightened her back. "I won't accept it if it's from Shorty Anderson, Luke, you hear? I won't take a penny," she said.

"I can't know for sure!" Dr. Blevins said, louder than before. "Besides, I asked Shorty, and he denied it all. Loree, I think God's bein' a father to the fatherless here."

A few places back in the line stood Graciela and a neat, well-scrubbed Rodriguez, who was nice-lookin' in a way I'd never before noticed. Graciela's friend Esmerelda Garcia nudged her and whispered, "Oh, your new pastor is so handsome!"

I saw she meant Clay, who was standin' near the altar in his new clerical robe, talkin' to a beautiful young hispanic woman in her early twenties whom I soon learned was Emerelda's daughter. Graciela must've seen too, 'cause I heard her say, "And I see he has already made the acquaintance of your lovely Felina."

"Yes, and he has asked my Raul permission to court her!" Esmerelda announced.

Next in line to speak with Mama was Will Hankins. "Lorena, I'm ashamed I didn't stand by Ethan," he said. "I'm thankful Shorty jerked the rug out from under them rascals, whatever his reasons." Then he glanced around, kind-ly secret-like and embarrassed both. "All I'll say is, biggest mistake of my life was lettin' the blasted government pay me not to grow crops and sucker me into sellin' my soul for fancy new equipment. You know they done it to men all over the county—all over the country, I'll wager you." He couldn't look at her any more. "Then the droughts and what-all. We been sinkin', Loree, and so much of it was Sallie Beth's money. Even when they offered me money though, I didn't take it. But when they threatened my family . . . " Now he looked in her eyes, tears fillin' his own. "But I took nothin' from nobody."

"Never you mind, Will Hankins," Mama said, "never you mind. You're a good father and a good husband and a good man."

Then he leaned over and she embraced his head as he began to sob. It still amazes me who-all cried that day whose husband or daddy hadn't just died.

That young man Jed Schumacher was next in line. "Coach McKay said Mr. Shanahan already talked to the OU golf coach about me and they have a scholarship for me even though they've never seen me play golf," he said. I was watchin' him real close and looked like his eyes sorta got misty then. "Coach is gonna drive me up there when school starts in the fall."

"That's mighty fine, Jed," said Mama. "Ethan always saw somethin' special in you, beyond what you did on the field. You help the younger ones, hear?"

"Yes, ma'am," he said.

I happened up just as he stepped away. The way Mama defined, this would prob'ly have come under the headin' of presumption rather than Providence. Anyhow, that young man nodded and smiled down at me, whereupon I just kind-ly broke out into one big embarrassed grin, which Mama described later as "goofy." For then, she just said, "Silly girl." Then she looked a few places back in the line and said, "Pastor Jasper, sir? Would you be so kind as to wheel me out into the sunshine?"

"Why, yes, ma'am," said he, who had helped Clay with the service.

As the line of folks followed them out, Rodriguez stopped by and stared, at me. At first I thought I'd done somethin' to make him mad, then I saw he was tryin' to talk, but no words would come."

"It's alright, Mr. Rodriguez," I decided to say. "My daddy loved you too, sir."

Eduardo Herrera Pancho Villa Rodriguez could not dare weep in front of a female, especially a little girl, so he clamped his hand over his mouth as tears streamed over it, nodded his head, and rushed out of there.

The good news I can tell you is that he came back to church again real soon, and he kept comin' back, even to now.

Not long after, ever'one but me had followed Mama outside. The sun splashed those fake stained-glass windows into a hundred dancin' rainbows all over the sanctuary and I thought how beautiful they made the real country where I lived.

I walked down the crimson-carpeted aisle to the altar and up to the pulpit where my daddy preached longer than I had been alive. Then I looked down and saw where years before he had 'em carve into the wood edgin' the top of the crescent-shaped pulpit stand, "Woe unto Him who preacheth not the Gospel of our Lord Jesus Christ." He said that was what the pulpit said that he once stood in at Suffolk County, England, where another of his heroes, the famous "Evangelical Bishop," J. C. Ryle, preached for 20 years before they moved him up to Liverpool or some such place, even though he scared the dickens out of "they."

My daddy stirred up a few ruckuses in one little town, but J. C. Ryle stirred up ruckuses in a whole nation, and I suspect that was one reason Daddy liked him. Daddy said the man who held that Suffolk pulpit now was a nice man, but he needed to read what was written on it.

Our pulpit seemed nine feet high, as I suspect it has to many a sinner, but—just as I was startin' to look out and pretend it was me preachin' to a full sanctuary—I chanced a peek over top of it and saw Shorty Anderson in the back of the room. He walked down the aisle toward me, needin' his cane ever' step of the way, which surprised me as so many things in life have. I had only glimpsed him a few times and never without a tent of cigar smoke hangin' over him.

Now I am proud to say that next to the Maid of Lorraine, Joan of Arc herself, I was about the bravest girl you ever saw that whole day, up to then. I obeyed what I considered would've been my daddy's direct orders on how to carry myself in such a situation. But now my eyes burned with tears as that—that man—came near, leanin' on his ole cane, and cleared his throat.

"Miss Shanahan. I am here to apologize personally to you for havin' so long been such a bore. Your father was a fine pastor and a great man," he said, his voice gravelly and his words kind-ly stumblin' out one at a time. But that didn't throw me off one mite.

"Then why?" I said, lookin' down on him from my daddy's pulpit, and grippin' it too, even though I had to stand on my tiptoes and look over the side of it to see him. My words kind-ly started slow like a train comin' out of the station, then just built up a mighty head of steam.

"Why were you so mean to my daddy? He only wanted to help you—ever'one else gave up on it and told him he was a fool even to care."

This time it was Shorty's eyes that watered over. It took him a long West Texas minute to say anything. "'Twas my daddy gave the very land this church sits upon after he come out from Mississippi," he said. Now this truly surprised me. "He and his mules dug out the earth where the basement sits," he said. "All growin' up, this church was mostly my whole world."

"Then how did you turn out so cur-dog mean, sir?" I asked respectfully.

"Well, your daddy and me, we had a fallin' out o' sorts," he said, lookin' at the gold-tipped head of his cane and turnin' it in his hands, "but it was my fault not his—"

"That's funny, he said it was all his fault," I shot in, assayin' I'd caught him for sure on this one.

"Oh? Well, I respectfully differ with him about that," Shorty said. "Anyhow, it wasn't there I went wrong, honey, 'twas a time long before. Somewhere along the way I started takin' the Lord for granted. That'll happen when folks get 'em some money. Then He didn't seem so grand and special. Then I got bitter." Now he was really hunched over that cane, which looked awful old and scuffed up. "Then when we lost our little Boo—" He looked up at me now. "—I would reckon her to have been about your age, honey; well, bitter wadn't the word for it after that."

I noticed as he began to gaze around the room, that the sun had turned to an angle where it was spillin' some of those pretty rainbows all over Shorty's head and shoulders. But he didn't even seem to notice like I did. "And that's how I stayed till I heard your daddy leadin' the Doxology after losin' that vote," he said. "Hadn't heard it 'n years. But . . . I remember singin' it when I was three years old."

He and his cane made their way to the altar like a calf comin' home without his mama. "The Reverend Samuel J. McCormack baptized me on this very spot three-quarters of a century ago yesterday," he said.

"I never knew, Short—Mr. Anderson," I said, comin' out from behind my daddy's pulpit.

"If only I'd have heeded the words o' my daddy like you have yours, I might've counted for some good," he said.

Just then Graciela shouted from the doorway at the back of the sanctuary. "Katie! Your mama wants you out here!"

Now I kind-ly smiled at ole Shorty as I came back down to ground level. "It's not too late for you, Mr. Anderson," I said, feelin' the rainbows against my own face and shinin' all through the land. "It's not too late for any of us."

Then I walked past him and out of the church. I remember he had a surprised sorta look on his face as he watched me.

After I was gone, he glanced around to make sure he was alone, then he hobbled over to the open doorway of my daddy's office. He looked in and saw my daddy's robe and one of his cowboy hats hangin' on the wall. Then he stepped to the desk, real slow.

He pulled an envelope from his inside pocket and took a money order from it made out to the Cotton Patch Presbyterian Church for one million dollars. The signer's name said "Samuel J. McCormack." Shorty slipped it back in the envelope and put it in a work bin on the corner of the desk.

After that, he stepped back to the door, where was a row of framed portraits on the wall, of which my daddy's was the newest and Samuel J. McCormack's the oldest. The men who pastored that church. Shorty kind-ly nodded at 'em, the way Texans do at men and ideas they respect, things that give 'em hope they can be a little better'n they are now, and he walked out.

A couple minutes later he was outside too. His eyes scanned the still-large crowd, which included future Oklahoma Governor Matt Cutter and his new wife, quite a few other OU football teammates of my daddy's, and a teary-eyed, rawhide-tough bootlegger's boy whose father was murdered and whose mother committed suicide and died in his arms.

Coach and Mrs. McKay were there, and Tater Tatum—who shot that new cougar two days before—and his family, Bubba Coltrane, Jefe, Jumpy, Jose, and many, many others, including Paw Paw Gremillion, who just cried and cried.

Now a sound we hadn't heard in a long time tolled forth as the bell atop the roof of our church began to ring. The entire startled host looked up to see the bell ringer high above was none other than Old Man Taggart.

How he ever got up there—or how he got down—I never knew.

And for the first time in years, a broad happy smile covered Shorty Anderson's face. It was even said later by some that he actually commenced to laughin', but not in a way that caused any there, includin' Mama, offense.

"Look how bright the sky is, Katie," Blanca said to me as her daddy tied her little brother's shoe. "It's almost as if heaven came down today to join us."

It was sure enough the bluest I'd ever seen too, with no clouds—no milkweed, no wisps, no nothin'—and I nodded my agreement as I saw Mrs. Posey drop to her knees and bury her head sobbin' into Mama's bosom. "You come over tomorrow *after*noon," Mama told her. "And we'll jar us some preserves together from the garden."

Amy stood nearby, embarrassed and alone. A couple other girls our age, of the richer and more popular sort, stood not far away, whisperin', gigglin', and pointin' at her. I walked straightaway to her, ignorin' 'em as they said their greetin's to me. "Hi, Amy. I've been thinkin' how we should get to be better friends than ever before," I said, meanin' it with my whole heart. "Think maybe your mama'd let you come go ridin' tomorrow, and spend the night at our place?"

Then Amy's face lit up like the rainbows had shown up in her country too. "No one's ever—oh I think I'd like that, Katie!" she said.

*　　*　　*

I never saw the home, but they say it was one of Highland Park's greatest mansions. If you're from Texas, I don't have to draw you a pitcher o' what that means.

The unmailed letter sittin' on the end table said, "Dearest Ethan, I hope this too-long-delayed correspondence finds you well."

187

You couldn't see the lady's face next to it, sittin' alone in a fancy parlor chair, but you could see mounds and mounds of kind-ly wild but silky raven hair tumblin' down her back.

"Please accept my most profound apologiess for all the pain I caused you when we were young," her letter went on, in the same flowin' hand that a long time ago—before me or even Mama—had charted so much of my daddy's course.

Alongside the letter were a quarter-full bottle of gin, an empty glass, and a pen.

Then the words said, "And for never having told you that dear Clay, whom I sent to you, is—your son, Ethan. Our son. After you wisely broke off our relationship, in my anger and hurt, and to my everlasting regret, I concocted the abortion story. Now you know why I really left school a year early. It was not for a modeling career in New York City. How can I ask you to forgive me for never before having told you, when I know your belief of that lie has been a dark cloud over your life ever since?"

You still couldn't see her face, you'd never see it, but you could see the old, old crimson scarf, frayed and faded, she held in her olive-colored hands.

And you could hear her as she began, again, to weep and the scarf fluttered from her hands to the fancy Persian rug.

Twenty-Four

I've never thought much on those months that followed. For one, they're mostly a blur anyhow, and second, I found there's enough hurt layin' around this world o' woe, that you're gonna get knee deep in it even if you don't try, so why bring it on yourself. Or like Paw Paw Gremillion used to say, "Don't go borryin' trouble."

And there isn't much about those next months that didn't have hurt attached to it, leastways for me. Without belaborin' it for you, I might just kind-ly summarize it by mentionin' our Cotton Patch girls grade school track team. Even though Mama continued home schoolin' me, we paid our property taxes like ever'one else to keep the state schools runnin'.

So, they let me run on the track team. Since I was tall and fast like my daddy, they had me runnin' all sorts of events. At first. But the longer we went, the more I lost heart. Seemed when it really startin' hurtin', which track is a sport where that happens early and often, it reminded me of how much I was hurtin' already, inside, and I just had a hard time keepin' goin'.

Fact is, I decided to quit the team. It was only 'cause Mama said she'd send me off to a girls reformatory school before she'd watch me quit anything, that I even kept goin' to practice.

That was about all I did, however, was show up. They were so excited to see me on the team at first, but then they pulled me off the 200-meter dash, then the 400, then the 400-relay, then the mile relay. Finally it was only the long jump, and that was just 'cause they had to have me workin' on somethin' at practice. If they hadn't felt so sorry for me, they woulda kicked me off the team, which was what I was tryin' to get 'em to do.

When Cotton Patch hosted the big all-county grade school track meet at the end of the season, which we had never won even once, they had the long jump in the mornin'. I did my three jumps, scratchin' on two of 'em, and finishin' eleventh on the other. I didn't care if I finished fiftieth, just as long as it was over.

That afternoon, the worst news hit me since my daddy left: almost our whole team was throwin' up, go-to-the-hospital sick from food poisoning they got from eatin' lunch at a hamburger place one o' their daddies took 'em to after the coach told him not to. Stupid me, I had been chicken to go and now only five girls were not headed for the hospital for IV's: Wendy Callahan, our discus thrower, who was slower than me even when I wasn't tryin', which I hadn't been the whole season; all the girls who ran on the mile relay team except Dorethra Jackson, the anchor and fastest; and me.

They weren't gonna run the mile relay. Then the voice of Mr. Hankins, the public address announcer, boomed out, "With only the final event of the day remaining for the girls, Waxahachie, Ennis, and Cotton Patch are tied for first place!" The crowd was shocked and so was I. Those two towns were both several times the size of Cotton Patch. So Mr. Langtry, the deacon, who was our volunteer coach, asked me if I'd run. I told him no, and I told the other girls on the relay team no when they asked me, and I said no to Mama when she came down out of the stands in her wheelchair. Then she looked me straight-on with those green eyes o' hers and she said, "I wonder what your daddy'd think o' all this?"

I shot back, "Well he idn't here, is he? And he idn't ever gonna be here again—'cause of some old stupid 'possum!"

That is when I ran off behind the stands somewhere, so's they could win or lose their lousy track meet without me.

*   *   *

Reverend Jasper stood talkin' to a group of black folks, mostly elderly and mostly female, in the cafeteria at the Cotton Patch old folks home. Leastways, that's what we all called it. It was pretty much the same group used to sing with Miz T in the little wooden church.

"So that's what I done them long years ago, brothers and sisters," Reverend Jasper said, lookin' down at the floor ashamed after a confession there's no reason now to tell you what it was. "And that's why Dr. and Miz Charles Tollett—honorable folk they was—left my congregation and up and started your little church." Then he kind-ly looked up at 'em, surprised-like. "You never knew?" he said.

"They never breathed one word of it," one old lady said.

He looked down again, swellin' up with feelin's.

"What do you want from us, Brother Jasper?" another old lady asked.

"Nothin' but yo' forgiveness, ma'am," he said, lookin' at 'em again.

Ever' one of 'em nodded in his or her own way.

"Yes."

"Amen."

"Yes."

"Hallelujah."

Reverend Jasper nodded back at them, over and over, his eyes fillin' up. "Thank you, thank you kindly. Now I can retires with dignity."

One more nod and he turned to leave. For the first time, a frail little fella in the back, the oldest person in the group, and prob'ly in Cotton Patch, spoke up. "Don't do that, suh," he said, risin' to lean his crooked stooped body against his metal walker. "You need a place to build back 'cause yo property's been condemned, and we need a pastor. We need each other, suh."

Ever' one of the others agreed right off with him, so that Reverend Jasper wondered if they hadn't talked it over ahead o' time.

But meanwhile, a hope spread through George Washington Carver Jasper that he had not known in a very long time, and a sense of forgiveness and freein' up that filled him with joy and gratitude so that he thought he might burst.

He couldn't wait to get home and tell Hannah. And best of all, he could look her in the eye again while he told her.

*   *   *

Just like I kind-ly hinted at earlier, folks sure aren't gone just 'cause they died. My daddy couldn't remember even one thing o' his daddy, yet that yellowed old pitcher with the uniform and the cap with the eagle on it, and stories he heard from his mama and others, why it was like he had him with him right along the way.

And I had lots more'n pitchers and stories, I had the real *him*, all those years, day in and month out.

Maybe that was why when I got under those stands, watchin' 'em sell their blue and red and green Sno Cones, he might just as well've been standin' right there with those blue eyes starin' a hole through me. It didn't matter if his body was in this life or the next, his memory was makin' me feel so guilty that next thing I knew I was standin' there waitin' to get the baton, and on the last leg of the relay too, 'cause all the other girls were so spent havin' to run extra races for the foolish ones went and ate those double bacon cheeseburgers and fries and onion rings they shouldn't of.

I was scared plenty, 'cause I knew I hadn't run hard as I should've all those practices, and I figured it served me right to get showed up bad in front of the whole county, which was pretty well there. But I was scared worse what he'd think, watchin' up there in heaven, if I didn't at least try, and I was afraid to embarrass him if God was lookin' on with him, case God had to see my daddy didn't raise him anything but a little coward.

So there I was, makin' up for some lost prayers and takin' that stick, at least seein' we were twenty yards ahead of the second place team, Ennis. Course I did note the best runner in the meet was their anchor. I figured just to run all-out the whole way.

It went pretty well the first couple hundred meters. I think I even stretched our lead a tad. But then it felt like I ran smack into a telephone pole. It was like my brain wasn't connected to my legs or even my arms any more, and after a minute, I don't think it was connected to anything.

Oh no, I fretted to myself, glancin' over my shoulder and seein' that fast girl closin' on me. *If I lose that lead, and we lose the race, then the meet, ever'body's gonna know it was 'cause I didn't try hard like ever'one else in practice.*

Comin' in to the last turn, I begged God for the strength to keep goin', but the only thing goin' were my wobbly legs as I staggered into the stretch run and felt that fast girl pullin' up almost next to me.

I figured it was all just more sadness and disappointment and that I couldn't win and didn't deserve to and it hurt too much anyway. I was tired of ever'thing hurtin' so much, so I just decided to quit right there. But then I saw that young man right at the front of the stands, watchin' me close, and when I gritted my teeth and tried to keep goin', I saw him stand up, like my daddy had stood up for him, and somehow I got my heart back and I didn't know if I could hold that fast girl off, but if I could just keep runnin', just keep puttin' one foot front of the other . . . I knew I didn't have to win, I just had to finish and not quit tryin' my hardest, even when it hurt.

I never saw folks scream that loud for little kids, even at the Cotton Patch softball and T-ball games, but I couldn't feel anything any more, legs nor arms nor nothin'. I only think I was prayin' my way down that final stretch, with that fast girl tryin' and tryin' to pass me ever' step of the way and me tryin' to hold' her off, my legs clompin' and droppin' but still movin' and folks screamin' somethin' fierce.

And sometimes the Lord doesn't let you win, leastways how folks keep score, but this time He did and when I fell down throwin' up after I broke the finish line string, I felt my daddy's arms holdin' me but I knew that young man had stood up for me, too.

*   *   *

I remember Annie Lee nickerin' as my daddy placed the bridle over her head. It may have been 'cause the horseflies were bitin' extra nasty that day, bitin' ever'body—horses, people, pigs, dogs, cats, cows, 'possums and snakes too, probably. But she stood true, all sixteen hands of her, when he threw the blanket and saddle over her back, and even when he buckled the cinches under her girth.

Then is when I watched him swing high up into that saddle in his jeans that always smelled of the land he loved, even when Mama just washed them, and his boots that looked the same the whole time I knew him, which wasn't long enough.

And I remember him smilin' that white smile that always made me feel safe, even though I knew it was not all smile behind his blue eyes but could turn hard and final as the twisters that came over from tornada alley.

Then he had my little hands in his rough big one—rough sure for a preacher—and I was flyin' up to that saddle myself and the butterflies were flutterin' in my tummy and somewhere a little girl was gigglin' with a delight she had no reason to think would never be quite be as full or free again.

I am not sure that if you have never galloped through a meadow of wavin' buffalo grass then over a rise to see an ocean of bluebonnets stretchin' far as you can make out in the sunshine that you have really seen the whole hand of God the Creator at work.

There goes that giggle again, almost a screamin' sort of giggle now as we go down the path between the bluebonnets, and this time my little boy's tummy is behind me as he hangs onto me, and it's tryin' by now to climb out of his mouth but I know he doesn't want it ever to stop.

Then up our hill we go, the one with the Indian paintbrushes glowin' red off to the side and the last live oak at the top. I don't even have to pull rein, ole Splash knows just where to stop, next to the live oak. I get down, then the eldest of my three children hops down on his own, and I grab a blanket from behind the saddle and a book from the saddlebags.

We walk over to the tree and I spread the blanket on the greenin' grass and my boy and I sit on it.

"Mama, did you and Grandpa Ethan used to come up here a lot?" he asks me.

I just nod.

"What was he like?" he asks.

I think about that a minute and I look around as a mourning dove coos and a scissortail lights out after a crow and one of our whitefaced Herefords calls from over in the east pasture. "Like here," I say.

My boy looks at me, then I am proud to see him smile and nod, understandin'. "Daddy says it smells like Texas perfume," he says.

Now my eyes fill up, in spite of myself. I look at him and I say, "Your Grandpa Ethan used to say that when the bluebonnets come in spring, then the red Indian paintbrushes, then those little yellow flowers, then the white ones, then the purple ones, then the dark red ones, then the brown ones in the middle with the red and yellow around 'em—why, that was God's way o' givin' us just a taste o' what it'll be like when we're all together in heaven."

He sniffs the air and says, "Don't see how heaven can smell much better than here, or even be much prettier."

Then comes the sound of dog barkin', lots of dogs.

My boy stands up and shouts, "Here they come!"

One, two, three, four full-grown white Labs bound up the hill toward us—followed by a pint-sized white Lab puppy. My boy runs toward them, the spring sun a-shinin' off his mop of orange-lookin' hair, orange like my daddy's mustache. I turn to the tree, where a redbird has lit. That which my daddy carved long ago is still there. I smile and open my Bible. Then my mouth drops open and I just stare at it. You won't hardly believe what I see.

I have opened the book right to a brand new bookmark—one radiant bluebonnet.

I just keep on starin' at it, 'cause I didn't put it there and no one's been near that book since I opened it this mornin'. I look this way and that, thinkin' maybe to spot someone hunkerin' down behind a mesquite tree or the like with a wadfull of bluebonnets in his hand.

But I know better really, and pretty soon my face lights up kind-ly like the sunrise breakin' over the Trinity Valley. My eyes misty, I look up, past the hangin' boughs of that ole live oak and into the blue, marvelin'. "Daddy . . ."

'Cause don't you know by now, God's the God o' the seen and the unseen.

Then comes the sweet harmony of the singin' voices, waftin' through the cedars and the pastures rollin' away to the east behind our place.

I hear 'em first. I smile and say, "Right on time." I listen close as the singin' fades with a shift in the wind, then gets clear again. *"In the Sweet Bye and Bye,"* I whisper.

Then I wave at that young man, my husband Jed, varsity football, golf, and track coach at Cotton Patch High School, and elder at the church, as he turns his Shivy off Shiloh Road and onto the gravel path.

Turns out he never stopped standin' up for me.

Ridin' with him is my smilin' half-brother Clay, husband of Felina, father of six boys and two girls, and pastor these twenty years of our Cotton Patch Presbyterian Church, which ever' week now's full as it was when Zig Ziglar came to town.

I expect Clay's got a brisket for Mama to cook us. You know by now she had her sad times, and it hurts me to know who gave her a lot of 'em. But she hung in there and 'cause of her wise counsel, lots of the younger ladies at our church and around Cotton Patch haven't taken near as many rough knocks as they would have.

Now I watch as my Splash grazes the good earth, Little Jed our son frolics with all his dogs, and the fields of bluebonnets and Indian paintbrushes stretch on and on through my country, across the land, toward the sky, even to heaven.

See you in the mornin', Daddy.

Printed in the United States
73464LV00001BA/1-144